
★

I blinked, trying to accustom my eyes to the gloom. There was something at the back of the cave.

"Don't move, Dorothy. Don't go any closer."

I waited there, hardly breathing, while he went to investigate. He touched nothing, looking carefully before he put a foot down on the rocky floor. When he had seen what he had to, he came back to me.

He looked sick as he took my arm and led me to a big rock just outside the cave.

I stared resolutely out to sea and tried not to think about the body in the cave. The body lying casually on its back, wearing calf-high boots and a miniskirt, the body whose long, honey-blond hair spread out in a little pool of seawater and moved as the wind reached the water, moved in a grotesque imitation of life.

The body of Alexis Adams.

★

"...satisfying...the panoramic scope of the Cornish landscape...mesmerizes."

— *Chicago Sun-Times*

"...a welcome addition to the series."

— *Publishers Weekly*

TO PERISH IN PENZANCE

JEANNE M. DAMS

WORLDWIDE®

TORONTO • NEW YORK • LONDON
AMSTERDAM • PARIS • SYDNEY • HAMBURG
STOCKHOLM • ATHENS • TOKYO • MILAN
MADRID • WARSAW • BUDAPEST • AUCKLAND

TO PERISH IN PENZANCE

A Worldwide Mystery/November 2002

Published by arrangement with Walker Publishing Company, Inc.

ISBN 0-373-26438-0

Printed in U.S.A.

Author's Note

Since I have used typical Cornish names for many of the characters in this book, I must stress all the more strongly that the only character who remotely resembles any real person is Lord St. Levan. Mentioned in passing, he really is the head of the St. Aubyn family and suzerain of St. Michael's Mount.

The landscape, on the other hand, is as real as I can make it, and all the hotels, pubs, restaurants, and so on, really exist, though the antique shops are fictitious. Moreover, though I've barely scratched the surface in describing Cornwall's smuggling history, such details as I have given are accurate.

My version of the Mousehole legend is based on the charming book *The Mousehole Cat* by Antonia Barber, delightfully illustrated by Nicola Bayley.

ONE

SEPTEMBER IN ENGLAND can be quite a lovely time of the year. The roses pretend that June is only just past, the trees cling to their green summer drapery, the flower beds delight both eye and nose with their extravagant profusion. Days have grown a bit shorter, true, but twilight lingers long in sweet, gentle melancholy, and when night comes, the air is still soft.

On the other hand...

"If it rains for another five minutes, I am going to go stark, raving mad!" I threw my book on the couch beside me, startling Esmeralda, my British blue, out of my lap. She skittered over to the hearth rug where Samantha lay dozing and cuffed her on the ear. Samantha, who is half Siamese, uttered sounds indicating she was being killed (diva fashion, dying on a high E-flat) and joined battle.

"Ah," said Alan placidly, shifting in his easy chair and turning a page of the *Evening Standard*. "In that case, I'd best ring up the asylum and arrange for you to be admitted straightaway. The *Standard* says rain for the next four days at least."

"Alan, for pity's sake put down that paper and talk to me. Quite honestly, if I sit here any longer listening to that miserable rain, I'm going to lose my temper. Enough is enough, and a week of steady rain is far too much. I'm going stir-crazy."

"Anything you say, my love. What would you like to talk about?"

There are certain characteristics that even the best of men share with their less pleasant brothers. They won't ask directions, they can walk right past a mess without seeing it, much less cleaning it up, and they don't understand that talk needn't be *about* anything.

One must make allowances. I sighed and pointed to the *Standard*. "Isn't there anything interesting in the paper?"

"I haven't finished reading it," he said pointedly. "Nothing in particular has struck me thus far. Politics and scandal and crime—the mixture as before."

"Crime. Now, there's a subject that ought to pique your interest."

For Alan, before he retired, was a policeman, and an exalted one—chief constable for the county of Belleshire, in southeast England. The story of how I, Dorothy Martin, an American widow, came to live in Sherebury, Belleshire's principal town, and meet and marry the widowed Alan Nesbitt, is a long and absorbing one, at least to me. But since Alan and I both knew it, it wasn't good conversational material. Crime was much more promising.

"Not the sort of crime in tonight's paper." He slapped it in disgust. Sam instantly abandoned her mortal battle with Emmy and jumped on the nice rattly paper. Alan stroked her absentmindedly. "An old lady's handbag was stolen in Canterbury, actually in the cathedral, which I suppose is a piquant touch. Football louts are at it again in Liverpool. Some poor soul jumped off Tower Bridge. They think he'll survive, by the way, if he doesn't die from the germs he swallowed along with several pints of the Thames."

"No juicy murders?"

Alan moved his hand in a dismissive gesture; Sam attacked it. "Now, now, madam! Sheathe those claws, if you please. One murder in London. Domestic. A drunken brawl. Man who'd been beating his wife for years finally killed her. Disgusting, horrifying, but not what I'd call interesting."

"No." I shivered. Alan dumped Sam out of his lap and got up to put another log on the fire, but my cold was internal and not so easily warmed. "What a lot of pain there is in the world, Alan."

"Pain and evil. It isn't fashionable these days to talk of evil as a noun, an entity, but it exists. Lord knows I've seen enough of it in my time." He poked the fire expertly and then came to sit by me, draping one long arm across my shoulders. "We're very lucky, my dear."

I snuggled nearer to his comforting bulk. "We are, indeed. I can't even begin to imagine what you must have had to deal with in your career. We've never talked about it much."

"Most of it doesn't make good listening. A policeman's lot is not a fascinating one. Long stretches of boredom alternate with short stretches of horror. Neither aspect is dinner-table conversation. Speaking of which, are we going to eat at some time in the near future? You may not be hungry, but the cats and I could both do with some sustenance."

I heated up some stew while Alan fed our two little tyrants, and we settled down to a homely but satisfying meal in our warm, cozy kitchen. As we were polishing off the last of the apple crisp, I broached the subject again.

"Alan, I'd be interested in your stories—if you don't mind talking about them, of course. I know you loved your job. There must have been at least a few interesting cases in—what, forty years?"

"About that." He stirred his coffee, staring at the Aga. I knew he was seeing, not a stove, but a life.

"I joined the force in the late fifties." He sat back and tented his hands, fingertips pressing to fingertips. It was his narrative pose. I sipped my coffee and prepared to listen.

"I lived in Cornwall then. I've told you that, haven't I? My father was a fisherman. I was brought up in Newlyn, where fish and crabs are the main source of income, and I suppose the smell of fish is one of my earliest memories. My mother couldn't get it out of Dad's clothes, no matter how hard she tried.

"And she did try. She was an educated woman, taught music in the local primary school, and she wanted us and our house to be clean and neat. I was the only child, and she had ambitions for me, too. I think she wanted me to go to university, but I had no inclination toward the academic life, not then, anyway. I'd wanted to be a policeman always. I can't remember making the decision; it was simply what I knew I wanted.

"So as soon as I left school, I joined the force as a lowly constable in Penzance."

"Penzance? As in *Pirates of?*"

"The same. But whatever Gilbert and Sullivan may have made you think, pirates are actually much less important in Cornish history than smugglers. Smuggling is an old and honored tradition in Cornwall, though there's far less going on there now. The glory days for Cornish smugglers were back in the eighteenth and nineteenth centuries. Nowadays it's airports we have to watch, mostly for guns, drugs, uncut jewels from Holland, the odd piece of art—prosaic stuff. At any rate, I had nothing to do with smugglers. I walked a beat, tried shop doors to make sure they were locked, saw the occasional drunk safely home, directed lost American tourists, the lot. Not exciting, but I learned the town and the people like the back of my hand.

"Gradually I worked myself up the ladder. I was keen on my job and was promoted to sergeant rather early on, and then, when I showed a bit of aptitude for working out puzzling situations, to detective inspector. And after a couple of years—murders aren't two a penny in this country, you know, the way they are in America—in due time, I was given my first murder case. And I came a cropper."

I expressed suitable astonishment and waited for him to go on.

"In sixty-eight, it was. We were beginning to have our hands full about then with drugs problems. Cannabis was the most popular, and the hardest to trace and eradicate. Still is, for that matter. But LSD was growing to be a serious problem, and we worried more about it than the cannabis. So many young people—it was almost always young people—were having bad trips and getting into all sorts of trouble. A few were badly injured from jumping out of windows, thinking they could fly."

I nodded. "That happened back home, too, only one student died in Hillsburg. Well, a student *from* Hillsburg. He was visiting some friends in Chicago who lived in a high-rise apartment. They had a party on the seventeenth floor, and…" I spread my hands.

"That, more or less, is what happened in Penzance, late one evening in July 1968. Or at least what was thought to have happened. A girl of about twenty apparently jumped off a sea cliff onto the rocks far below. No one saw her jump, and her body wasn't found until several days later, but from the nature of the injuries it was easy enough to deduce what had happened.

"We were inclined at first to consider it a suicide, but

when the autopsy turned up large quantities of LSD, it looked like death by misadventure." Alan got up and made more coffee.

"Wait, I thought you said it was a murder."

"I'm still convinced it was, but we were never able to prove anything. In the end there was an open verdict. The case was never closed, so far as I know. I used to look it up now and then, throughout my career. Turn over what we knew, see if there was anything we'd missed. Never came up with a single lead."

"What made anyone think it was murder, then?"

"There were anomalies. For one thing, we never identified the girl. She wasn't local, that was certain. We circulated her description, of course, but we couldn't circulate a meaningful photograph."

I made a face. "Fish, I suppose, if the tides had gotten at the body."

"Fish, and crabs, and simply the abrasive action of water and rock. All in all, there wasn't much left of her face. We tried to match her up with all the missing-person reports, but nothing came of it. When we learned about the LSD, of course, the investigation slowed down."

"Yes, it would." I thought for a moment. "Why the delay in finding her body? I'd have thought she'd have been found right away. Isn't Penzance something of a seaside resort, with people all over the place?"

"Very much so, but she didn't go over actually in Penzance. I've misled you. The Penzance police dealt with the case because we were the nearest town of any size. She jumped, or fell, or was pushed at a place called Prussia Cove, about five or six miles east of Penzance. Fetched up in a smuggler's cave, rather a famous one used by a gang of brothers in the nineteenth century."

"Oh, so there must be a village or something there. At

the top of the cliffs, I mean. A place where the smugglers could take their booty.''

''Actually, no. A few farmhouses, widely scattered, and an abandoned hut. That's all. In fact, that's the main reason I was never satisfied about the case.''

He sat down, poured out fresh coffee, and tented his fingers again. ''The weather had been wet for a solid week when she was found. Everyone was upset about it; bad for the tourist trade. Anyway, the pathologist said she'd died probably four to five days earlier. Now why, I said to myself and anyone else who'd listen, why would a girl dressed for a party go clambering about on cliffs, miles from anywhere, on a wet night?''

''Oh, she was in party clothes? You didn't tell me that.''

''Well, they hardly looked festive when she was found, but one of her boots was still more or less intact, and it was white patent leather, calf-length. Enough of her skirt was left to show that it was a Mary Quant knockoff—remember Mary Quant?''

I nodded. ''Carnaby Street, miniskirts, all the girls wanting to look like Twiggy—all that.''

''This girl did in fact look like Twiggy. At least her figure did, or the lack of it. She might have weighed all of six and a half stone—that's ninety pounds or so to you Yanks—and that despite the fact that she'd borne a child, according to the autopsy, only three or four months before she died. I could never see the appeal in the starved look, myself, but a lot of chaps did. Her hair had probably been beautiful, long and blond and I suppose ironed straight before the sea snarled it. I remember she'd been wearing beads, a long strand of rather pretty, carved red ones, old-fashioned looking. They'd been strung by hand, and the string had broken, of course. The beads were scattered about the cave. Rather pathetic, that.''

''Poor child! All dressed up, and the only place she ended up going was over a cliff.''

''Yes, and how did she get there? That was the other thing. We could never trace where she'd come from or how she'd got to Prussia Cove. No car left behind, no bicycle. She couldn't have walked far in those boots; three-or four-inch heels they had. We were never able to turn up a taxi driver or anyone else who would admit to driving her out there.''

''No one saw her that night?''

''Well, remember we couldn't say for certain which night it happened. Too much time had passed by the time she was found, and the sea and the rocks had changed the body too much. The pathologist could narrow it down to only a two-to three-day span, and that made things much harder. Besides, asking at a seaside resort in the late sixties about a tall, slender blond in a miniskirt, white boots, and scarlet beads was like inquiring after a particular seagull. Everyone had seen someone who might have been our corpse, but no one could tell us anything useful.''

We sat in silence listening to the rain dripping dispiritedly from the stopped-up gutter. ''I applied for a transfer not long after that,'' Alan said finally. ''No one blamed me over the case. There was no blame going, actually. The whole thing was too nebulous for that, but I couldn't quite get the taste of what I considered a failure out of my mouth, and I wanted away. So I did a stint with the Metropolitan Police, then went for a command course at Bramshill, got one of their scholarships for university work—one thing led to another, and I ended up in Sherebury as chief constable.''

He finished his coffee and started clearing the table.

"I'll do the washing up, my dear, if you'll choose a video we might enjoy."

I chose one with lots of sunshine in it and lots of laughter, but as we sat and watched I brooded, and later, after Alan had drifted off to sleep, I lay awake and made plans.

TWO

I TACKLED MY HUSBAND the next morning, just as soon as he'd ingested enough caffeine to be reasonably alert.

"I have an idea," I announced brightly.

"Mmm?" He was deep in *The Times*.

"I'd like to get away for a little while. This weather's getting to me."

He put the paper down and looked at me consideringly. "I suppose the budget would run to a week or so in the south of France. No rain there this time of year. Or Spain might be cheaper."

I've lived in England for several years, but this notion of casually taking off for France still leaves me breathless. He was suggesting a trip no longer than, say, from southern Indiana to somewhere in Iowa, but Going to Europe sounded to me like a wild, exotic adventure. It also sounded appealing, but I stuck to my plan.

"I was thinking of somewhere much closer. Like, perhaps, Cornwall."

Alan's eyes narrowed.

"I've never been there, and I've always wanted to see Land's End up close. Frank and I used to see it from ships or airplanes, sometimes, that lonely spit of land with the lighthouse. It looked so romantic, one's first glimpse of England after an eternity of ocean, and it was always a welcome sight because it meant we were almost back in the place we loved.''

"Dorothy, you'd hate Land's End now. They've Disneyfied it, put up 'attractions.' It isn't a bit the way you imagine it.''

"Well, St. Ives, then. Who knows, we might meet a man with seven wives. Or Mousehole. I've been looking at the map, and I'd dearly love to visit a place called Mousehole.''

"It's pronounced Mowz'l, not mouse-hole, and it's about as big as our Cathedral Close.''

"Well, I didn't exactly expect Manhattan, did I, not with a name like Mousehole—or Mowz'l—and anyway, who cares? It sounds picturesque. And St. Michael's Mount is nearby, too, I've heard a lot about that, and—''

"Dorothy.''

I closed my mouth.

"What do you think you're up to?''

I tried to look innocent. "I'm tired of rain, and we were talking about Cornwall last night, so I looked up the weather in the paper this morning, and it isn't raining there, it's lovely and warm, and I just thought—''

This time he simply looked at me.

Then he sighed. Heavily. "My dear, I appreciate your concern, truly. Yes, I do still worry now and again about that old case. Yes, I do still wish I'd been able to solve it. But the thing happened over thirty years ago, love. There is nothing more to be done. Some things in life must simply be accepted, and I long ago accepted the fact that we will never know who that girl was, or what happened to her.''

I ought to have known better than to try to put anything over on Alan. The bells of the cathedral, ringing almost over our heads, reminded me that honesty is often the best policy. "All right. It's your call. But everything I said about Cornwall is true, you know. I have honestly wanted for years to visit the West Country, and I do honestly have a bad case of cabin fever. And the sun really is shining there, according to *The Times*. Besides, it was your home, and I'd like to see it."

He smiled. I love Alan's smile and the way his eyes crinkle up at the corners. He put a hand on mine. "Very well. As soon as we come home from church, I'll book us into a hotel you'll like in Penzance, if you'll talk to Jane about the cats. And if you can get leave from your job, of course. But we're going for a holiday. Right?"

"Right," I said solemnly, and if my fingers were crossed, it was only metaphorically.

After church I cornered Mrs. Williamson, my boss at the cathedral bookshop. "Willie, Alan and I would like to go away for a few days, two weeks at most. Do you think you could get along without me? We'd like to leave tomorrow. I'm sorry to give such short notice, but something came up rather suddenly." I was a little uncomfortable about asking. It's a volunteer job, and I put in only a few hours a week, but I do try to be reliable.

Willie was nice about it. "I think we can manage. Business has been a trifle slow. Nothing's wrong, I hope?"

I thought of the incessant rain, and then I thought about Alan's face when he talked about the old murder case. "Nothing serious. Thanks so much. I owe you one. Several, in fact."

"Oh, I shall collect, never fear!"

My next task was easy. Jane Langland, our crusty, lovable next-door neighbor, has often looked after our cats, though she's more of a dog person. When I knocked on her back door that afternoon, I was announced with assorted barks and snufflings from her tribe of bulldogs.

Jane's spent so many years with the breed she actually looks a good deal like them.

"Come in, Dorothy," she called. "I'm up to my elbows."

She was, almost literally. Her hands, sticky and floury, were in the pastry bowl, scraping a batch of bread dough onto the board to be kneaded. She took my request in stride, as I'd been sure she would.

"Always happy to oblige with the moggies, you know that. Where are you off to this time?"

"Penzance. I talked Alan into a little holiday where the sun's shining."

Jane snorted and gave the lump of dough a sharp jab with a powerful fist. "Don't know what's got into the weather. Ought to be fine, this time of year. My chrysanths have gone all scraggy in this rain, heads down in the mud, most of them. Time to cut them off and start again."

"If the rain stops long enough to get out. Jane, is there a way to look up old police records? I mean really old, from years ago?"

"Quarreled with Alan, have you?"

"Of course not! What a question."

"Why're you asking me, then? He'd be the one to know."

"I don't want to tell him what I'm doing. I'm trying to find out something about an old case of his, one that was never solved. I think he's worried about it, and I'd like to try to help."

Jane worked at her bread for a few seconds, every punch and thump an eloquent comment. "No curing you, is there?" she said eventually. "Have to poke your nose in. Suppose the murder or whatever it was happened in Penzance."

"Near there, over thirty years ago. Alan was talking about it last night. He says there's nothing to be done, and that he's accepted the fact, but he isn't happy about it, Jane. I'm not, either. It isn't just nosiness, though I admit to my share of curiosity."

Jane gave the bread dough another eloquent thump.

"All right, maybe more than my share, then. I know I tend to get mixed up in things that are none of my business, but it's because I believe in justice. The thought of someone getting by with a crime eats at me. It's not *right!*"

Jane gave the bread one last pat and covered it with a cloth. "Have you ever thought," she said deliberately, capturing my attention with a complete sentence, "that there are some stones better not turned over?"

"I—what do you mean?"

"If there's a criminal out there who's not been caught in thirty years, you could go stirring up more trouble than you dream of, lass, and not just for yourself."

I filed that sobering thought away as I went back home to pack.

WE GOT A LATE START Monday morning, drove slowly through blinding rain and snarled traffic, and put up for the night in Dorchester. It was as rainy there as in Sherebury; we didn't linger on Tuesday, but set straight out for the promised delights of Cornwall.

The promises were true. Penzance, when we arrived in late morning, was a miracle of hot sunshine, sparkling blue sea, and flowers in brilliant profusion. The tourists were taking full advantage of the weather, too. The Queens Hotel, an elegant Victorian hostelry just across the street from the beach and the promenade, was crowded with vacationers, many of them retired couples like ourselves. Alan had stretched the budget to indulge me, so we had a lovely room, luxuriously furnished with a four-poster bed and a bay window overlooking the busy street below and, just beyond it, the sea.

If his intent was to take my mind off old crimes, he succeeded. I looked out the window and was instantly enchanted.

"Oh, Alan, look! That has to be St. Michael's Mount. Way over there to the left, see?"

He joined me and peered. "Yes, indeed. It's quite near, you know. Two miles, two and a half, something like that. We could easily walk it this afternoon if you like. We'll want to take our sticks; it's rather a stiff pull up to the castle. How is it that you know St. Michael's Mount? Most Americans I've met have never heard of it."

"Frank and I had a friend who went there, years ago, and took pictures. One of them was published in the *Hillsburg Herald,* and somebody wrote in, very indignant, and said it ought to be called by its proper name, Mont St. Michel."

Alan laughed. "It does look very similar, of course. In fact, the house on it was originally a priory, founded by the Benedictines as a daughter house of the French abbey. So the mistake is understandable."

"Anyway, I've seen Mont St. Michel, and I can't wait to see this one. Let's go right after lunch."

We changed to more summery clothes and went down to the dining room ready for a meal of local crab or fish or lobster, all of which Alan assured me were excellent. Unfortunately, there wasn't a table to be had.

"I'm so sorry," said the headwaiter, sounding as if he actually was. "Everyone came down in a body, it seems. I'm afraid it might be rather a long wait."

An elderly woman and a much younger one had just

sat down at the table nearest the door. They looked at each other and nodded slightly. The older woman spoke.

"We'd be happy to share a table, if you'd like to join us."

"That's very kind of you," said Alan. "If you're sure it isn't a bother..."

"Not at all." The waiter pulled chairs out for us and we sat down.

We sat for a moment studying our menus in a sort of stifled elevator silence, everyone pretending that the others didn't exist, until I couldn't stand it any longer.

"Perhaps we should introduce ourselves, since we're all staying here at the hotel. That is, you *are* staying here?"

The woman and her—surely, granddaughter—nodded.

"Well, then, I'm Dorothy Martin, and this is my husband, Alan Nesbitt."

They took the different surnames in stride. "My name is Eleanor Crosby," said the older woman. "My daughter, Alexis."

I hoped my face didn't show the shock I felt. I'm nearer seventy than sixty, and I'd have sworn Mrs. Crosby was my age, or older. Her hair was completely white, her face scored with deep lines. The girl Alexis didn't seem much more than twenty, though her eyes were troubled. She was also quite beautiful, with a perfect oval face that was innocent of makeup and needed none. Her eyes were dark blue with long, thick lashes that were plainly real. Her honey-colored hair, worn in a simple French twist, was smooth and glossy, and her figure was perfect. She was, in short, one of those classic beauties, so familiar in type as to make one think one had met her before.

Mrs. Crosby, on the other hand, looked like a pleasant-enough woman, perhaps attractive before age had taken its toll, but she must have married an extraordinarily handsome man to have hatched a chick as stunningly lovely as Alexis.

However, one couldn't express such thoughts. I smiled brightly and made the usual small talk as we ate. Where are you from (London), how long are you staying (only for a few days), do you know the area (not well), et cetera, et cetera. They replied courteously, but with an air of constraint that made me wonder a little. They had, after all, invited us to sit with them. Why, if they didn't want to talk?

"My husband and I are planning to walk to St. Michael's Mount this afternoon," I said as the waiter took our plates away, "if we *can* walk after all that marvelous food. I must say you two were much more sensible." Actually, they had eaten almost nothing, and I wondered about that, too. Alexis, who had spent most of the meal drinking one bottle of water after another, might be considering her figure, but her mother was so slender as to be verging on gaunt.

None of your business, Dorothy, I reminded myself, as I frequently have to do. I continued. "If you've never been there, maybe you'd like to come with us?"

Mrs. Crosby smiled. "What a good idea, but not for me, I'm afraid. I plan to be very lazy and have a nap. A walk would be good for Lexa, though. What do you think, darling?"

"We'd really love to have you," I said hastily, as Alexis looked about to refuse.

"Thank you, but I believe I'll stay in, too. Perhaps another day. Shall we go up, Mum?"

Mrs. Crosby took her daughter's arm as they left the dining room and headed for the elevator. It seemed to me that Mrs. Crosby was leaning quite heavily on Alexis, and that they were both trying to hide it.

"Something odd there," I said to Alan when they were out of earshot. "Mrs. Crosby must be forty years older than her daughter if she's a day."

"The woman's ill," he said bluntly. "That was a wig she was wearing, did you notice?"

"No, I just thought she had beautiful hair. Oh, dear, you're right, though. She's so thin, and her face has that awful gray look to it. You don't think… ?"

"I do, I'm afraid. Let's hope she's come to the seaside to recover from the chemotherapy, and that it's done its job properly."

"Maybe that's why they're so quiet. They're worried about her health. But if they didn't want to talk, why did they invite us to their table?"

"Perhaps they were simply being courteous?"

"Well, there's that," I acknowledged. "But there's more going on there, Alan. I can feel it. It's almost as if there's some tension between them, though they're plainly fond of each other. I think maybe they asked us to sit down so they wouldn't have to talk to each other."

"Or perhaps you're imagining things, and they're quiet people. Not everyone can keep up your conversational pace, you know, my dear."

I stuck my tongue out at him and we went upstairs. I donned a sensible sort of hat, Alan got our walking sticks, and we set off for the tiny town of Marazion and the remarkable pinnacled island off its coast. We said little as we walked. I kept thinking about the Crosbys, and my own phrase of a few days before kept replaying in my mind, over and over again: "What a lot of pain there is in the world."

THREE

ENGLAND IS A SMALL country. One forgets that, living there, but how else does one explain the fact that Alan sees someone he knows nearly every place he goes? We met no one on our seaside walk to Marazion, but when we went out to the island of St. Michael's Mount itself (on foot, since the tide was at its lowest and the causeway therefore negotiable), the first person we encountered was one of Alan's old friends.

The tall, rather stout man who strode toward us as we climbed up the ramp from the causeway was sixtyish, silver haired, nice looking, and well dressed in a tweedy, English country gentleman sort of way. His figure reminded me of Sir Robert Morley, the old English actor, though he was much better looking than Morley. We exchanged impersonal nods, and then both Alan and the man stopped for a second look.

"I do beg your pardon, but surely—" said the man.

"Forgive me, but I believe—" said Alan at the same moment.

"It is—yes, Nesbitt, isn't it?" The man darted a glance at me, a question in his eyes.

"It is, and you must be Boleigh. Allow me to present my wife, Dorothy Martin. John Boleigh, my dear."

I shook the extended hand, noting with appreciation the instantly suppressed flicker of surprise in the man's eyes.

Obviously the man knew nothing of Alan's second marriage, possibly not even of his first wife's death, but torture would not have made him break the Code of the English Gentleman and ask a personal question. "How do you do, Mr. Boleigh," I said demurely. Let Alan deal with it.

Which he did, after sharing my amusement in a quickly exchanged glance. "I was a widower when Dorothy and I met a few years ago, and she a widow," he explained. "She kept her former name; it seemed simpler. And how is your family?"

"Ah, well, it's grown a bit since we last saw each other. Good Lord, it must be all of thirty years. The children are married, both of them, and one of the grandchildren, as well. Twenty-three, she is. I'll be a great-grandfather one of these days, I suppose. Makes you think, doesn't it?"

We all clucked a bit about how time speeds up as one grows older. Then we ran out of conversational matter, as one does on these occasions.

"Well, we don't want to keep you," I finally said with great originality. "We've just arrived on the island, and you seem to be leaving."

"Yes, I was in the neighborhood, so I nipped up to see Lord St. Levan for a moment."

I raised my eyebrows in question. Alan supplied the information. "St. Michael's Mount, though it's owned now by the National Trust, is the home of the St. Aubyn family, of whom Lord St. Levan is the head."

Well, of course that made everything perfectly clear. Sometime I'll get around to asking why the English nobility have so blasted many names that a conversation about them is like reading a Russian novel. I have a private suspicion it's done on purpose to confuse foreigners.

At the moment I simply nodded and tried to look intelligent while Mr. Boleigh went on talking.

"Yes, but look here, old man. I take it you're visiting hereabouts?"

"Not visiting, just a little holiday in Penzance. Dorothy seemed to think the weather would be an improvement on the steady rain we've been having back in Sherebury, and I must say she was quite right. We'll be staying for a few days, at least."

"Well, then, you must come to my party tomorrow. Short notice, but then I didn't know you would be here, did I? I simply won't take no for an answer. It's to be a musical evening. That's why I was here, actually, asking Lord St. Levan if there was anything in particular he'd like played. He and his lady wife have been gracious enough to say they will attend, and they are, of course, great music lovers. I seem to remember that you also enjoy music?"

"Very much, and it's a kind invitation, Boleigh, but neither of us brought evening dress with us."

"Of course you didn't, not for a holiday at the seaside. Don't give it a thought. We'll see you at about seven-thirty, then, shall we? A bit of a buffet and then some rather nice chamber music, I hope. You remember where I live?"

"I remember," Alan replied with a hint of a smile. "Seven-thirty tomorrow, then. Thanks so much, Boleigh. You'd best hurry, hadn't you—unless you want to take the boat back. The tide's coming in."

"Indeed, indeed." He waved and marched smartly down to the causeway, where little waves were beginning to lap against the outer edges.

"So," I said as Alan and I approached the ticket office,

"tell me about Mr. Boleigh. I have the feeling there's a story there."

"You're quite right. John Boleigh is what he'd probably call a self-made man. In fact, as I understand it, it was an inheritance from one of those proverbial rich uncles we all wish we had that started him on his present career of philanthropist and patron of the arts."

Alan purchased our tickets and we began the walk up to the castle. If you've ever seen pictures of Mont St. Michel, the famous island off the coast of Normandy, just shrink it down and you have St. Michael's Mount. The island was nearly pyramidal to begin with, and the priory built in the twelfth century put the point on the top. I don't know how the present St. Aubyn family get themselves to their home in that remodeled priory—I strongly suspect a hidden elevator somewhere in the mountainside—but tourists walk up, and a precipitous walk it is. There are stairs in places, carved out of the rock, but most of the way is a steep and somewhat rocky path. With arthritic knees that are unpredictable at best, I would never have made it without my stick and Alan's strong arm in the toughest stretches. I soon began to ration my breath, asking only short questions. Alan, who is in better shape, was able to reply in longer snatches.

"How do you know him?"

"He joined the Cornwall police two or three years before I left it. We never worked together, except in the most general sense. I outranked him by a good deal, you see. But it's a small force. Everyone knows everyone else. He was a good policeman, as I recall, nothing spectacular but a good, steady worker. I never had the feeling he was fond of the work, though, so I wasn't entirely surprised when he gave it up, having come into his money. That was—oh, I suppose about a month or two before I left Penzance.''

"You've stayed in touch?" I lost my balance and clutched at his arm.

"Careful! All right, love? Good. Steady as you go. No, I wouldn't say kept in touch, but one hears things from time to time. He's become quite a big bug in Penzance, has old Boleigh. Someone told me he'd given up his house and bought Bellevue. It's quite an impressive villa, up on the hill."

He waved vaguely back toward Penzance. "You'll see it tomorrow evening, of course. I've never been inside the place, but it probably lives up to its name. The view from the terrace ought to be rather fine."

"It sounds intimidating. And what was that remark about evening dress? You surely weren't talking about black tie?"

Alan groaned. "I'm afraid so. We do that sort of thing more often than Americans do, you know, and poor old Boleigh's a bit of a snob, I'm afraid. He's pleased as punch that Lord St. Levan's agreed to turn up, but that makes evening dress more or less de rigueur. I can't possibly organize a dress suit at short notice, but I suppose you'll want to do some shopping?"

"Well—I could use something new, at that." I stopped talking then and concentrated on keeping my footing while thinking about new clothes. It's true that the English, at least of our generation, are a good deal more formal in some ways than Americans, and I had worn my party clothes nearly to death. I wasn't sorry to have an excuse to replace them.

The last part of the climb to the castle really was a climb, with a bit of rock scrambling at the end. I was more than ever convinced that the resident family, St. Aubyn or St. Levan or whatever they called themselves, got in some other way, but I had to admit that the castle was worth the effort. The best part was the topmost terrace, which afforded a glorious view all around the island, truly an island now, the causeway shimmering faintly under a foot or so of seawater. Alan pointed out a white spot among the trees on one of the hills above Penzance.

"That's Bellevue, what you can see of it."

"Oh, dear. Just how big is it?"

Alan heard the trepidation in my voice and smiled at me. "Only a fair-sized house. Quite posh, but not a patch on Bramshill."

We had lived for a few months at Bramshill, an enormous manor house in Hampshire which now houses the police staff college. Alan served as interim commandant during part of the first year of our marriage. The idea of playing the "lady of the manor" role had terrified me at first, but I'd coped, almost enjoyed it, in fact. I still worried a bit, though, about my social skills as an American married to an Englishman, so I appreciated Alan's reassurance.

"Well, then, we can hold our noses just as high as they can. Oh, Alan, look at the sun sparkling on the waves! And the gulls riding the air currents—it's almost too beautiful!"

WE DINED AT a good pub in Marazion that evening and then, far too tired to walk, took a bus back to Penzance. Next morning when we went down to breakfast, Mrs. Crosby and Alexis were just leaving the dining room.

"Good morning," I said brightly, careful not to make any comments about what a beautiful day it was. Mrs. Crosby's face was pinched and her eyes shadowed, and Alexis had been crying.

She made a gallant effort, though. "Good morning, Mrs. Martin, Mr. Nesbitt." She gave us a smile that took my breath away, even forced as it was. "Did you enjoy your walk yesterday?"

"We did, though it wore us out. We were sorry you couldn't come, too." I hesitated a moment, then plunged ahead. This girl needed some cheering up. "Look, Alexis, I need to go shopping this morning, and shopping isn't really Alan's thing. If your mother doesn't need you, how would you like to come with me? It's no fun to shop alone." I didn't include Mrs. Crosby in the invitation. I didn't want to make her invent an excuse.

Alexis exchanged a glance with her mother. It was full of meaning, but a meaning I could not interpret fully. Partly it said *She knows,* or so I thought, but there was more than that, and I didn't know what. At any rate, Alexis didn't look happy. "Thank you, but I think my mother—"

"Now, Lexa, we're here on holiday." Mrs. Crosby spoke with some determination, though her voice was soft. "I will not have you dancing attendance on me. If I choose to sit by the fire like a pampered cat, that's my decision, but there's no reason for you to hang about. I shall be perfectly comfortable, darling, and you're entitled to a little treat."

Her look this time was one of clear command. Alexis closed her eyes for a moment and then smiled at me, a charming smile that didn't reach her eyes.

"Thank you, Mrs. Martin. I'd like to go shopping with you."

"Good." I spoke briskly, before she could change her mind. "The lobby in forty-five minutes? And you might ask one of the staff the best place for evening clothes."

"Evening clothes? In Penzance? Well, I'll ask. See you later, then."

She smiled that perfectly manufactured smile again, but as she turned away, her face fell into shadow.

FOUR

AN HOUR LATER we were walking down the oddly named Market Jew Street looking for dress shops. Lexa was carrying her ever-present bottle of water; I was burdened only with a large handbag. I stopped to look at my reflection in a shop window and adjust the tilt of my hat. It was a cheerful one, black straw decorated with cherries, and I was moderately pleased with my appearance until I caught a glimpse of Alexis's reflection next to mine.

I turned to her. "My dear girl, I must say I'm beginning to have second thoughts about shopping with you."

She looked puzzled.

"You have such a perfect figure. Whereas I—well, I enjoy my food a little too much. I admit I'm very much looking forward to a cream tea with real Cornish clotted cream, but it all has to go somewhere, doesn't it?" I patted my tummy ruefully. "You give me a complex. I should imagine you live on lettuce and air—and water, of course."

She laughed a little at that. "More or less. I've had to, really, for so many years it's second nature. Rabbit food, regular exercise, no drinking, no drugs—it's a bit of a bore, actually."

"Had to?"

"For my job, yes."

"I'm sorry, you've lost me."

She smiled. "Oh, yes, I forgot you didn't know. I'm a model. I have to look after myself properly or my income's gone. My professional name is Alexis Adams."

I smote my forehead. "Oh, goodness! That's why I've had the feeling we'd met. I don't read the fashion magazines anymore, but I must have seen your face on magazine covers at newsstands, and I've certainly heard your name. Heavens, you're right up on the top of the heap, aren't you? You must think I'm an idiot, not recognizing you."

"Actually, it's—this sounds terribly conceited and sort of world-weary—but it's rather refreshing. I was pleased when you didn't take any particular notice of me yesterday at the hotel. I don't care for being treated like a celebrity, at least when I'm not working. On a shoot, of course, it's part of the image."

I let it go at that, but I was still confused. Alexis Adams had been a top fashion model for years, in *Elle* and *Vogue* and the rest. This girl didn't seem more than twenty-two or -three. Had she begun as a precocious adolescent?

Whatever the case, she was famous. Shopping with her might be rather trying.

As it turned out, it was great fun. Either the salespeople didn't recognize Alexis in blue jeans and no makeup, or they had better manners than to say anything. She was, as I ought to have anticipated, an absolute expert where fashion was concerned, and knew immediately what would look good on me and what wouldn't. I tried on one outfit after another, many of them things I wouldn't have looked at twice, and loved them all. I finally bought the two most beautiful of all, stifling conscience pangs at the prices.

"You won't be sorry, Mrs. Martin," Alexis assured me with the confidence of one who knows what she's talking about. "They're excellent style and they suit you. And they're not extreme. You'll feel pretty in them for years."

"I'd better. My credit card is going into meltdown. But what about yourself? Didn't you see anything you liked? Or—how silly of me. I suppose you buy originals."

She laughed softly. "I wear them for a living, but I don't buy them. They're too far out for me. I did actually see one frock I rather liked, but I've no need for it here, and it would be a bore to pack."

"Show me!" I demanded, a plan beginning to stir in the back of my head.

She tried it on. It was a floor-length evening slip of burgundy satin, meant to skim the figure, touching it in all the right places. What made it spectacular was the black chiffon overdress that floated on top. Embroidered with a lush, black baroque border at bust and hem, it moved beautifully over the slip, creating beguiling patterns of light and shadow as it swirled.

It cost three hundred pounds, more than I've ever paid for a garment in my life, and quite possibly less than Alexis spent on her blue jeans. Never mind. On her it looked like a million dollars. Of course, on Alexis a flour sack would have looked like a million dollars.

"It's you," I said flatly. "Buy it."

"But it's silly. I don't need it."

"Yes, you do." I made up my mind. "Alan and I are going to a party tonight. We were invited at the very last minute, so it's plainly the sort of thing where it doesn't matter if a few extra people show up. Buy that dress and come with us."

"Oh, but I couldn't! Not without an invitation—and I don't know the people—"

"Neither do I. Neither does Alan, really. We ran into the host at St. Michael's Mount yesterday, and it turned out they're old cronies, but they haven't seen each other for thirty years. Oh, for charity's sake, Alexis, come.''

''For charity's sake?''

''Yes, in aid of me. If you come, there'll be one person, besides Alan, that I can talk to. Besides, Alan's put out because he doesn't have his tux with him, but if you come with us in that dress, nobody will give him a second glance. Or me, or anyone else in the room, for that matter.''

She grinned, not the famous model's smile I had seen earlier, but a genuine, mischievous grin. ''I haven't crashed a party since I was a teenager,'' she said, a dimple deepening in her left cheek.

''Oh, I'll call, for form's sake, and ask if we can bring you. No one will mind, I'm sure. It's not as much fun that way, I admit, but I try to behave myself, being a foreigner and all.''

''Are you Canadian? I wasn't sure—you haven't much of an accent—''

''American, but I've lived in Sherebury for several years. I suppose I've lost some of my native tongue.''

''I've been educated out of mine,'' she said, and there was a tinge of regret in her tone. ''I was born in South London. 'Sarf Lunnon,' I used to say. But a posh model is expected to sound posh, as well, so I learned to 'talk proper.'''

''Eliza Doolittle,'' I said. ''She had her problems, too. But Alexis—''

''Call me Lexa. Mum's the only one who does, nowadays, and I like it.''

''I was about to say, your mother has an Oxbridge accent, more or less.'' I was being nosy, I supposed, but Lexa had brought up the subject herself.

''She's my adoptive mother, actually, and she was my

Professor Higgins. She taught me to speak well, and to stand up straight, and—well, everything, really.''

Her voice shook a little and she turned her face away.

Should I offer sympathy over Mrs. Crosby's illness? I wanted to, but if Lexa didn't want to talk about it, and apparently she didn't, I wasn't going to trespass. I'd said too much already.

''Well, it's plain that you're the apple of her eye,'' I said cheerfully. ''Come on, have them wrap up that dress for you and then let's get back. I'm starving and it's time for your lettuce leaf.''

''Perhaps two,'' she said gamely, all trace of distress smoothed out of her voice. ''We've had a bit of exercise this morning.''

FIVE

THE PARTY WAS Old Home Week for Alan. All the world loves a lord, so everyone who was anyone in Penzance had turned up to mingle with Lord St. Levan and his wife. It was unfortunate that the lord and his lady had, at the last minute, found themselves unable to attend. Mr. Boleigh, upset about the defection of his prize guests, and trying not to show it, fell back on making a big fuss over Alan. What made it especially awkward for me was that most of the town remembered him and his late wife, and had never heard of me. Alan did his best to help me fit in, but I felt quite a lot like a third wheel, and Lexa, though she tried her best, wasn't actually much help.

For if Alan made a stir among the more mature guests, Lexa was the center of attention for the younger crowd from the moment we arrived, and no wonder. She had all the beauty and elegance of Grace Kelly and all the gamine charm of Leslie Caron, and every man in the room missed a heartbeat or two when she walked in. It being an English crowd, they were polite about it, at least at first. They followed Alexis's progress around the room only with their eyes as the three of us, champagne glasses in hand, trailed after our host.

John Boleigh introduced us first to his wife, Caroline, who remembered Alan, or pretended to, and then to all the other luminaries. The mayor, a tall man with slick black hair (probably dyed) and a hail-fellow-well-met air, was cordial. The rector of St. Martha's, much smaller and with the stoop and earnest manner of overworked clergymen everywhere, asked Alan if he was still a great music lover, and reminded him of the St. Martha's concert series. The string quartet had to delay their warm-up while the cellist asked Alan if he remembered him. The superintendent of the Penzance Constabulary, a youngish man with a ruddy face, shook Alan's hand warmly and said something about his retirement being a great loss to law enforcement. And so on. I smiled until my face hurt and tried to say the right things, but when Mr. Boleigh finally let us off our leashes and the buffet dinner was announced, I was glad to tug Alan to the serving line. Alexis, at that point, was captured by five of the youngest men in the room and borne off to a small table, where she sat with two of them while the other three went off to fetch food and get back as soon as they possibly could.

Mr. Boleigh's "bit of a buffet" was set out on long tables at the end of the ballroom. Gigantic ice sculptures reflected the hundreds of lightbulbs in the chandeliers. Huge silver trays of roast beef and shrimp and smoked salmon and cheese and fruit and dozens of dishes I couldn't name overwhelmed the senses.

"Bearing up, love?" Alan asked quietly.

"Just about," I replied. "I'll be better when I get some food in me. It's hot in here, and I drank too much champagne too fast."

"You're not finding much to eat," he said, observing my plate.

"I know. There's too much to choose from. After a while it stops being tempting. Like working in a chocolate factory."

"Have some Stilton, then. Cheese is good for counter-

acting alcohol. I'm sorry about the Old Boy reunion sort
of thing, by the way. I ought to have known.''

So he saw it the same way I did. That was comforting.
''It's all right. But were all these people really your dear-
est friends?''

''Heavens, I barely remember any of them except Ben
Clarey. The cellist,'' he amplified. ''He was only fourteen
or fifteen when I left Penzance, but already playing with
the local quartet and making a name for himself as something of a child prodigy. Now he's with this London
group. If the other three are as good as he is, we've a
treat in store.

''The rest, well, they simply think I'm a local boy made
good, and they're basking in a reflected glory which is
purely imaginary, I assure you.''

''The superintendent was very complimentary.''

''He's a nice chap,'' Alan admitted. ''From a police
family. His grandfather was the super here when I first
joined the force, and when the old man retired, the job
passed on to his son. Now young Colin holds the reins,
and I suspect he'll make as good a job of it as his father
and grandfather did before him. I beg your pardon, but
are these seats taken?''

The last was addressed to the others at the nearest table.
They shook their heads and smiled, and then one of the
women took a closer look at Alan as we sat down. ''I
don't imagine you'll remember me, Mr. Nesbitt, but—''
And he was off again, trying to keep afloat on a tide of
reminiscences, many of which might have existed only in
the mind of the teller.

That was when Lexa drifted away from her tableful of
admirers, pulled up a chair next to me, and sat down with
her glass and plate. The men at our table, including Alan,
leapt to their feet at her arrival. Most of them were

roughly our age and would probably have stood up for any woman, English manners being what they are, but I doubted they would have moved quite as fast for anyone but the ravishing Lexa.

She distributed dazzling smiles all around and then devoted her attention to me. "I thought you looked stranded," she murmured.

"I felt that way. But weren't you having a good time?"

She shrugged delicately. "I suppose. Men are all alike, aren't they?"

"No," I said.

"Oh, well…" She glanced at Alan, who was once more submerged in conversation, and made a face. "Perhaps not all." She picked up a fork and toyed with her food.

"Cheer up. You're too young to be cynical about life."

"What would you like to wager on that?" She turned to her champagne glass, which was filled with something that looked like her usual water, sparkling this time. Her mood had changed; she was suddenly withdrawn. I looked at her averted face and applied myself to my plate.

With one silent companion and one all too busy with other people, I had no recourse but eavesdropping, which is, I confess, one of my favorite entertainments. You can sometimes hear amazing things, especially in a place where there's enough noise that everyone has to shout, and where most people have a little alcohol in their systems.

This evening the noise level was almost too high. I could hear little that made sense except the conversation immediately behind me, a diatribe delivered by the rector of St. Martha's to the police superintendent—I couldn't remember their names—about the escalating drug problem in Penzance.

"It's these raves!" shouted the rector. "As if the parties weren't bad enough with that frightful noise they call music, there's this dreadful ecstasy taking over the minds and bodies of our young folk. It's a scourge, and it's got to be stopped.''

I was briefly startled until I remembered that ecstasy was the street name for a drug popular among teenagers, especially at the all-night dance parties called raves. I didn't know much about any of it, except I'd heard that ecstasy could be dangerous. Had some kids died of it, or was I imagining that part?

"It's the clubs," said the superintendent patiently. "If we could shut them down, we'd be streets ahead of the game, but they move from place to place, and even when we find them it's not easy to get proof of illegal activity."

"Hmph! Shouldn't think you'd have trouble finding them, the amount of noise they make."

"We can't be everywhere. If no one complains about the noise, we may never know. Then, too, our young people haven't much to do here in Penzance. We'd have more juvenile crime if we took away their music and dancing. It's a knotty problem."

"It always was," Alan murmured, as much to himself as to me. He had freed himself for a moment from conversation with our table partners. "The drugs change with time, the kids involved change. The problems don't. One is amazed at how people forget."

I knew he was thinking about his old case and tried to give him a comforting smile, but he wasn't looking at me. His eyes were on his plate, but he was, I thought, seeing the body of a young woman in a cave.

"You're right," said Lexa unexpectedly. Her voice was low, but intense. "About drugs, I mean. They destroy people. I know. I could tell you—'' She broke off and bit her lip just as Mr. Boleigh appeared at my elbow.

"Do help yourselves to more food if you'd like, but the musicians are ready to begin. I hope you're having a pleasant evening, Miss Adams?"

Lexa murmured something appropriate and smiled her practiced smile, but I went on worrying over her remarks about drugs.

Could we be wrong about her mother? Could she be an addict? The thought flashed through my mind, followed by another even more horrific. Not Lexa herself?

I glanced at her and immediately dismissed the thought. No. That perfect skin, those clear eyes—those spoke of health, of youth uncorrupted by poison. She looked tired just now, and worried, but she was no addict, not even a moderate drug user. She had said she took no drugs, and I was prepared to believe her.

Well, *could* she have been thinking about her mother?

I couldn't ask. She had moved away from me. Oh, she was still sitting there at the table, her chair crowded close in to mine, but Lexa herself was somewhere else, even as Alan was.

I moved my hand over to Alan's. I needed to know that he was there, warm and alive and with me, even if his mind was remote.

THE EVENING DRAGGED to its conclusion. The musicians were excellent, but string quartets are not my favorite entertainment, I confess. I've always preferred brass. Alan, who is something of a musical snob, tells me my taste is low, but given a choice between Schubert and Sousa, I'll choose the marches anytime.

Of course, I didn't say so to Mr. Boleigh when we were saying good night. I mouthed polite insincerities, certain that he was paying no attention, anyway. His eyes were on Lexa, for which I couldn't say I blamed him.

"You sounded," said my loving spouse when the three of us were tucked into our car, "exactly like a little girl at a birthday party. 'Thank-you-very-much-I-had-a-lovely-time.'"

"I was well brought up," I said, and yawned. Lexa said nothing.

A dispirited drizzle began before we reached our hotel.

I HAD WANTED, next day, to go to Mousehole, but the good weather had deserted us. We woke to pouring rain, with a fierce wind that blew the rain into horizontal sheets and raised monumental waves. We sat sipping coffee at a window table in the dining room and watched the high tide crashing over the seawall.

"So much for getting away from the weather."

"It's the hurricane," said Alan, turning a page of his newspaper.

"A *hurricane?*" My voice rose to a squeak and I pushed back my chair. "Alan, if a hurricane's coming, what are we doing here? Hadn't we better go somewhere inland?"

"Not our hurricane, love." He tapped the newspaper. "The backlash of South Carolina's. American coastal weather usually reaches Penzance a few days later. Gail, I believe this one is named. Appropriate."

"Oh." I collected myself and poured some more coffee. "So when is this particular gale going to blow itself out?"

"Late tonight, probably. We'll plan on Mousehole tomorrow, shall we?"

"It isn't much fun walking around in the rain," I said doubtfully.

"It won't be raining. I can virtually guarantee it, and not just because *The Times* says so. Don't forget, I spent a fair part of my life in Cornwall. I know how these things behave."

"Of course you do. Sorry. Alan, should we ask Lexa to go to Mousehole with us, or do you think she's tired of our company? She didn't have a good time last night."

He shook his head. "No, but I don't think that had anything to do with us. There's something wrong with that girl, more than simply her mother's illness. I can't put my finger on it."

"I had an awful thought last night." I lowered my voice. "You don't think her mother has a problem with drugs, do you?"

"Only legal ones. They're certainly bad enough, the chemotherapy drugs, nearly worse than the disease, but they don't make a person look the way cocaine does, or heroin, or any of the street drugs."

He looked bleak, and I was sorry I'd raised the subject. "Well, you'd know. I think I'll try to get Mrs. Crosby talking today, since we'll all have to stay in the hotel. Maybe I can find out what's wrong with both of them. Now, don't look at me that way. It isn't prying! I'm concerned."

"I know you are, love, but be careful how you go. They're friendly enough, those two, but they value their privacy, all the same."

"I'll try not to go stomping in with both feet, then." I looked out the window. The storm was getting worse. "But it's a long day ahead, and everyone will be bored. If I can't get her to talk at all, I'm losing my touch."

As it turned out, I didn't get the chance. I saw neither Lexa nor her mother all day. And by the next day it was too late.

SIX

THE RAIN ABATED gradually as the day passed, but the wind and waves increased. Alan and I sat in the sun lounge (woefully misnamed on such a day) and watched the violent motion of the sea and the clouds. Hoping to find Mrs. Crosby or Alexis, I made forays from time to time into the other lounge, the lobby, and the bar. After a listless lunch at which neither woman appeared, I went upstairs to read and fell asleep over my book, waking in midafternoon in a panic lest I had missed the Crosbys. Alan assured me he had seen nothing of them.

By dinnertime I was heartily sick of the hotel and wanted a change.

"There must be a decent restaurant somewhere nearby," I suggested. "Let's go out to eat. I'm going to scream if I have to stay indoors one more minute."

"Dear me," said Alan calmly. "Can't have that, can we? There's a nice little tandoori 'round the corner, or there used to be an Italian cafe on the promenade, just down the street from here."

"Italian," I decreed. "We'll be able to see the waves from there, and I like to watch them. Just not from the hotel."

"I'll go up and get our coats."

"And umbrellas, in case the rain starts again!" I called after him.

He returned sans umbrellas.

"My dear," he said at my reproachful look, "can't you see the wind! They'd be torn inside out and snatched from our hands the moment we set foot outside the door."

"No, I can't see the wind, and neither can you. Shades of Christina Rosetti! 'Who has seen the wind? Neither you nor I.' Et cetera. But I take your point." It was reinforced the minute we stepped outside. I had to hold on to my hat with both hands, and we were pushed along so briskly I was almost running when we got to the restaurant.

Inside it was warm, cheerful with red-checked tablecloths, and pleasantly redolent of garlic and herbs, but not very busy. The storm was discouraging patrons, I surmised. We sat at the bay-window table, ordered Chianti and food, and sipped our wine, watching the tempestuous sea just across the street.

The waves seemed higher than ever. As they battered the seawall, foam leapt up, spraying the promenade just this side of the wall and even, sometimes, the cars parked along the curb. Small groups of children ran along the promenade, deliberately trying to catch the spray. When a wave broke over the wall and spray drenched them, they would duck, scream, and run a little farther to do it again.

The waitress brought us our dinners. "They look like they're having a wonderful time," I commented with a nod out the window.

She smiled. "I used to do the same thing when I was a kid. I'd get dripping wet and my mum would have a fit, but I had fun. Enjoy your meal."

"Not such fun for the owners of the cars," Alan remarked as he started on his veal parmigiana. "Salt water's death to the coachwork, not to mention what it'll do if it finds its way under the bonnet." He gazed out the window, shaking his head.

"Don't tell me about salt damage to cars," I said. "They use it on the roads back home when it snows, and—"

"Dorothy!"

There was a very odd note in Alan's voice. Urgency, even fear. I caught my breath and reached my hand out to his. "What? What's the matter?"

"No, it's nothing," he said. "That girl—I thought—but I'm only seeing things."

"What girl, where?"

He pointed. "Just passing the window now—no, she's out of sight."

"For you, not for me." I craned my neck, looking over Alan's shoulder at the figure just disappearing around the corner. All I could really see was a pair of dark, high-heeled boots, a short, dark skirt, and a swirl of blond hair tossing madly in the wind. "What about her? You sounded so—I don't know. I thought something was wrong with you."

"Sorry, love. It's just—well, I'm seeing things, as I said. The wind, the waves—I've not seen a storm like this since I left Penzance thirty years ago. I suppose my mind was wandering, but I saw that girl walk down the street toward me, and just for a moment—" He waved his hand. "Never mind. Stupid of me."

Boots. Miniskirt. Long blond hair. "It reminded you of that girl. The one in the cave."

"It was in a storm something like this that she went over the cliff, that's all. I'm going 'round the bend in my dotage."

"Dotage, hah!" I picked up my fork again and attacked my lasagne. "Funny, she reminded me a little of Lexa. Though I can't imagine Lexa in an outfit like that. She dresses more conservatively."

"What I can't imagine is where Lexa would be going on a night like this, all by herself. One would think she'd stay in and eat her dinner with her mother at the hotel."

"We came out."

"Together. It makes a difference."

"I only got a glimpse, and from the back, at that. It was probably someone else. Forget it. Do you suppose there's any tiramisu? I'm still hungry."

I ate my dessert, and we both had some espresso, and then we walked back to the hotel. The wind was in our faces going back, sweeping up from the coast of South Carolina over thousands of miles of cold Atlantic, and the rain had begun again. I'm not a lightweight, and Alan is a tall, solid man, but we were nearly blown backward. By the time we'd covered the two blocks to the hotel, I was exhausted from the chill and from fighting the wind, and we were both soaked to the skin. We went straight to our room. I took a hot bath and then climbed into the inviting four-poster bed. Alan stopped reading his book and put out the light.

He was snoring softly in a few minutes, but I couldn't seem to sleep. The wind and rain battered the windows, howling through the chinks and rattling a loose pane. Wind has always frightened me, and even Alan's comforting presence couldn't quite still my vague fears. Or maybe it was the espresso. I kept seeing that girl, her hair blowing wildly, her short skirt and tall boots, going through the storm to—where?

When I slept I dreamed of her, wishing I could see her face, but it was always hidden from me.

ALAN, HAVING SLEPT soundly, awakened early. He lay quietly in bed, but he woke me by his very wakefulness. I turned over and buried my head in the pillow, but it was no use. Morning was definitely upon us. "If you love me," I muttered, yawning, "make me a cup of tea."

Once my eyes were properly open, I could see it was a beautiful day, and I began to scheme. We ate breakfast in a dining room that was nearly deserted, the hour being so early, and as we were finishing I made my suggestion to Alan.

"I've been thinking," I said as he sipped his second cup of coffee. "Would this be a good day to go exploring those smugglers' caves you've been telling me about? It all sounds very romantic, and very unlike anything one would find in America."

He smiled. "Oh, I'm sure there's something similar in America, if one knows where to look. England never had a monopoly in smugglers. Most of them were, and are, your run-of-the-mill criminals, nothing romantic about them. But there was a certain bravado about some of the Cornish ones, I suppose, and once a criminal passes into legend, the more grisly aspects of his career are often forgotten.

"Yes, we'll go and see some of the caves, if you like. You'd best dress warmly. I know the sun's shining, but the wind's still fierce and the seas are still high. You're apt to get wet, clambering about over rocks. And don't forget your sunscreen."

I was not to be deterred by all the recommended precautions. If Alan was seeing dead girls walking down the street, there were ghosts to be exorcised. I had no intention of allowing my husband to go on stewing about a crime long past. If, as I hoped, an expedition to the caves would give him a chance to open that murky corner of his mind and spirit and let daylight in, I'd clamber till I dropped. I pulled my only pair of blue jeans out of the drawer, added a sturdy shirt, a lightweight, waterproof jacket, and a pair of clunky running shoes. With a pull-on denim hat, I was ready to go.

"We might as well do the most famous ones first," said Alan when we got to the car. "The three little inlets that make up Prussia Cove."

Where the dead girl was found, I remembered. I didn't mention it. "Oh, yes, you talked about some brothers who plied their trade there."

"A trade it was, too. Almost, by the standards of the day, an honorable one. The brothers were the Carters, three of them: Harry, John, and Charles. It was John, in fact, who named the place Prussia Cove and called himself the king of Prussia."

Alan negotiated a tight curve. "He *was* something of a king, I suppose, or he and his brothers were, between them. They were born somewhere around the mid-seventeen hundreds, and by the 1770s they were famous throughout Cornwall. Not only as smugglers, mind you. They were staunch Methodists, and Harry, the leader of the bunch, had quite a name as a fiery preacher. He wouldn't let his crew swear, I seem to remember from the old stories. Oh, and once when one of their shipments was seized and locked up in the customs house, John organized a raid and got it back. There were other goods in there as well, but John wouldn't let his men touch them. He didn't consider that honest."

I giggled. "I suppose even the devil has a conscience."

"Oh, the Carters weren't devils. They provided a service, according to their lights. I must say they had something of a point. The duties on tobacco, brandy, sugar, and tea were iniquitous, often running to several hundred percent. Men like the Carters reckoned that if they could buy a pound of tea for two shillings in France and sell it in Cornwall for five, they made a reasonable profit for their trouble and risk and at the same time acted as public benefactors, because the duty alone ran something like six shillings.''

"Yes, I see. All the same…''

"Yes, all the same, it was a dangerous game, and not only for the smugglers who died when ships were wrecked on the rocks or revenue officers put a musket ball through their heads. Society in general suffered, because widespread defiance of even a bad law leads to disrespect for law in general. Eventually, 'round about 1850, parliament saw the wisdom of that argument and reduced the duties to reasonable levels, which took away the smugglers' profits and put them out of business. Amazing, really, how long it took the government to grasp the fact that collecting a small duty all the time would net them more income than never collecting a large one. Not to mention paying good money to customs agents into the bargain.''

"Well, it's a good, full-blooded story, anyway. I can just see them, sailing into the cove on a moonlit night—''

My loving husband snorted. "Not if they knew what they were about, they didn't. You're thinking of those romantic old pictures. Sensible smugglers landed when there was no moon, and preferably clouds to veil even the starlight. And in most of Mount's Bay, *this* was the coastline they had to contend with on those pitch-dark nights.''

We were driving along the top of a cliff, the sea visible from time to time through trees and brush. Alan pulled the car into a turnout, a place where there was a break in the undergrowth, and stopped. "Get out and take a look at Piskie's Cove, the first inlet of Prussia Cove.''

"I thought you said it was Mount's Bay.''

"That's the whole area, Porthgwarra or so right 'round to The Lizard."

"Oh."

"Never mind. I'll show you a map later. Just look."

I stepped out into the wind, moved close to the edge of the cliff, and gasped.

The sea was far below me, but its noise was loud, even up here. Waves rolled in and broke on the rocks in ceaseless tumult. The rocks were sharp and cruel, tossed down as though to lay a trap for an unwary sailor. Landing a sailing craft there would be the act of a madman in broad daylight, let alone on a moonless night.

"Alan, how did any of them survive? It looks impossible."

"We'll drive a little farther, to Bessie's Cove where we can park, and I'll show you."

Bessie's Cove turned out to be a rough half-moon carved out of the cliff by centuries of wind and water. At the top of the cliff was a lovely green meadow that afforded a tiny parking place. A farmhouse or two stood far back from the cliff, and near its edge there was a small, deserted stone building that might at one time have been a shepherd's hut.

Down below there was a broad, fairly flat, rocky shelf sloping up gradually from the water's edge. After fifty feet or so, though, the shelf met the body of the cliff and rose almost straight up in a series of uneven ridges.

The rocks were nearly black and must have been very hard, for they didn't seem to be very much weathered. They had broken off here and there and left boulders at the edge of the sea. Basalt, perhaps, I thought, for the edges looked sharp.

"Well, it's bigger than Piskie's Cove, but it looks just as dangerous to me."

"Let's go down," said Alan. "There's a path that's not too bad, but I'll go first. Give you something soft to land on."

"I hope it won't come to that," I said, gritting my teeth and grasping my walking stick so tightly my knuckles were white. With my unreliable knees, going down is always much worse than going up. Ah, well, if I had to do any slithering, at least my jeans were tough.

Alan paused about halfway down to give me a chance to catch my breath. When I had, I pointed. "Alan, what are those grooves in the rock? On the flat part, see? They look for all the world as though railroad tracks had been there and been taken up at some point."

"You've got the track part right. Those were made at least two hundred years ago by the wheels of the smugglers' carts. They didn't sail their cutters right up to the rocks, of course. You were right about that; it would have been impossible. They anchored as close in as they dared and then took the cargo off in small boats, or, in the case of rum, floated the casks right in to shore. Once they got the cargo to the rocks, they loaded it into carts and trundled it to the caves, where they'd store it until it could be taken up the cliff."

"Good heavens." I sat on a convenient rock and looked, and listened. The hypnotic clamor of the waves, the cry of the gulls, the smell of salt water and seaweed. A sky so blue it looked like a touched-up photograph, bright sunshine warming the rocks. Such a peaceful scene, but this place had been the site of dangerous, desperate activity, night after moonless night, for enough years to wear permanent tracks in the rock, tracks that another two centuries of high tides had not yet worn away.

"Are you game to go on down to the caves? The tide's

coming in, but I should think we've a bit of time before the footing gets sloshy.''

"Sure. I came to see everything, and I'd better do it now, because I guarantee you'll never get me down this path again. I may not be able to go inside the cave, though, or not very far. It depends on how big it is. I managed Fingal's Cave all right, but little ones..."

He nodded. He knew about my unfortunate quirk. I'd had to explain to him once, when we'd visited a wonderful castle, why I couldn't see the dungeons or climb the narrow, winding, enclosed staircase to the roof.

"I hate it. It's stupid and irrational and it keeps me from doing a lot of things I want to do, but a phobia's a phobia, and I've been told there's very little, short of hypnotism, to be done about claustrophobia.''

So I followed Alan down with some trepidation. I was eager for him to revisit the cave, but I personally wanted nothing to do with it.

The path soon reached the flattened rock shelf. The footing was uneven and slippery, but my stick helped a good deal, and Alan's arm was useful more than once. Still, I was panting again, and not entirely from exertion, when we rounded one last point and stood just inside the entrance of the biggest cave.

I blinked, trying to accustom my eyes to the gloom. There was something at the back of the cave. I thought at first it was a large bunch of seaweed, carried by the tide to the back of the cave.

Alan's stillness told me, just a second before my own senses did.

"Don't move, Dorothy. Don't go any closer."

I waited there, hardly breathing, while he went to investigate. He touched nothing, looking carefully before he put a foot down on the rocky floor. When he had seen what he had to, he came back to me.

He looked sick as he took my arm and led me to a big rock just outside the cave. He made me sit, and he watched me for a little while before he said anything.

"Can you bear to stay here, do you think, or is the cave too troublesome? We must get help, and the mobile's in the car. I can climb the rocks faster than you can."

"I'm fine. The cave doesn't bother me as long as I'm not actually in it. The sooner you go, the sooner you'll be back."

He looked hard at me and pressed his lips together, then turned and loped off across the rocks.

I stared resolutely out to sea and tried not to think about the body in the cave. The body lying casually on its back, wearing calf-high boots and a miniskirt, the body whose long, honey-blond hair spread out in a little pool of sea-water and moved as the wind reached the water, moved in a grotesque imitation of life.

The body of Alexis Adams.

SEVEN

IT SEEMED A LONG TIME before Alan came back down. I sat on my rock, shivering a little in the chill wind from the sea, but grateful all the same that Alan had remembered about sunscreen. I burn very easily, and skin cancer is not high on my list of Things I Want to Experience. I tried not to move much. We'd already compromised the crime scene, if crime scene it was, simply by being there. I didn't want to add any more extraneous evidence, or ruin any that might be there.

Not that there was likely to be much. The floor of the cave was solid rock, no good for footprints, and anyway, a line of seaweed many yards up the rocky beach showed how far the last high tide had reached. The floor of the cave, the rock where I sat so restlessly, the cart tracks—all would have been covered by two or three feet of water at high tide.

Would it have reached the back of the cave?

No, I wouldn't let myself think about that. I would think about waves, hypnotic waves rolling in, creaming over the rocks, retreating, rolling in…the ageless rhythm of the sea.

The gulls cried, screaming harshly, swooping, fighting over choice tidbits of something on the rocks.

Dear heaven! Were gulls scavengers?

In a panic, I stood and ran at them with a shooing motion. Those birds mustn't get into the cave!

They wheeled away, jeering. I stood and took deep breaths, trying to stop shaking, trying not to be sick.

Alan had looked sick when he left the cave, caught up in his own personal nightmare. This body, so like the other, in the same cave…this couldn't be real, it couldn't be happening. I was in the nightmare, too. I'd wake soon.

But I wouldn't, and neither would Alan.

I went back and sat on my rock, staring this time at nothing. I was very much afraid Alan was going to worry himself to a frazzle over this, fretting all the more because he could play no active role in the investigation of this crime. He'd blame himself for not solving the first murder, all those years ago. He'd wonder if this death was related, and he'd turn everything over in his mind, trying to force from his memory some tiny fact that would help. He'd feel old and ineffectual and useless.

Well, I wouldn't let that happen! I slapped my hand on my knee. "I will not have it!" My shout startled a gull that had once more ventured too close. It flapped away with a scream that, in turn, startled me.

Where *was* Alan? I looked at my watch, but since I had no idea when he'd left, the time shown on the dial told me nothing. I felt as though he'd been gone an hour, but common sense told me that probably no more than fifteen minutes or so had elapsed. We'd taken—what?—about ten to come down from the head of the path, but we'd moved slowly on my account. Alan would have gone up faster, but then he had to get to the car, make the phone call, wait for the police to arrive, and escort them down.

Another twenty minutes, then, at a bare minimum. For the first time in my life I wished I were a smoker. A cigarette would at least give me something to do, and maybe a nicotine hit would keep me from thinking too much?

I had never smoked. That dubious comfort was denied me. I sat and watched the waves.

The tide was coming in.

Fast.

I stood, in an instant panic again. What did I know about tides?

Precious little. I'd spent my first sixty-odd years living in southern Indiana, many hundreds of miles from the nearest ocean. I had a vague idea that there were two high tides a day and two low tides, but that they were not at exact six-hour intervals; that's why seaside places issued tide tables. The figure of half an hour stuck in my mind. Was it six and a half hours from high tide to low, more or less? Or twelve and a half from one high tide to the next? Or did the variation work the other way? Could I somehow work it out from when low tide was three days ago, at Marazion?

Well, no, I couldn't. I was too ignorant. All I knew for certain was that each powerful wave that swept into the cove came up a little higher than the one before. Where Alan and I had walked dry shod to the cave, wavelets now lapped. Water licked at the base of what I had come to think of as "my" rock. As I watched in horror, an especially large wave rolled into the cave, going back a few inches before retreating.

It couldn't—it mustn't—

I took deep breaths again. *Think,* Dorothy!

I could do nothing about the tide. King Canute couldn't stop it, and neither could I. Nor could I blunder into the cave to try to rescue Alexis, and not only because of my ridiculous phobia. Much as I was sickened by the idea of the water reaching her, I tried to be reasonable. The sea couldn't harm her now, and if it destroyed evidence, well, that was a serious matter, but I would certainly mess things up much worse if I tried to move her. When someone has died, the very first rule of investigation, as I knew from the hundreds of mysteries I'd read, was "Don't move the body."

Mysteries. A thought was swimming to the surface, struggling for attention. Don't force it. Think about something else. I closed my eyes and concentrated on my breathing, recited the multiplication tables, tried to remember state capitals...

Have His Carcase, that was it. Dorothy L. Sayers. The body on the big rock, on the remote beach. Harriet Vane found it and then worried because the rising tide might wash the body away before she could get to a telephone and summon the police.

So she took pictures.

I reached in the pocket of my jacket. Yes, it was still there. Only a throwaway camera, but it had a flash. Considerably better than the thirties model Harriet had had at her disposal.

Clutching my stick and gritting my teeth, I splashed through the water, much deeper now, and entered the cave.

How far in would I have to go? How far in could I force myself to go?

There's no danger, I told myself. The tide will never rise anywhere near the roof of the cave. You won't drown. There is no reason whatever to be afraid.

I was sweating profusely, and I couldn't seem to get enough air in my lungs.

You are a photographer, a technician. You have no emotions. You are a recording device. I repeated the phrases over and over in my mind like a mantra as I pointed and shot, pointed and shot, working almost blind in the dimness. The body first, from as close as I could make myself go. Then the cave, pointing the camera in all directions. The rocky, rapidly disappearing floor. The walls. The area behind the body—I wouldn't think of it as Alexis—from two different angles.

When I had run out of film, I secured the camera in the breast pocket of my shirt. It made an odd bulge, but it would be safe and dry there, with the jacket zipped shut. Then I waded out of the cave, staggering as a wave reached nearly to my knees and tried to knock me off my feet.

Once I was out on the rocks I sought a secluded corner, far enough up the shore to be out of the water at the moment, but close enough to the sea that the tide would reach it soon. Having found an appropriate spot, I was able to relax and let myself lose my breakfast.

I stood taking deep breaths of the lovely, cool air that surrounded me and looking at the vast sea, the ocean that stretched out without an enclosed space between here and France, or so I supposed. I couldn't seem to stop shaking. It wasn't the body, I thought as I wiped my mouth. That wasn't so very awful, if I could forget for a while that it was someone I had known and liked. No blood or other obvious horrors. And the cave was actually just a cleft in the rock, not really a cave, not a deep, dark cavern with the earth pressing down on one's head…

My body discovered that there was a little more in my stomach, and purged itself anew.

When it was all over, I had to rinse my mouth with sea-water. It tasted terrible, and the salt burned my lips and cheeks, but it was better than the other taste. Then I found a higher rock and sat to wait for my husband.

HE CAME ABOUT ten minutes later, accompanied by the scene-of-crime officers, several men in uniform and plain clothes and two in wet suits. He showed them the cave and then hurried back to me.

"All right, love?"

"I was sick," I said. "Over there. I thought maybe I should tell you, so if they find it, they'll know it was me."

He sat and reached an arm around my shoulders. "I'm sorry. I was afraid you'd be upset."

I leaned against his arm. "My dear man, sometimes you are so very English! Of course I'm upset about Lexa, but that's not what made me sick. I had to go back into the cave."

I explained about the tide and the pictures. "I have no idea whether they'll do any good. I don't even know what they'll show. It was dark in there. I hope the flash gave enough light, but of course when it flashed I was blinded and couldn't see what I hope the camera saw. I'm sorry I had to go tromping around in there, but I couldn't just let the sea take away evidence, in case there's any to take away."

"I'm glad you went in, Dorothy, and I must say it was very brave of you. It took much longer for Penzance to organize a team than it ought to have done, and I was concerned about the tide, too. They're going to have a job getting her out, now, without getting her wet."

"Will it matter so much? I mean…" I had to swallow before I could go on. "Was—was the body dry when you first looked at it? Or had she been there for the last high tide?"

"I don't think so. Her clothing looked dry. Her hair was in a little pool, but that's probably a tidal pool that's more or less permanent."

"So no—no fish?" I hated to ask, but I had to.

"No. Nothing like that."

"Thank God!"

"Yes."

He had been watching me, but now his gaze shifted. He focused his whole attention, his whole being, on what he could see of the working scene in and around the cave.

I could feel his tension. Oh, how he wanted to be there with them!

"I'll be all right here, Alan, if you want to go down."

"I'd only be in the way."

His voice was oddly distant, and I could have bitten my tongue. Of course. They wouldn't let him in, would they? It wasn't concern for me that kept him by my side, it was fear of rejection. He was out of the loop, and he was hating it.

There was a question begging to be asked. I wondered if I dared. Would it make him feel even more useless, or would it distract him from his situation?

I made up my mind and cleared my throat. "I'm almost afraid to ask, but did you see enough, when you first went into the cave, to tell how she died? I tried not to look when I was taking the pictures, but of course I couldn't help seeing that there wasn't any blood. Though I suppose it might have been washed away."

"I don't think so. I didn't go near enough to make any sort of examination, but I saw no injuries or wounds of any kind. No bruising or lacerations as if she'd somehow fallen down the cliff. No gunshot wounds, at least not unless there was an entrance wound on her back, with no frontal exit wound. That's possible, of course, but a cave is a foolish place to use a firearm."

"Because of the ricochet problem?"

"That, yes, but these sea caves are unstable, as well.

The roof, the whole lot for that matter, could come down.''

I shuddered. The thought of a cave-in raised my claustrophobic sensibilities by several orders of magnitude. I took a few very deep breaths, trying not to let him notice, trying not to think about the cave.

They worked as fast as they could, I'm sure, but it was some time before they brought out a stretcher with a body bag lying on it. An ugly, shapeless black bag. It was horrible that the beauty that had been Alexis was reduced to this.

"Oh, heavens, Alan! Has anyone told her mother? She'll be frantic. She'll know that Lexa's missing—''

"I told the constable who answered the phone that I could identify the body positively, and that someone needed to notify Mrs. Crosby. I'm sure she knows by now.''

He spoke with a remote courtesy, his gaze still fixed on the police activity. I stood up. "Then I think we should go back to the hotel. Now. Someone needs to be with that poor woman until family can get here. Alan, let's go.''

He looked at me then, looked as if he wasn't quite sure who I was, and then made a curious little gesture and said in an almost normal voice, "Yes, of course. If you'll give me your camera, I'll just speak to the DCI for a moment.''

The detective chief inspector was nearby. I heard Alan tell him about the pictures, and about the little pile of unsavory evidence I had added to the scene. Then my husband, the former chief constable of Belleshire, very formally handed over my camera and asked if he was still needed as a witness, and was very formally told that he might leave.

We climbed the cliff path in silence.

EIGHT

WITH WHAT I THOUGHT was commendable restraint, I made no further comment on the situation until we were on the road back to Penzance.

"So. What have you told them?"

"Only that we found the body, who it was, under what circumstances we found it. Later they'll ask us a good many questions about when we last saw Lexa, her frame of mind at the time, how well we knew her, and so on."

"How well we knew her! That sounds like something you'd ask a suspect."

"No, it's just routine. They have to establish the facts about her before they can even begin to establish whether they're dealing with a crime or an accident."

"But it's perfectly obvious—"

"Nothing is obvious, Dorothy, except that Alexis Adams is dead. She hadn't been happy; even we could see that. We've seen her worried, upset, depressed. This could be anything."

"Are you saying she committed suicide?"

Alan didn't reply for a moment. I looked at him and saw an expression on his face I'd never seen before. When he did speak, his voice was tightly controlled. "I have no idea whether she committed suicide, suffered an accident, or was murdered."

It was the sort of voice I'd used, back when I was a

teacher, to a fourth-grader who had pushed me almost beyond the limit of endurance.

I, too, was silent for a time. Long enough to call myself seventeen varieties of idiot. Would I never learn when to keep my mouth shut?

When I did speak, I tried very hard to sound calm and sensible. "Alan, I'm sorry. That was stupid and insensitive. I'll leave it alone, I promise."

He sighed, but said nothing the rest of the way to the hotel. I was back in the room with a brooding husband, and had changed into clean clothes, before I ventured a question. "Do you think I should go see Mrs. Crosby? I hate the thought of her being alone, but I don't want to intrude."

"I can't see that it would hurt to try." His voice was neutral; I could gather nothing from it. "If she doesn't want company, I imagine she'll tell you so."

"Yes. Well. I guess I'll call her room and check."

An unfamiliar voice answered the phone. I identified myself, said I was an acquaintance and was aware of the tragedy and asked how Mrs. Crosby was feeling.

"Not very well, Mrs. Martin. I'm WPC Danner, and I'm staying with her for a little while, but she did mention your name, and I believe she'd like to see you."

"She hasn't been given a sedative?"

"She refused one."

"I'll be right there, then. What's the room number?"

MRS. CROSBY'S ROOM was immediately above ours and was almost identically furnished. It should have been as pleasant as ours, sea view and all. But the draperies had been drawn, shutting out air and sunshine, and the gloom of sorrow made the dim atmosphere even darker and drearier.

If Mrs. Crosby had seemed ill when we first met her, she looked like death itself now. She was sitting up in the big four-poster bed, very small and somehow naked without her wig. Her scalp was thinly covered with gray down. It would have to grow a lot to be a crew cut. Her eyes were red and swollen, her cheeks pale as wax. In a pair of faded pajamas, she looked more like an old man than a woman. Her hands, fretting at the bedclothes, seemed almost transparent.

She cried out the moment she saw me.

"Mrs. Martin! Do you know what's happened? No one will tell me what's happened, only that Lexa's dead!"

"Now, Mrs. Crosby, you don't want to upset yourself—" The young policewoman tried to soothe, but Mrs. Crosby's voice rose in fury.

"Go away! Get out! I don't want you! I want someone who will tell me something!"

WPC Danner was really very young. She looked uncertain.

"I think she really does need to talk," I said quietly. "Would you be disobeying orders if you were to wait in the hall?"

She bit her lip. "I'm meant to stay here and try to help."

"Could you stay in the bathroom, then, with the door open? I promise I'll be careful."

The policewoman shrugged. "I'm not here as a police spy or anything of that sort, you know. We simply try to stay with bereaved families as long as we're needed. Please don't upset her, if you can help it." She removed herself, and I pulled a chair up to Mrs. Crosby's bedside.

"Now. What do you want to know? I promise I'll tell

you the truth, but you must stop me if you begin to feel worse.''

''I'll never feel anything but worse. It doesn't matter. Do you know what happened to Lexa?''

I took a deep breath. ''I only know that we found her, my husband and I, in a sea cave at a place called Prussia Cove, not far from Penzance.''

''No! Not that!'' Her hands clenched; tears rolled down the waxen cheeks. She made no effort to stem the flow, or to control her sobs. I hadn't expected quite this reaction. She had already been told of Lexa's death. Maybe she hadn't fully taken it in, since apparently no one had given her any details. I waited for her to regain control of herself. This was no time for meaningless consolation. When she began to sniffle, I handed her a tissue.

''But I don't understand,'' she said when she could speak, and there was a peculiar intensity in her voice. She raised herself on one elbow and stared at me out of those pitiful eyes. ''Why was she there? It's miles from anywhere, isn't it? Why was she there, of all places?''

''I don't know, Mrs. Crosby. No one knows, yet. But— you sound as if you know the place. I thought you were a stranger to Penzance.''

She sank back to her pillow. ''I am, but yes, I know the place. I've never been there, but I know about it.'' Her hands clenched again. ''I'm not Lexa's real mother, you know. Her real mother died in that cave over thirty years ago.''

Her mother!

No wonder Alan had been seeing ghosts. That unknown girl in the cave so many years ago...

''But—but I thought Lexa was in her twenties.''

''She looks—she looked much younger than she was.

She was thirty-three. She was only a few months old when her mother died. In 1968, that was.''

I took a deep breath. ''If you're up to it, Mrs. Crosby, I'd like to hear the story. It may be very important.''

Mrs. Crosby settled herself. A little color came to her face. ''It's a sad story, but it brought me Lexa, and that's been nothing but good. Until now.''

She wiped her eyes, blew her nose, and began.

''Her name really is Alexis Adams. I mean, it's not an assumed name. Her mother, Elizabeth Adams, was my best friend. I was older than she was, but when she first moved to London in 1966 I was advertising for a flatmate. She answered the advert, moved in, and we hit it off from the first.

''She was young, and always wilder than I had ever been. I was almost thirty then, and she was only just twenty. I had a steady job, nothing glamorous, just working as a secretary, but I was independent and living in London, happy enough to do my job and have a little fun at weekends, go to the cinema, go dancing with friends, that sort of thing. I never had any real boyfriends, just couldn't seem to find someone who really appealed to me. It was a silly sort of time, the sixties, and I was always serious-minded. I never much cared for rock music and I thought drugs were a waste of money.

''Betty Adams—she was always called Betty—she was different. She was quite bright, but she never could seem to stick to a job. Both her parents had died, and she had no other family. I don't know if they'd been strict, her parents, I mean, and she was off the leash for the first time, or what, but she couldn't seem to settle down. She flitted about from one thing to another, but she never caused me any worry over the rent. She never brought boyfriends back to the flat, either, though she had plenty of them, I knew. Sometimes she tried to arrange dates for me, but they never seemed to work out. She played about with drugs a bit, too, I knew, but not much, and again, never at the flat. She knew I wanted nothing to do with that sort of thing.

"You might think I'd have been jealous, or disapproving, or whatever, but I never was."

I had been thinking that very thing. I looked at Mrs. Crosby closely, but she seemed to be telling the truth. "You would have had reason, it seems to me. How did you avoid those feelings?"

"Partly, I suppose, because she never flaunted her success with men. She took it for granted. She was very pretty. Well, you've seen Lexa. Betty wasn't quite as beautiful, but if you could see her now, you'd take the two for sisters, they're that much alike. Betty's hair was nicer than Lexa's really, so blond it was almost white, and ironed smooth as satin, the way girls used to do then.

"There was another reason why I got along so well with Betty, though. She was always so gay—I mean in the old sense—that she brought sunshine into the place. You might say I was one of those people who was born middle-aged, but she was gay and giddy and carefree, and fun, at least on the surface. Underneath, though, there was something else. It was as though she was running from one job to another, one boy to another, trying to find something and never able to. There was a sadness, a kind of longing—no, I can't put a name to it, but it was there, and it made me put up with her when she was annoying. Maybe it was because she had no mother. I was almost a mother to her, though I wasn't all that much older. We were very close."

She dabbed at her eyes and coughed. I poured a glass

of water from the bottle of Evian that stood on the bedside table, and Mrs. Crosby took a sip.

"Now, I don't want you getting funny ideas. We weren't lovers. Betty was definitely a man's girl, and I was, too, or would have been if there'd been any men about that I could fancy. We were friends, and more than friends, almost sisters, or mother and daughter, as I said.

"Then Betty got pregnant."

Mrs. Crosby paused. "It happened in June. She'd been to Penzance for a few days with some friends, just having a good time, and a few weeks later she realized.

"It could have been a disaster. In those days that sort of thing wasn't supposed to happen, and it could have sent her into a tailspin, but it had just the opposite effect. It steadied her, seemed to give her a purpose in life. She cut out all the drugs the moment she suspected, stopped smoking and drinking, got a better job, started saving her money. We began to buy baby things, get the flat ready. She'd offered to find another place, but I told her I'd love having a baby about.

"It was the truth, too. When Alexis came, she was the best thing that had ever happened to me. I'd more or less given up hope of ever marrying and having babies of my own, and here I was with the most beautiful baby there ever was and caring for her almost as if she were mine.

"Betty left her job for a few weeks to look after Lexa, but of course she had to start working again soon, and then things were harder. Good care for the baby was expensive, and Betty was very choosy. She wasn't going to let just anyone mind her child. I thought she was quite right, too, but once she'd paid that bill, there wasn't enough money left over to pay her share of the expenses. It began to be a worry. We thought about finding a smaller flat, or getting someone else in to share, but neither alternative was very attractive.''

Mrs. Crosby stopped talking, coughed, drank some more water.

"Stop if you're tired," I said. "You look as though you need some rest, and it must be hard for you to talk about all this."

"No, I need to talk about it. It's only that I'll never forgive myself for what happened next. If I'd managed better, somehow, Betty would never have died."

NINE

I DREW IN MY BREATH. Should Alan be here? Was I about to learn what had happened on that stormy night in 1968? It took Mrs. Crosby a few minutes to compose herself. Whatever was coming, it wasn't easy for her to talk about.

"I blame myself, you see. I was worried about the money, and I let Betty see it. If I hadn't fretted so, she might never have gone."

"She went to Penzance," I prompted.

Mrs. Crosby nodded. "She'd made up her mind she had to ask Lexa's father for money."

"Who was the father?" I asked, scarcely daring to breathe.

"She would never tell me. She didn't know him well, I know that. It was just a weekend fling; there'd been a party where everyone was smoking pot, and things went a little too far. To tell the truth, I don't think she even remembered him all that clearly. She'd never have thought about him again if it hadn't been for Lexa."

"Didn't she tell you anything about him at all?"

"Only that he was the sort you'd never think would have anything to do with drugs. She'd giggle when she said that. I got the idea he was a very respectable type, maybe even someone important."

"And that was all she said."

"That was all. But when the money started getting

scarce, she got it into her head that she'd take Lexa to show to him, and ask him for some help.

"Well, I argued with her. He didn't even know about the baby; Betty'd never wanted to tell him. She said he didn't matter to her and why should he know? I think she was afraid he might want to marry her, and she didn't want that, even when things were so hard. I told her he wouldn't like it if she suddenly turned up with a baby and claimed it was his, and finally I persuaded her to leave Lexa with me."

"You must always have been grateful for that."

"Yes, at least I did that right, if nothing else. I tried and tried to tell her to write to him first, not just appear and make demands, but she said she didn't know his address. Anyway, she said, he'd find it harder to say no to her in person."

She sighed, a long, shuddering sigh that broke my heart. Her gaze turned inward. She was remembering, I knew, remembering the long wait for Betty to return, the worry, finally the newspaper stories of the girl in the cave, the terror...

I didn't want to make her live through that again. I cleared my throat. "Mrs. Crosby," I said gently, "I know the next part. I may know more than you do. You see, my husband was the investigating officer on that case. All his life he's worried because he never solved it, never even knew who the victim was. Why did you not report Betty missing?"

I knew the question would hurt her, but it had to be asked, though I thought I knew the answer.

"I was afraid," she said, after a long pause. "Not for myself, for Lexa. I'd got the idea, you see, that the man Betty'd gone to see was someone important, influential. And if he'd—well, if Betty's death hadn't been an accident, what might he do about Lexa? Would he want her, try to take her away from me? Or would he try to—to do something to her, too? I couldn't take the risk.''

Years of worry for Alan, years of agonizing over what he'd thought was a failure, and all because a woman had been afraid. I took a deep breath. ''Why were you so sure it was Betty? I know you didn't think she'd just run away, but you said she was a bit giddy.''

''Not anymore, she wasn't. If I've made her sound irresponsible, I haven't told the story properly. She liked to have fun, and she'd made some mistakes, but she had her head on straight, and she adored Lexa. She would never have run off and left her baby. That wasn't what made me sure, though.''

She paused for another sip of water.

''I gave her those beads. There were pictures of them in the papers. The police could never trace them, because they were old. Carved cinnabar, they were. They'd been my mother's, back in her flapper days. I restrung them myself and gave them to Betty. She loved bright colors. There was no way I wouldn't recognize them, even in a newspaper photo. I knew it was Betty from the moment I saw those beads.''

There was so much I wanted to say, but I could find no way to say any of it. There was no point in berating this grieving woman for what she had left undone so many years before.

She could see what was in my mind, though. People often can, with me. I'm no good at hiding my feelings.

''And don't you think I've carried that burden all these years? Don't you think I know they might have caught the man if I'd told what I knew? Over and over I've asked myself if I did the right thing.

''But I couldn't risk it, don't you see? I couldn't bear

to lose Lexa. She was only four months old, and so precious! She was the only baby I'd ever have, and I loved her as much as Betty had. I couldn't lose her!''

And now you have lost her, I thought. That might not have happened if you'd gone to the police when Betty died.

But I didn't need to say that, either. The pain of it was etched in Mrs. Crosby's face forever.

I LEFT HER shortly after that, promising to come back later and check on her. I had let her talk too long, about things that were too painful. I didn't know if I had done more harm than good, but I knew that I had to tell Alan what I'd learned, and that it might not be easy.

''You were a long time,'' he said when I walked into the room. He was sitting at the table in the bay window. There was no reading matter in front of him. I suspected he had been staring out the window, caught up in unhappy thoughts.

''Yes, I'm sorry. I only meant to stay a minute, but she wanted to talk.''

I sat down beside him. ''Alan, I have a story to tell you.''

I told it as simply as I could, but it still took quite a while.

When it was over, Alan shook his head. ''That poor woman.''

It was the last response I expected, but for once I had the sense to keep still.

''Now she's lost everything, and she's floundering about in a sea of 'what if ?' It's a great mistake, playing 'what if?'''

''But— don't you ever wonder—?''

''Of course. Everyone does. It's a mistake, all the same.

'What now?' is the only question that's ever worth asking.''

''And are you asking yourself that?''

''I am.'' He frowned.

''You're wondering whether to take this story to the police?''

''No, of course not. I must take it to them. It gives a whole different spin to the investigation into Lexa's death. They must know.''

He frowned again. ''No, the question is what I'll do then. It rather depends on the tack they take.''

I wanted to jump in. I wanted to say that he—we—should investigate this thing ourselves, no matter what the police said or did.

I kept silent. This time, it had to come from him.

''Well, there's no point in speculating about that, either. If you don't mind, love, I'll give them a ring. They'll probably want to send someone down to get the story straight from Mrs. Crosby.''

''I don't think she's up to it right now. And WPC Danner heard it all from the bathroom, anyway. Won't that do?''

''I believe,'' he said, ''that you forgot to tell me about WPC Danner.'' He turned to the phone and didn't see my sigh of relief.

He was in! He wanted to make this report himself, constable or no constable, so he could gauge the police reaction. He had the bit between his teeth and intended to run with it.

And whether he realized it yet or not, I intended to run right beside him.

He was on the telephone only a short time, and told very little of his story. I could make almost no sense of his end of the conversation, and when he hung up he had an odd expression on his face.

"Bad news?"

"I'm not sure. The DCI isn't in, but the chap at the switchboard recognized my name and shot the call up to the super. He wants to see me straightaway."

"Oh, dear."

"I'm not sure. He sounded—well, I'll know more when I talk to him. Will you be all right for a little while?"

"I think I'll take a nap. This morning was a little— shattering."

"You do that. I'll be back soon." He straightened his shoulders and left the room, and I lay down on top of the bedspread to worry.

I did eventually doze a little, though when I woke I wished I hadn't slept. My dreams had been troubled. I could remember only vague snatches of content, but I knew my heart was pounding and the bedspread badly rumpled.

Alan had not yet returned. I put on my glasses and looked at the clock. Nearly two hours! Was he in trouble? Maybe he had been reprimanded for interfering. Well, they couldn't actually do that, could they? He wasn't a member of the force anymore. But they could act snooty, and make him feel terrible, and—

The door opened, Alan entered, and my anxious speculations dissolved. The man who walked in was ten years younger than the one who had left. His step was jaunty, his smile broad.

"What happened?"

"All in good time, my dear, all in good time. We've missed lunch, you know, and your breakfast is feeding the fishes. Let's go out and find a good cream tea, and I'll tell you all about it."

There's no hurrying him when he's in that sort of mood. He enjoys springing surprises, and he does it in his own way and takes his own sweet time. I sighed ostentatiously and reached for my hat.

There was a tea shop not far from the hotel. Small and unprepossessing, it nevertheless promised "Genuine Cornish Cream Teas." We went in and were pleasantly surprised.

The scones were homemade. So was the strawberry jam. The tea was delicious, and as for the clotted cream—well, let me just say that cholesterol never came in a more delectable form. One could positively feel it clogging up the arteries, but what a way to go!

I was, of course, in a mood to enjoy anything. True, Alan and I were delving into "old, unhappy, far-off things" centering around more than one tragedy, but we were doing it together and he was happy again. Soon, I hoped, he'd tell me why. Life was good.

When we'd eaten every last crumb of the wonderful, fattening stuff, Alan not having uttered a word except "More tea, dear?" and "I could do with a bit more of that jam," I put my foot down.

"All right," I said. "If you don't tell me this minute what's got you looking like a little boy with his first electric train, I'm going to make a public scene."

There were enough people in the shop to make any scene very public, indeed. They also served a more useful purpose; their babble of conversation acted as a screen to keep our talk private.

He leaned back, felt in his pocket for the pipe he no longer smoked (on his doctor's orders), made a face, and then settled down to his story.

TEN

"THE GIST OF IT, since you're so impatient, is that I'm to have a reasonably free hand in helping to investigate Lexa's death."

Well, that took my breath away, as he'd known it would. I simply looked my questions, and he grinned. "Oh, well, if you want the whole story, that will take a bit longer. It seems that young Colin has an exaggerated opinion of my prowess as an investigator. He called me into his office as soon as I got to the station..."

"SUPERINTENDENT CARDINNIS will see you immediately," the constable at the desk had said. "You'll remember where his office is, I don't doubt."

"I remember," said Alan, and walked the length of the brown-linoleumed hallway with growing apprehension.

"Chief Constable, come in, sir!" The superintendent sounded welcoming, even cordial. Confused and wary, Alan went into the office and sat down.

"Just Mr. Nesbitt nowadays, you know, Superintendent."

"Not in these parts, sir. Here you're The Chief, and always will be. We're very proud of you, you know."

Alan had not considered matters in quite that light.

"You're the only local man who's ever risen to the

very top, and we're not likely to forget it," continued Cardinnis.

"Your SOCOs seemed a bit stiff this morning," said Alan dryly.

Cardinnis shook his head. "I was afraid it might have struck you that way. Embarrassment, pure and simple, mixed with not a little awe. And, of course, fear that they might make great fools of themselves in front of you."

"I see." Alan's tone was noncommittal.

Cardinnis looked at Alan and seemed to hear what he wasn't saying. "You'll be wondering why I had the effrontery to ask you here. The fact is, I'd have come to you, but I wanted to put a proposition in front of you now, today, and I simply hadn't the time to leave the station. That's why I don't intend to beat about the bush. Chief Constable, I know you're retired. I know you've come here with your wife on holiday, and I've a lot of cheek to ask. But the fact is, I'd like your help with this Alexis Adams mess."

Alan said nothing, just kept his eyes focused on the superintendent's.

"Unofficially, of course. I can't hire you, and I can't pay you, but what you began to tell me seems to confirm the first idea I had when I heard about your call this morning."

"And that was?"

"That there's a connection between the two cases, the unsolved murder from your time, and this one.

"My grandfather and my father, both, used to talk about that old murder. Like you, they were convinced it was murder. And they said that if anyone ever found the key to it, it would be you. Now, maybe it's just coincidence that you found the body of the Adams woman, and that you've learned of her link with that old case. Myself, I don't believe in coincidence. I think it was meant.''

The old superintendent of his time, Alan thought, young Colin's grandfather, had been a strong Methodist. It sounded as though Colin might be following in his footsteps.

''So I'd be a fool—wouldn't I, sir?—to ignore all the connections. Your intimate knowledge of the earlier case, your acquaintance with the present victim, your reputation as an investigating officer. And I'm not that much of a fool.'' He sat back and waited.

Alan chose his words with some care. ''I am, as you say, on holiday. What exactly is it that you propose?''

Cardinnis sat up. ''An exchange of information. You tell me what you know and what you are able to learn in further inquiries. In return, I keep you apprised of the progress of the case from our end. Autopsy results, interview transcripts, the lot. No official sanction or authority. Unofficially, any help that an understaffed operation can provide.''

Then Alan had sprung what would, he was sure, be the undoing of the proposal. ''You should know, Superintendent, that my wife is no mean investigator herself. She has been of great help to me on several occasions. I would insist that she be included in this matter.''

To his great surprise, Cardinnis had laughed, loud and long. ''My dear sir, I never had the slightest idea that she could be excluded. Her reputation is well known here, as well.''

''AND WITH THAT,'' Alan concluded, ''we agreed.''

''Well, it's all very exciting, and I do think it was noble of you to deal me in. But I'm dying to know, what did he tell you about what they've found out? You were there forever. I was getting worried.''

''They don't know much yet, of course. A list of Lexa's effects. There was nothing in the least interesting, by the way. A preliminary report on a possible cause of death, which boils down to, they haven't a clue. Nothing obvious; there are no wounds, no obvious symptoms of poisoning. We'll have to wait for the autopsy. They haven't yet traced her movements last night. In fact, they've barely begun to check anything. No, what took the time was less what Colin told me than what he wanted me to tell him: my recital of your version of Mrs. Crosby's story. They want it from the horse's mouth, of course, and they'll probably ask you to retell it, as well, but Colin wanted to know what struck me about it, if anything.''

''And?''

''Oh, the drugs angle, of course. Colin was onto that, too, straightaway. And then he said something very interesting.'' Alan picked up his cup, found it empty, and put it down again. ''He said, Dorothy, that something odd is going on in Penzance. 'There's too much money about' was the way he put it. When I asked him to be more specific, he couldn't. He only said that far more money was being spent in Penzance than he could account for by any lawful activities.''

''Drug money?''

''That's just it. He doesn't know. He can't put his finger on anything, only his feeling that, somehow, too much money is in circulation. And that would fit in very nicely with a drugs operation, wouldn't it?''

''THERE'S A LOT MORE we need to ask Mrs. Crosby,'' I said, after Alan had ordered us a second pot of tea.

''Yes. Colin agreed to let us, or more probably you, do

most of the talking to her, on the grounds that she's ill and frail and less likely to be upset talking to someone with whom she has established a relationship. There's a condition, though: We'll have to tape all the conversations, unless a policeman is there to take notes. They lent me a tape recorder for the purpose. Colin doesn't want any more second-or thirdhand accounts. Now, have you a notepad in that valise of yours?''

"Of course." My purse is large, true, but I want to be able to put my hands on whatever I need, and one never knows when a little spiral notebook may come in handy, or a flashlight or a bag of cough drops or a deluxe Swiss Army knife, or…

I rummaged, found the notebook and a pen, and sat, ready to record whatever brilliant insights we might develop.

"Ah. Good. First off, then, we have to know why the Crosbys came to Penzance."

"I can guess."

"So could I, but I'd rather ask."

"Right. 'Queries for Mrs. Crosby. 1. Purpose in visiting Penzance.' Next?"

"We don't know what they did while they were here. That's going to be extremely important."

"I shouldn't imagine Mrs. Crosby was feeling up to doing anything much. But Lexa—yes, we'll have to know what her movements were. I should think the police will be working on that, though."

"Of course. We'll be retracing their steps with most of what we do, but we might have some ideas they don't. That's the whole point of involving us, isn't it?"

Obediently, I wrote it down. "'2. Trace Lexa's movements.' What else for Mrs. Crosby?"

"I'm not sure at this stage. She'll have to identify the body, of course."

"Oh, Alan, that poor woman! Is she really well enough, do you think?"

"She strikes me as a strong person. Not physically, not now, but of strong character. When she realizes it is something she must do, I think she'll summon up the courage to do it. We'll want to go with her."

"Of course, if she wants us." I turned back to the pad and considered for a moment. "Okay, this may strike you as a silly idea, but I think we ought to go back to the cave."

"Can you? And I thought you hated the cliff path."

"Well, as to the path, I didn't like it, but I managed it once, I can do it again. And the cave—well, I don't know. Maybe if I concentrated very hard on what I was doing, it wouldn't be so bad. I think I have to try, anyway."

"We'll need to let the SOCOs finish. The last thing they need is someone contaminating a crime scene, if in fact it is a crime scene."

"Well, I think we're operating on that assumption, aren't we?" I retorted. "Anyway, I didn't mean now. They ought to be finished in a day or two, and then I'd like to take another look. With a good, big flashlight along. There may be nothing for us to see, but I'd feel better about it. Even if I get stupid and can't go in myself, you can, and you're a trained observer. Who knows, there might be something that would ring bells for you, from the old case."

"A bell would have to be extraordinarily resonant to sound for thirty years. Very well, add it to the list."

I looked at my pad. "Only three items, but they each involve an awful lot of time and work. I think we need to get started. Oh, by the way, did the police get my pictures developed?"

Alan smiled. "Yes."

"And?"

"Colin was polite about them."

"Oh, dear. That bad, huh?" I began to giggle at the look on Alan's face. The giggles turned into snorts and then, I'm sorry to say, to hiccups.

It's amazing how inebriated I can become on tea.

ELEVEN

WHEN WE GOT BACK to the hotel, a detective was just coming in the door with Mrs. Crosby. We looked at each other in some alarm and Alan took the detective aside to have a word.

"Has she been to the morgue already?" I asked anxiously when he returned to me. "I really didn't want her to have to face that alone. How is she?"

"Doing fairly well, considering. The chap interviewed her here first, and she said much the same thing she told you, apparently. Then he took her for the formal identification. He did ask if she wanted someone with her, but she refused. She seems to have stood it as well as could be expected. She'll rest now. By the way, when they get the interview transcribed, they'll probably want you to have a look at it. It might be just as well if you were to write down all you remember of what she said."

"Heavens, Alan! You know how easily I forget things."

"Then you'd best do it now, before any more of it gets away."

So I spent the next hour noting down in my little notebook the main points, at least, of that extraordinary conversation with Mrs. Crosby. When I had finished, the thing was so crossed out and interlined as to be indecipherable, so I copied it neatly and handed it to Alan.

"There. That's the best I can do. Your memory is a lot better than mine. Can you think of anything I told you that I've forgotten to write down?"

He read it carefully. "No, it seems reasonably complete. Here, take a look at this."

He handed me what he'd been working on while I'd been racking my brains. It consisted of two lists on several sheets of hotel stationery. Alan's handwriting is neat, very English, and almost impossible for me to read.

I studied it for a minute or two, shook my head, and handed it back to him with a grin. "You'd better just tell me, dear."

"Ah, yes, your peculiar inability to read perfectly legible writing. Very well, then. I've been engaging in your favorite habit of making lists."

"I could tell that much. Give me some credit."

He ignored that. "I've listed, you see, the steps the police will be taking. Then I've made a separate list of things we might usefully do, either dogging their footsteps or launching out on our own."

"Sounds reasonable. If anyone ought to know what the police are up to, it's you."

"One would hope. The procedure is absolutely cut and dried, you know, once they decide it's murder they're dealing with. HOLMES and all that."

HOLMES stands for Home Office Large Major Enquiry System. The first time Alan told me about it, I meekly asked if "Large" and "Major" weren't somewhat redundant, and got him to admit that one of the adjectives was thrown in at the last minute. He wouldn't tell me which, but I doubted anyone had ever contemplated HOLES. No. HOMES would have worked all right, though, so I strongly suspected that someone with a sense of humor had added "Large" purely for the sake of the delightful acronym.

At any rate, I'd known for some time that HOLMES laid down procedures to be followed in the investigation of any major crime, including exactly what information was to be entered into the nationwide computer database, and how. The standardized methods have made it much easier to track criminals who repeat themselves, as well as those on the run, and if followed properly, they ensure that details aren't lost or forgotten, details that might make all the difference in eventually nailing the villain.

But I'd never known exactly what the specific procedures were, so I listened carefully as Alan spelled them out for me.

"Good grief, Alan," I said when he'd finished, "it sounds only slightly more complicated than organizing D day."

"Certainly it often felt that way to me. The paperwork is unending."

"But, with such a lot being done by the police, what on earth can we contribute?" I had never been made to feel such a rank amateur. The police operated a well-oiled machine. I could see no reason why they should want the assistance of a complete outsider. Alan, yes, possibly. He knew the ropes, knew the area, had all the sharpened instincts of a topranking policeman.

But a retired American schoolteacher?

He put an arm around me. "All that cumbersome mechanism exists only to manage the data, coordinate efforts. Somebody has to gather that data. Somebody has to make those efforts. And the fact is that in the great majority of cases that require investigation, the crucial piece of information doesn't come as a direct result of the patient plodding. People start to talk, you see. One person tells another about the case, and it gets passed on, and on, and the rumors and innuendos stew in the community, and eventually an idea floats to the surface, a memory of something that seemed odd at the time, and someone goes to the police with it.''

''Yes?'' I said, frowning.

''Our job is to keep that pot stewing.''

''So we talk to people.''

''That's always been the beginning of police work, you know. The physical evidence, forensics procedures, all that sort of thing, they're usually a matter of proving what the police already suspect. We have to make a case, you know, a watertight one that will stand up in court.''

''The cigar ash, the footprint. Or nowadays, the microfibers, the DNA sample.''

''All Sherlock's bag of tricks, brought up to date. But we know where to go looking for the cigar that deposited the ash or the coat that matches the fibers because we've talked to people, and they've said they saw X behaving suspiciously at the crime scene.''

''Except that it usually isn't quite that simple.''

Alan sighed. ''Almost never, in fact. But we have to try. Hence, the second list, our tasks.''

It was quite a lot shorter than the first. I tried again to read it. '' 'Mrs. Crosby.' Yes, of course, we'll be talking to her right along.''

''And the important thing to remember is the verb.''

I frowned and cocked my head.

'' 'Talking' to her. Not interviewing her, not questioning her, or not a lot. Just talking, or listening, actually. Let her talk about Lexa and Lexa's mother. You'd be surprised what might come out.''

''Right. Then—what's this?''

Alan looked. '' 'Lexa's room.' We'll want to look it

over. Yes, I know what you're about to say, and of course the police will have examined it already. But we'll look it over as people who knew her, at least slightly, and we'll take Mrs. Crosby with us. Not to question, again, but simply to let her talk.''

"That'll be very hard for her."

"Of course. But the crying will be good for her, I imagine, and she might just mention something—"

"Okay, I get the idea. Then is this—oh, I see. 'Boleigh.' No, don't tell me. She went to his party. She talked to people. Mr. Boleigh might know who, might be able to tell us something about them. And even though the police will have been there ahead of us, you might get more out of him because he's known you for years."

"And because I won't be asking a lot of questions."

I sat back and began to laugh. "Alan, I love it. You've just set down, very precisely and formally, exactly the sort of thing I've been doing for ages. Going out and talking to people. It's the only way I ever 'get my man.'"

"You see," he said, dropping a kiss on the top of my head, "I'm learning to be an amateur detective."

There were more entries on the list. I made out a few of them, something that looked like "Polwhill" and "Pen" something.

"Polwhistle," Alan said in response to my questioning look. "The rector of St. Martha's, remember?"

"I didn't ever catch his name. And the other?"

"Pendeen. The Lord Mayor."

"'By Tre, Pol, and Pen/ Ye shall know Cornishmen,'" I recited. "I read that once in some old English mystery, but I didn't think it would still be true."

"Oh, Cornwall doesn't change much. There've been a lot of outlanders moving in, of course, and many of the old Cornish names never did have the traditional prefixes.

Cardinnis, for example, the superintendent. His family are Cornish down to their boots. But you still find Tre, Pol, and Pen everywhere hereabouts.''

I shook my head admiringly. "There'll always be an England. Alan, your father must not have been a Cornishman originally. Or is Nesbitt one of those other Cornish names that don't fit the pattern? It doesn't sound like it, somehow.''

"No, you're quite right. Father was born in Kent, not too far from Sherebury, actually. He was a hop farmer. But Mother was Cornish—Trethewey, so that ought to keep you happy—and she missed the sea. Father was besotted with her, couldn't deny her anything, so they moved back to Newlyn, her old home, shortly after they married. Father had to learn the new trade, but he became a very good fisherman.''

He fell silent then, remembering, and I thought ruefully about the vast things I would never know about my husband or my adopted country. There are some things that are in the blood, sprung from the home soil, things that an outsider can never, never truly understand.

I stood and stretched. "I don't know about you, love, but I could use a drink. It's been a trying day.''

"And you accuse the English of understatement. Our two hearts beat as one, my dear. After you.''

WE DIDN'T TALK MUCH about the murder over drinks or later, as we poked at our dinner. Nor did we eat much. Not only had we had a hearty tea, but I, at least, was suddenly very tired, and so full of our problem I had little room for food.

"I hope Mrs. Crosby's finally taken a sedative," I said with a sigh as I pushed away my plate.

"I doubt she'll sleep much in any case.''

"No. Poor woman. She doesn't deserve this."

"Only a monster could deserve what's happened to her. Twice. Her best friend and then that friend's daughter."

"It's the old question, isn't it? Why are such things allowed? Why is there such evil?"

He shook his head wearily. "There's never a satisfactory answer, Dorothy. One can read the books and talk to the preachers, and the answer still comes down to 'We don't know.' Perhaps, one day, the other side of the great divide, we will. Meanwhile, all we can do is try our best to combat evil, try never to give in to it ourselves."

"That's what you've done all your life, isn't it?"

"I've tried. I've often failed."

I looked at him anxiously. "You're not blaming yourself over the old case again, are you? Because—"

"No, I'm not talking about that. I'm talking about the number of times when I've given in to anger, to hatred. The number of times I've wanted to take a murderer, or a child rapist, or a wife beater, or even a stupid, arrogant little twit of a drugs dealer, take them in my own two hands and beat their heads against the wall, or choke them senseless, or—" He broke off. His voice had remained low, but his hands were clenched into tight fists. They were shaking.

He took a deep breath. "I'm sorry, my dear. I've frightened you."

"No—well, not exactly." I lifted my wineglass and took a hefty swig. "You don't often show that side."

"I've tried never to bring it home with me. I'm not proud of it. I've never let that anger loose, not quite, but it's there. And every time it rises to the surface, I know I'm no better than the devils I've spent my life putting behind bars. I've wanted to hurt them just as badly as they hurt other people, and that's not justice, Dorothy. That's revenge.''

"But you didn't do it!" I leaned across the table, intent. "That's the difference between you and them, between any person of integrity and any criminal. You wanted to do harm, but you didn't. The restraints held. That's what civilization is, Alan. That's what morality is. Maybe we can't always keep our emotions in check, but so long as we control our actions, we'll stay on the right side of the line.''

"I'm not so certain. Every time the emotions get off the chain, there's the risk that the actions will, too.''

I poured a little more wine in both our glasses and tried to smile. "That's just the Englishman talking. If you'd let 'er rip a little more often over little things, you wouldn't build up such a head of steam over the big ones.''

"Kick the cat and swear at the motor mechanic and you'll never murder your boss, is that the idea?''

"More or less.''

He smiled a little, and I grinned back, and the talk eased back to trivialities, but I'd been shaken. I knew my husband to be a man of conviction, and I knew why being a policeman had been so important to him. His sense of right and wrong was strong. He'd wanted criminals out of society and in prison, where they could do no more harm, at least temporarily. He had known, of course, that they wouldn't stay out of circulation forever. He'd been sensibly aware that his work had been more like house-cleaning than demolition, that there was no permanent solution to crime, only a day-to-day effort to keep the savages at bay.

All that I'd understood, and admired, about Alan, but I'd never known the strength of his passion against evil.

In a sober mood, I followed him back upstairs.

TWELVE

I WOKE FILLED WITH dread the next morning. Today I would have to try to talk to Mrs. Crosby. There were things we needed urgently to know. Alan and I had agreed that I should be the one to approach her, since she seemed to have some degree of trust in me. Then if it appeared that Alan needed to probe for some details that only his trained policeman's mind could analyze, I would ask if she was willing to talk to him.

No matter how much we needed to know, though, no matter how much she might trust me, it meant intruding on someone in the first stages of unbearable grief, and someone who, moreover, was extremely ill.

"Alan, I feel like a brute."

"One always does, talking to the families of victims. I hated it myself until I learned to develop a certain amount of distance. It helps to remember, every moment, that you're on their side, that you're doing the only thing that can help at all, and that's to learn the truth. They want the truth, Dorothy, the families do. They want, more than anything, to know what's happened. And then they want the person responsible to be captured and punished."

He seemed about to say something else.

"What?"

"I was about to say, they want them hanged."

"But that doesn't happen anymore."

"No."

I wanted to ask him how he felt about that, but something in his face closed up. There would be another time, perhaps, for a philosophical discussion of capital punishment. Not just now.

"I hope the police didn't tire her too much yesterday. I wonder if they still have a WPC with her."

"Probably, if they have enough staff. In cases like this, they try to have someone stay for a day or two at least, especially when the bereaved person is alone, like Mrs. Crosby."

"I think," I said, finishing the cup of indifferent tea we'd brewed in the room, "I'll skip breakfast. Mrs. Crosby will have spent a horrible night. If I get there early, maybe I can offer her a crumb or two of comfort. Besides, I'd like to get it over with for today. I'll probably have to keep going back to her, over and over. She'll be sick of the sight of me."

"It's all part of the job. But you're not going to tackle it without your breakfast. You ate next to nothing for dinner."

"Alan, I'll be all right. I'm not exactly melting away." I gave my reflection a disgusted look and pulled in my stomach.

"Perhaps not, but the mind doesn't function well when the blood sugar is low. I was always adamant that my officers get their meals regularly, even if it had to be ham rolls or sandwich packets eaten on the fly. The same rule applies here. Toast and juice, at least. I insist."

Well, I could just face that, though the thought of a full English breakfast nauseated me. Reluctantly, I followed Alan down to the dining room. I added coffee to the menu, gulped it all down as soon as the waitress put it in front of me, and rose. "Alan, go ahead and finish your meal, but I can't sit still any longer. The toast is fighting with the butterflies in my stomach, and the only way to calm everything down is to get on with it.''

"I'll go up to the room in a few minutes. Ring up if you need me.''

I called Mrs. Crosby from our room. She answered on the first ring. She sounded exhausted, but there was no sleep in her voice.

"This is Mrs. Martin. I thought I might come up for a few minutes, if it's not a nuisance.''

"No, it's no bother. I'm in bed, I'm afraid, but I'd like to see you.''

I hung up, found the tape recorder Alan had brought home from the police station, and walked to the elevator.

A different WPC was on duty, a quiet, serious woman who looked Indian. She stopped me just inside the door, a finger to her lips.

"Mrs. Crosby is very ill, I think, Mrs. Martin.'' She spoke in a near-whisper, with a clipped accent and precise grammar. "I have asked the police surgeon to come and see her. I am not sure she should not be in hospital.''

"Should I wait and come back later?''

"No, she wishes to talk to you, but please try to be careful. She is under great strain.''

I nodded, grateful for the woman's concern, and went on into the bedroom.

Someone, probably the policewoman, had opened the draperies in Mrs. Crosby's room, letting in the sun, but the windows were still tightly shut. The room felt stuffy and smelled vaguely like a hospital. Mrs. Crosby, making some effort with her appearance, had put her wig on and wore a robe or bed jacket over her pajamas. She looked terrible, but she was composed. My guess was that the frenzy of grief had, for the moment, totally drained her of emotion.

"Please sit down, Mrs. Martin." Her voice was subdued.

I wished we could get to first names, but I felt awkward about suggesting it. Under the circumstances, maybe it ought to come from her. "Can I get you anything, Mrs. Crosby? Some tea? Have you had breakfast?"

She made an odd little sound that might almost have been a snort. "Breakfast? No. But I've had tea, thank you. Sujata takes very good care of me."

"Did you sleep at all?"

"I dozed a little. I sleep very little nowadays, even before…" She made a futile little gesture and trailed off.

"Are you sure you're up to talking to me? You've had a terrible shock, and I'm afraid you don't look very well."

"Now, Mrs. Martin." The soft voice was chiding. "I'd have taken you for a truthful woman. You know perfectly well what I look like."

I waited, afraid to reply.

"I look," she went on calmly, "like someone who's dying. Which is reasonable, since I am."

"Cancer?" I asked after a deep breath.

"Of course. I'm glad you don't protest, pretend that I look wonderful."

"Some people prefer euphemism. Some don't want to face unpleasantness. I didn't know what sort you were, but now that I do, no, I won't pretend. My husband made a diagnosis the moment he saw you. It took me a little longer. Would you like to talk about it, or not?"

"I don't mind. It's in my colon. I fought it as hard as I could, but it refused to be cured. It doesn't cause much pain now, and I found at some point that I had accepted it. Now I welcome it. I think I'll die soon. They say one dies when one gives up the will to live. I have no reason now to fight anymore.'' She looked away.

I hesitated for a moment, and then took the plunge. "I'm sorry, Mrs. Crosby, but I'm going to have to argue with you. You may think I'm awfully rude, but I have to tell you you're wrong about having no reason to live.''

"Am I? You're not going to preach to me, are you? If so, please don't. I'm really not strong enough for that sort of thing.''

"No, I'm not going to preach. What I mean is that you still have work to do.''

She made a sound that might almost have been a laugh. "Mrs. Martin, I can barely get out of bed. Soon I won't be able to do that. You can hardly expect me to work.''

"You can do this work in bed. You can start right now. You can tell me everything about Alexis, everything that might help us, Alan and me, to find her killer.''

She pushed herself up on her elbow and really looked at me for the first time since I'd entered the room "You? Why you? Are you working for the police? I've talked to them already. They made me look—'' She couldn't finish.

I spoke quickly, to get that image out of her mind. "We're working with them, in a way. You remember I told you that my husband was the investigating officer when Lexa's mother died?''

"Yes.'' Her voice was flat. "And that he never found out a thing, never caught anybody.''

That was unfair, but I swallowed my anger. "Quite true. What I did not tell you was that he, Alan, I mean, went on to a distinguished career, became a chief constable, in fact, and then commandant at Bramshill for a time. He might not have solved Betty's murder, Mrs. Crosby, but he's solved many, many others in his time, and the police superintendent here has asked him to assist unof-

ficially in this inquiry. And now that he knows more about
Betty's murder, knows who she was, knows why she
came to Penzance, he thinks he may have a chance, finally, to resolve that case as well.

"It's important to him, Mrs. Crosby. And it's important
to me, first because he is very dear to me and I hate to
see him feeling like a failure. And second, because I grew
very fond of Alexis in the short time I knew her. I never
had any children either, you see."

She lay back and closed her eyes. I was afraid I'd tired
her too much. Should I leave? I stood and was about to
tiptoe out when she opened her eyes and looked at me,
curiously intent.

"Yes, I think I do see. I'm sorry if I snarled a moment
ago. Please call me Eleanor. And ask me anything you
like."

I hid my sigh of relief. "Thank you. I'm Dorothy. Are
you sure you're strong enough for this right now?"

"No, but I'll try. You're quite right. This is important.
I'll keep talking as long as I can. Though you do realize,
don't you, that I could die at almost any time, perhaps
even today? I don't want to frighten you, but it's nothing
more than the truth."

"Death doesn't frighten me, Mrs.—Eleanor. We both
know you're dying. I don't think it will be today, though,
nor yet tomorrow. I simply thought a little rest might re-
fresh you, give you the strength to give me the answers I
need, that's all."

"No, we'll do it now, if you don't mind."

This was a remarkable woman. If I'd guessed it before,
now I knew.

"All right, then. I'll be quick, if I can, though I'm
afraid I'll ask a lot of the same things the police did. And
do you mind if I tape the conversation?"

She shook her head. I started the tape and murmured an introduction into it, feeling silly: the date, the time, and our names. It felt like an amateurish imitation of an interrogation, as seen on a third-rate cop show.

I cleared my throat. "For a start, why did you come to Penzance? And when, by the way?"

"On Monday, just the day before you arrived. Is it only five days ago? It seems a lifetime."

She bit her lip, conquered her tears, and went on. "It was Lexa's idea. You see, I hadn't told her anything about her background, not until—but I'd better begin earlier than that."

Eleanor's eyes stared into the past; her voice fell into a smoother pace.

"She knew she was adopted; I'd told her that. She knew that her mother had died when she was tiny, but I'd lied and told her that her father had died, too. She knew she was illegitimate. I'd had to tell her that, because she began to want to know about her medical history. Well, I could give her Betty's, but I made up a story to explain the rest.

"Somehow I didn't want to tell her that I didn't know who her father was. It made Betty sound promiscuous, and she wasn't. So far as I know, Lexa's father was her one and only one-night stand. Ironic, isn't it?"

She picked up the glass of water on the bedside table, sipped at it, and continued.

"So I told her, when she was old enough to know, that Betty and her boyfriend—I called him Bill, just to give him a name—that they had gone away to be married, but that they'd had an automobile accident on the way to get the license. I had to say that, you see, or Lexa might have looked up the license for her father's name. I claimed I never knew his surname, and made it sound reasonable.

It was the Swinging Sixties, after all. Everyone tossed Christian names about; I genuinely didn't know the surnames of half Betty's friends.

"I'd been afraid to tell her the real story, what little I knew of it. I didn't want her growing up thinking that her mother'd killed herself, or been murdered. That's a horrible idea for a child to have to deal with. And when she was older, I didn't want her looking for her father. I was afraid. I told you that before. I was quite sure he'd killed Betty, and I was terrified of what he'd do to Lexa."

"But you did tell her, eventually, didn't you?"

Eleanor took a sip of tea, set the cup aside, and stared at nothing.

"I knew I was dying, you see. Lexa had made me move in with her. She'd had a posh flat in Knightsbridge ever since she'd first made such a success of her modeling, but I'd been quite content to stay in my little one. I never married, you see. Crosby is the name I was born with. I started calling myself *Mrs.* Crosby, and told her I was a widow, when Lexa went to school. It would have been awkward, in those days, for people to know her adoptive mother was an old maid.

"We stayed close, but I never wanted her tied to my apron strings. She was a beautiful, successful, famous woman, and I was as proud of her as if she really were my daughter, but she had her own life to live, and so did I.

"Then I became ill, and then I got worse, and Lexa worried about me. She insisted that I move in with her. She couldn't always be there, of course. She travels—traveled—all over the world for her photo shoots, you know. But when she was out of town she'd have someone come in, a housekeeper, to keep the flat clean and cook for me. I could have done it myself, then, but Lexa could afford the help, and she liked to spoil me.''

She stopped talking and closed her eyes. This time I sat still. I didn't know if she was ready for sleep or just remembering.

She opened her eyes. ''The day I went to the doctor and he told me the cancer was still there, and growing, I came home and thought for a long time. Lexa came home early that day, and over tea I told her everything. I couldn't live with the lies any longer. Dying, a person comes to have a terrible passion for the truth.''

A person like you does, anyway, I thought.

''I never thought that at this stage of her life she'd want to find her father. I don't know that I'd have told her if I'd known how she'd take it. But it was all she could think about. 'My father's alive!' she kept saying. 'He must still be alive!' I explained, over and over again, why I didn't want her to look for him. I told her there was danger, but she was young and beautiful and famous. Nothing was ever going to happen to her. 'It'll be all right,' she said. 'You'll come with me, and you'll feel better. You know sea air is good for people.''

''But surely she knew how ill you were! You *had* told her?''

''I'd told her, but she refused to accept it. For people like her, the golden people, there is no such thing as death. She was quite wealthy, you know. She was sure that if we could find the right specialist, he would cure me. She had heard there was a good man living in Cornwall. He was retired, but she intended to persuade him to look me over. 'Just as soon as you're rested,' she'd say. 'And while you get your strength back, I'll go and find my father.'''

She lay back on her pillows. "Find her father! I think she found him, right enough." She closed her eyes.

There were so many questions still to ask, but Eleanor had had enough. I stood up.

"I'm tired," she said faintly.

"I know. I'm leaving. Try to rest."

Before I left the room, I spoke again to the police-woman. "Look, tell me to mind my own business if you want to, but in America we have organizations called hospices. They specialize in the care of people who are dying, especially cancer patients. Is there such a thing here?"

The woman smiled. "Of course. The hospice movement was, I believe, founded in England."

"Oh. Sorry. Anyway, when the doctor comes, could you ask him if he could set up visits by hospice people? I agree with you. Mrs. Crosby is very ill indeed, and I think she needs skilled medical care, but there doesn't seem much point in tying up a hospital bed, does there?"

She smiled again. "I will talk to the doctor, Mrs. Martin. I had already planned to do so."

Feeling more than a little useless, I slipped out of the room.

THIRTEEN

I MADE ALAN join me in a walk. I'd had enough of sitting inside a stuffy sickroom. The tide being out, we walked along the beach while I told him the whole story.

"So she was looking for her father," Alan said.

"Yes. I'd guessed as much."

"Of course, but it's useful to have it confirmed. And I think I remember that she thought, or at least her stepmother thought, that he was someone important, influential."

"Yes, but Eleanor could be quite wrong. It's not much to go on, Betty's tone of voice, her laugh when she talked about him."

"No, but it isn't to be dismissed out of hand, either. You say she's an intelligent woman, Mrs. Crosby. She struck me that way, too, although I have only a glancing acquaintance. And we mustn't forget that she knew Betty Adams very well."

"Ye-es."

Alan quirked an eyebrow at my tone, and I tried to explain.

"It's just that she's so prejudiced in Betty's favor. In the gospel according to Eleanor, Betty could do no wrong. She had a lot of boyfriends, but she wasn't promiscuous. She liked to have a good time at parties where there were drugs, but she never did anything really wrong. She couldn't hold down a steady job, but she was really a dependable kind of person. And so on. I'm not sure she, Eleanor, I mean, is entirely reliable on the subject of Betty's feelings and insinuations.''

"Hmm. I see what you mean. Were they lovers, do you think, Betty and Mrs. Crosby?"

"Eleanor said not, remember. Without my asking."

Both of Alan's eyebrows rose at that. "Protesting too much, perhaps?"

"I don't know. The number of Betty's boyfriends, and the fact of Lexa's existence, would seem to suggest that Betty, at least, wouldn't have been interested in a lesbian relationship. If you want my honest opinion, I think that Betty looked upon Eleanor as a mother figure, and Eleanor, a lonely woman, was pretty well content with the role. All the same, I intend to take Eleanor's character judgments, of either Betty or Lexa, with a large helping of salt. Mothers are notoriously biased toward their children, especially daughters.''

"Right. However, I say again, I don't intend to dismiss her intuition about Lexa's father. For one thing, the number of influential men of the right age, while large, is far smaller than the number of men without that distinction. Anything that narrows the field of search is useful, even if it's only a working hypothesis."

"Okay, I'll buy it, for now. So how many influential men would there have been in Penzance in 1968?"

"Nineteen sixty-seven. That's when Lexa was conceived. And don't forget, the man must still be here."

"Only if we throw in another working hypothesis, that the two murders were by the same hand."

"Confound it, Dorothy, you're beginning to think too much like a policeman." He grinned, but shook his head. "We can't examine the universe all at once. If we define

the problem narrowly and get nowhere, then we can ex-
pand our definition.''

"All right, all right, I'm just trying not to jump to conclusions. A habit of which you often accuse me, I might
add.''

"A hypothesis is not a conclusion. All right, then, influential men between the ages, at present, of—what,
would you say?''

"Let's see. Betty would have been twenty-one, or
thereabouts, when she got pregnant, twenty-two when
Lexa was born. She'd be fifty-five or so now if she'd
lived. I wouldn't think she'd have had much to do with a
younger boy. The difference between twenty-one and
nineteen, say, is vast. So the boy was probably at least
her age.

"But an upper limit? Oh, dear, I remember myself at
that age, falling head over heels for a visiting professor
at Randolph who was at least thirty years older than I
was. He was English, and I thought he was so suave and
sophisticated. And he could dance like Fred Astaire.''

I smiled reminiscently and then shook my head. "I
hadn't met Frank yet, of course.''

"Yes, love, I get the point. Back to the problem in
hand. We're looking for someone at least fifty-five, then,
up to—well, still able to totter about.''

"Better than that. Someone reasonably fit and mobile.
That cave isn't at all easy to reach.''

"Except by water.''

"Oh. I hadn't thought of that.''

"To continue. Someone, mid-fifties or older, who lived
in Penzance in 1967 and still lives here—''

"And who might have known Betty Adams,'' I added.

"That doesn't narrow it much. How do we know whom
she might have known?''

"Well, we know what kind of parties she liked to go to."

"Yes, but if we're talking about a respectable type, he'd probably have disguised his interest in that kind of party. So it could still have been anyone."

"You're right. Golly, it's going to be a long list."

"Not necessarily all that long," said Alan. There was an odd edge to his voice.

"You've thought of something."

"You say the Crosbys arrived on Monday."

"That's what Eleanor said. The day before we got here."

"And they didn't know Penzance."

"They both told us that."

"Then what was the best opportunity for Lexa to meet people?"

"Well, we don't know what she did on Monday or Tuesday—oh! The party, with us, of course."

"The party. And there may have been a fair number of influential people there, but it's a shorter list than the entire upper-class population of Penzance, especially when one weeds out those who weren't living in the vicinity in the late sixties. It'll certainly give the police something to run through their computers."

"I shudder to think how they used to do that sort of thing before there were computers."

"The old-fashioned, slogging way. And missed out on a number of possibilities, probably. When I remember the hours I used to spend as a constable—ah, well, it doesn't bear thinking about."

I dismissed that. "Well, there's nothing we can do about that list until the police get busy. Are they already working on it, do you think?"

"Probably. I told them about the party, of course."

"Yes, of course. By the way, shouldn't I get this tape over to them?"

"I'll do that. I want to ask them a few things, as well."

"Like what?"

"For example, we saw Lexa that night, walking past the restaurant. I could bear to know where was she going, and I suspect Colin's people have begun that trace, as well."

"Goodness, I don't envy them that job. It wasn't a good night for people to be looking out their windows, was it? And after the rain started in again, I wouldn't have thought anybody'd have been on the street who didn't have to be."

"Such are the frustrations of a policeman's life. But let's do some thinking, Dorothy. It was, as you say, a ghastly night to be out. So why was Lexa?"

"Search me. We agreed at the time she probably wasn't going to dinner."

"She certainly wasn't going for a nice walk, not in those high heels."

"Or that weather. Lexa took a lot of exercise, but even she wouldn't have felt obliged to do it then. So I give up. Where *was* she going?"

"Lexa," said Alan thoughtfully, "was a very single-minded young lady. She had come to Cornwall to find her father. At a guess, I'd say Lexa had managed to locate a fertile source of information."

"Oh, stop being mysterious and tell me!"

"You haven't taken her age into account, Dorothy, her single condition, her glamorous profession, any of that, or you'd have thought it out for yourself. And think how she was dressed. Where, these days, does a young, beautiful, single woman go to meet and talk to people?"

I frowned. "Not a pub, surely. No—no, wait, it's coming—a place where there's music. And, oh, she knew there were some places like that around here somewhere, because the superintendent and the rector were going on and on about it at the party, right behind us. Yes, and those young men she captured that night of the party— they'd have known exactly where to go. You're thinking of a rave club, aren't you?''

Alan's face was grave. ''I am. I may be wrong, of course, but it's the most logical conclusion, given her clothes and everything else. She was a little old for that sort of thing, but she appeared much younger. She was looking for someone who, once upon a time, gave her mother LSD. She knew he'd be middle-aged by now and perhaps no longer into drugs, but she needed to try to find a link to him. What more sensible place to begin than by finding a distribution center for the modern drug that's taken its place?''

''Ecstasy.''

''Or MDMA, as it's more formally known.''

I tried to remember what I knew about the drug. ''It can be very dangerous, can't it?''

''It can, for many reasons. Its proponents claim it induces peaceful, happy feelings, so no one on an MDMA high would ever harm anyone. There may be some truth in that, but it's not the whole truth. Part of the trouble with the drug is the reaction, the crash, which in some people can be severe. But even worse, MDMA is often adulterated with a similar drug called PMA, or para-methoxy amphetamine, if I have it right.''

''I'll stick to PMA, thanks. What is it?''

''It's a copycat drug, sometimes added to or substituted for MDMA, and it's a killer, Dorothy, really diabolical stuff. It elevates the body temperature, as ecstasy does. It makes the victim feel warm and pleasant and happy. The trouble is, the body temperature carries on climbing, and climbing some more, until the person dies. The temperature can get to 107 degrees, 108. The victim virtually cooks from the inside.''

I shuddered. "What a terrible way to die!"

"Yes. And if Lexa did go to a rave club, and did find out who her father might be, I'd lay you long odds that the autopsy will find club drugs of one sort or another in her body."

"She wouldn't have taken them, Alan! She didn't use drugs."

"She said she didn't."

"She was a model! She had to keep herself looking wonderful, and she knew the best way to do that was to stay healthy."

"All right, all right, now *I'm* thinking like a policeman. If she didn't die of something obvious, and we've agreed she probably didn't, then she died of something else. I'll concede that she probably would not have taken ecstasy or a look-alike. At least not knowingly."

As that one sank in, I dug the toe of my shoe into the sand, found a pebble, and kicked it with all my strength. When I spoke, my voice was shaking.

"I understand now, Alan. About you and those murderers and rapists and drug dealers. I didn't before, not quite, but I do now. I'm not going to rest until we find the man who did this to Lexa, and when we do, I'd better be physically restrained or I'm going to hurt him very badly."

We stood for a while looking at the sea before turning back toward the hotel.

FOURTEEN

I LOOKED IN ON Eleanor when we got back to the hotel and found the police surgeon with her. The three of us chatted for a moment, and then I followed the doctor out the door.

"How is she? And before you answer, I should tell you that I do know she's dying. I don't mean that. I mean, is she in pain, and how is her mental and emotional state?"

The doctor, thank heaven, wasn't the self-important type. He answered readily enough, "Mrs. Crosby suffers very little physical pain now. The disease has passed that stage. She is strong mentally, quite alert, even a trifle combative. Her physical strength will vary from day to day, though naturally the slope will be downhill in the long run. Emotionally, of course…well, she's suffered a very great loss. Just now I would say she's drained, or 'numb' might be the word. That's a mercy, of course, but unfortunately it won't last. She'll go over the tragedy in her mind again and again, until she either comes to terms with what's happened, or else—"

"Or else the strain kills her," I finished.

"It might well do. The will to live is a far more powerful force than many people realize, and of course the opposite is equally true. When someone is terminally ill, it is often the will *not* to live, rather than any definitive physical change, that will bring about the end."

"Yes, I understand. That's why I'm so glad you came to check on her. How did she react to you? Does she resent your coming?"

"No, she was quite gracious about it. She's realistic about her illness, as you've probably realized."

"Yes, but she's pretty prickly right now. Now let me ask you something. You probably know that my husband and I are—well, if I said 'assisting the police,' I'd give the wrong impression, but in fact that's what we're trying to do."

"Yes. I should also add, Mrs. Martin, that I knew Mr. Nesbitt slightly back in the old days, and I've followed his career with interest. I live in Newlyn, you see."

And that, given the tightly knit English sense of community, did explain his interest.

"Well, then, you know that Alan and I are going to need to talk quite a lot to Mrs. Crosby, ask her questions from time to time, painful questions, searching ones. Is she strong enough to stand that sort of thing?"

"You're asking, I think, how long she has to live."

"More or less."

"I can't tell you that. I don't know, and even if I did I wouldn't say. There is such a thing as confidentiality, you know. I can, though, tell you what you probably know much better than I, and that is that Mrs. Crosby seems to be a woman who knows her own mind. If she wants you to solve the question of how her daughter died, she'll not take kindly to anyone—me or anyone else—who tries to interfere. Furthermore, she'll almost certainly live until the case is solved, unless it drags on forever. That driving need to know what happened, to find the villain, gives her a powerful incentive to keep going. I'd say, go ahead and ask your questions whenever she feels up to talking. If it's too much for her—well, she'll die doing what she wants to do, and that's more than most of us can say, isn't it?''

"Indeed. Is a policewoman going to stay with her?"

"No, she's said she'd rather be alone, and she seems able to look after herself, more or less. We have notified hospice. I understand that was your suggestion.''

"Well, I mentioned it, but the policewoman had already thought of it.''

"Yes. At any rate, they'll be popping in from time to time, making sure she takes her pain medication when she needs it, helping her with bathing if she needs help, that sort of thing. I suggested that she'd be better off at home, but she doesn't want to leave Penzance, and I can understand.''

"That all relieves my mind a good deal. I'll look in again this afternoon and make sure she's had some lunch.''

We shook hands and I went to join Alan for lunch.

We had decided there was little I could do until Eleanor was able to talk to me again. Alan, however, set himself the task of tracking down the rave club.

"I'll go and have a chat with John Boleigh. The police will certainly have talked to him already, but I want to get the names of the men who whisked Lexa off at the party. One of them is likely to have been her date Thursday night. Once I find him, it ought to be fairly easy to find the club.''

"Then what?"

"That's the sticky part. I can hardly go charging in myself, asking all sorts of awkward questions. I'd get no answers, and I'd terrorize the wildlife.''

"True. You look an awful lot like a policeman.''

"It was a great handicap to my career, and in this case I don't think you can help, either. You don't look like a policeman, but I'm afraid you don't look like someone who would frequent a rave club, either.''

"No, I doubt that gray hair and flowered hats feature prominently among the patrons there. Anyway, my hearing's not so good that I'm prepared to risk it on the decibel levels in a place like that. I don't understand why all teenagers aren't deaf.''

"Many of them are, actually, or on the way. At any rate, let me try to find out what I can about the club, or clubs. We'll work out a plan to infiltrate it later.''

So I sent him off with a hug, and sat down to figure out what I could do for the good of the order. After fifteen minutes of sitting in our room with a blank pad of paper and an equally blank mind, I had achieved nothing but frustration. My strengths are with people, talking to them, gaining their confidence, sometimes learning their secrets. But here in an unfamiliar setting I could think of no one to talk to—except for Eleanor, and she needed her rest.

Very well. I slapped the pad and pencil down on the desk and stood. If I was exiled from my natural habitat of tea tables and cozy kitchens and other breeding grounds of gossip, I'd go to my other home away from home, the library, and see what I could learn there.

Back in my teaching days, I was often guilty, I admit, of the favorite academic cop-out: "Well, Johnny, I don't know the answer to that myself, but let's look it up.'' The funny thing was that it often worked. The whole class would go with me to the school library at the first opportunity and descend like locusts on reference books, history books, science books, biographies, even works of fiction that dealt with the question at hand. They found out the answer, and they also learned how to use a library. A few learned to love libraries almost as much as I did.

It took me only a few minutes to reach the one in Penzance, and when I got there, the librarians were kind and helpful.

I had decided on the way that my most useful strategy at this point was to learn all I could about the terrain, if that's the right word for an area that includes far more than its fair share of water. There had to be a reason why the bodies of two women had been found in a particular cave miles from anywhere. Maybe I could get some sort of clue from books about the Mount's Bay region.

There were a good many books. I filled most of a reading table with them and sat down to my task.

At the end of three hours, my eyes were tired and both my head and my back ached, but I had acquired knowledge.

I knew, for one thing, a great deal more than I had about the geography of the southwest extremity of England. I had figured out exactly where Mount's Bay was, and its relationship to Prussia Cove and its components, Bessie's Cove, Piskie's Cove, and King's Cove. I knew more about the history of Bessie's Cove, and its topography, than I was ever going to remember. I had learned (with a shuddering thought of Betty Adams's body) that the shore currents often brought flotsam to the caves of Bessie's Cove. I could reel off, with great fluency, the names of famous Cornish smugglers and something of their histories.

I knew about the tin and copper mines that had flourished of old, their shafts extending out under the sea, and the flooding that had often put an end to operations and, occasionally, to miners' lives.

I had read, too, about shipwrecks along the treacherous coast, and the extent to which Cornishmen profited from the plunder of the doomed ships' cargoes. (There was disagreement among various accounts as to whether those same Cornishmen might, perhaps, have *caused* some of the wrecks by the placing of misleading lights on a rocky shore.) I had read of famous wrecks, including that of a German ship in 1944, and had learned, with some astonishment, of the spectacular wreck in 1997 of a container-ship, the *Cita,* in the Scilly Isles a few miles off Land's End. That one provided bounty for the Scillonians for months, though one did wonder what they had done with the container full of fifteen hundred wooden toilet seats.

There were books about famous rock formations out on the moors, about valuable china-clay deposits. About saints, holy men, legendary figures. There were quite a number of books about King Arthur at Tintagel, up on the north coast: myth or history? The chroniclers quarreled about that, too. There were books about Cornwall's historic industries, about her ancient and now almost defunct Celtic language, with its strong links to Welsh and Gaelic.

It was all engrossing stuff. One could understand why books and books and books had been written about it.

What it was not, as far as I could tell, was helpful. There was nothing in the masses of material I had read to give me any idea why two women, mother and daughter, had gone out on stormy nights over thirty years apart, never to be seen alive again.

I noted down a few books I'd like to buy, if I could find them, thanked the librarians for their help, and trudged back to the hotel, better informed but no further enlightened.

Alan hadn't come back yet. I sat down on our lovely, comfortable four-poster bed and thought about a nap. My head did ache, after all, and a nap might help. Afternoon naps are a sad waste of time. Unfortunately, as one grows older, they become more and more attractive. At home, with the cats always willing to curl up beside me, the temptation is often irresistible.

I stood up and shook myself, rather like a wet dog. This would never do. Eleanor Crosby might be awake, and my convenience took second place to hers. I would, I had every reason to hope and trust, have many more years to take naps at my leisure. I might have only days to talk to Eleanor. I let myself out of our room and walked up the single flight of stairs to hers.

She answered my tap on the door almost immediately. Not only was she up, she was dressed, casually but elegantly, in trim beige slacks and a silk shirt. She even wore a little makeup: rouge, lipstick. It only emphasized her pallor, but it showed she was making an effort, for which I was grateful. If there really was anything in the "will to live" theory, Eleanor wasn't going to die just yet.

"What progress have you made?" she asked eagerly. "Oh, sorry, please do sit down."

I drew up a small chair and conscientiously turned on my tape recorder; she sank down in a comfortable armchair. "Very little, I'm afraid. Alan is out right now trying to get a line on where Lexa might have gone that night, and with whom."

"The night she died," Eleanor said, her voice perfectly steady and somewhat dry. "I try not to avoid the word, Dorothy. I prefer to call a spade a spade, and in my present circumstances it would be idiotic to do anything else. Please don't feel you must be diplomatic around me."

I swallowed hard. "I'll do my best. I'm pretty much of the spade school myself, but I do try not to cause anyone pain, if I can help it."

"Pain." Eleanor smiled bleakly. "It means little anymore. I have felt every kind imaginable in the months past. Dorothy, are you a religious woman?"

I never know how to answer that question. "My beliefs are important to me. I don't know how well I live up to them in practice."

"Do you believe there is a life after this one?"

"Yes." About that, anyway, I had no need to temporize. "I can see no sense to this life if it all ends after such a brief time. And I believe, profoundly, that the universe is meant to make sense."

"I've never been able to make up my mind. If you're right, then I'll see Lexa again, and Betty, too. And soon. Even if you're wrong, I'll soon be beyond pain. That, even if there is nothing else, is a great comfort."

Eleanor dismissed the matter, coughed, drank a little water, and settled down to the business at hand. "The night she died, you said. You want to know where she went."

I nodded.

"It's the obvious question, of course, and the first thing the police ask me. I could tell them no more than I tell you. I don't think they believed me, but I don't know where she went. She wouldn't tell me."

"I'm not surprised, actually. She knew you disapproved of this whole quest. She wouldn't want you to know the details."

"You see that, do you? I wasn't sure the policeman understood. He seemed to think I was trying to keep something from him. As if I wouldn't do anything in my power to bring her murderer to justice!"

I didn't mention the fact that Lexa's death was not yet officially classified as murder. Eleanor knew that, just as we both knew we were treating it as such. "What, exactly, did she tell you? You did know she was going out, didn't you?"

"Yes, she would never leave the hotel without telling

me. She had the adjoining room, and she knew I liked the idea of her being there. Not to play nursemaid, mind! I didn't want her to feel under any obligation. It was only that her very presence, nearby, was comforting.''

Eleanor turned her face away, blew her nose. I feared she would apologize for letting her grief show, but she was evidently past that, as she was past the need for polite evasions. When she looked back, tears were still on her face; she made no attempt to wipe them away. I hoped I could live up to her terrible need for honesty.

''So she said—what?'' I prompted.

''I can tell you her exact words. I will never forget them, for they are the last words she ever spoke to me. She came in to me, in this room, dressed like a teenager. Well, almost like a tart, truth to tell. I didn't know she owned such clothes. Short skirt, tight top, high-heeled boots, and her hair hanging loose and wild. She'd over-done her makeup, too. She really didn't look at all like herself, and I must have looked disapproving, because she laughed at me.

'' 'I'm off to a masquerade party, Mum,' she said, and twirled around to show me the full effect. 'You didn't know I could look eighteen again, did you?'

''Well, I didn't say what I thought. I couldn't say any-thing for a moment. She looked and sounded so much like her mother, I—oh, it terrified me. I felt foolish, though, and I couldn't find the right words. I wanted to tell her not to go, or not looking like that, but she's—she was a grown woman. I'd left off telling her what to do long since.

''But she saw what I was thinking, I know, for she said, 'Don't worry. I've no intention of doing anything foolish. I'll leave all that to the others.' And then she told me she'd probably be very late getting back, perhaps nearly morning, and I was not to wait up. Then she kissed me good night, and..."

The tears were open this time, and I admit I shared them. It was a poignant picture, the vibrant young woman, the older one so desperately ill, the casual, affectionate leave-taking...

"You have one good thing to remember," I said when I could speak easily again. "You parted on happy terms. I always think it must be terribly hard when there has been an argument and there's never a chance to make it up."

"It's terribly hard, no matter what the circumstances." Eleanor's voice was flat, emotion ironed out of it once more.

"Yes, of course." I tried to regain my own self-control. "What do you think she meant when she said she wouldn't do anything foolish?"

"Drugs, I thought at the time. I thought she was going to a rave, dressed that way so as to fit in. She almost never does that sort of thing. She has to get her rest; if she's tired the camera sees it. And she's never taken drugs in her life, not even medicinal ones. She's never ill. I doubt she's ever had so much as an aspirin. She can't; it would show. Her image has always been healthy, the girl next door."

"Yes, that's the impression I had of her. Clean, healthy skin, shining hair, a figure kept slender by exercise as much as diet. So she'd never been to a rave?"

"Well, I don't know, of course. Until I moved in with her, she led her own life. I didn't know the details. I'd say not often, if ever. She didn't really have the time for much social life."

I pondered that. "So she wasn't the glamorous international celebrity of her publicity?"

"She was a celebrity, but the glamour was more sham than real. Her job paid her a small fortune, but it was hard work. She hardly had the time to spend all that money."

Money! I hadn't considered that aspect of it. It was a touchy question, but Eleanor had asked me to forget about diplomacy. "So she must have left quite a lot. Who gets it, do you know?"

Eleanor hadn't thought about it, either, apparently. I could see the shock on her face. "I've no idea at all. I don't know if she had a will. If not, I suppose I would get the money, as next of kin. Though I don't know if adoption counts in that sort of thing. How ironic if I should get all that money. If the law moves at its usual speed, I'll hardly live long enough to see a penny of it."

"Do *you* have a will?"

"Of course. There's little enough to leave, but it was all to go to Lexa."

Well, it would have to be checked, but it looked as though one possible motive had just vanished in a neat little tail-chasing circle.

"I think I have only one more question, then, at least for now. What did Lexa do on the Monday when you arrived, and on Tuesday? How did she spend her time, I mean?"

"On the Monday I was very tired from the journey. She spent her time getting me settled in. But on Tuesday morning she went off to the library. She said she wanted to learn something about Cornwall."

The library! Suddenly my afternoon seemed less likely to have been a waste of time. "And did she learn anything of interest?"

"Not that I recall. Tuesday afternoon—when you asked her to go to St. Michael's Mount?"

I nodded.

"She wanted to stay with me. I wasn't feeling very well, so she sat and talked to me about what she'd read, until I was able to fall asleep for a nap. I wasn't really very interested; I just liked to hear her voice. All I remember is something about a shipwreck. Not very useful, I fear."

A shipwreck. Would it have been the famous one, the wreck of the *Cita* in the Scillys?

It might be of no importance at all, but I intended to do all I could to find out.

FIFTEEN

I LEFT ELEANOR THEN, telling her I'd be back soon. There was a good deal I wanted to talk over with Alan, so I was pleased, returning to our room, to find that he was back.

"Any luck?" he said when he had released me from a bear hug. "How did you spend the afternoon?"

"You first."

"Well, for a start I found an off-license and laid in supplies." He reached for the plastic bag on the table and pulled out a square bottle with a familiar black label. "Care for a spot?"

"Yes, please."

I took a sip and then put my glass down. "All right. What did you find out?"

"I found the club."

"You did! Oh, that's wonderful, Alan! How did you manage it?"

"I went to see Boleigh. He didn't seem best pleased to see me; I got the feeling I'd interrupted an afternoon nap."

"I can't say I blame him. I very nearly succumbed to one, myself. Then what? Was he cooperative?"

"He was civil enough, considering I'd disturbed him, and full of distress about Lexa's death. He seemed to be as confused about her real age as we were at first, by the way. He went on a good deal about the dangers teenagers are exposed to these days.''

"Did you tell him Lexa wasn't all that young?''

"No. Policeman's habit, I suppose. I don't readily part with information the other fellow doesn't have. One learns more by listening than talking. I thought he might mention some specific dangers, and he did, said he fretted about his grandchildren, what with drugs so readily available at dance parties.''

"Aha!''

"Well, no, worse luck. I asked, of course, if he knew of any rave clubs in Penzance or environs, but he said there weren't any, to his knowledge. He was rather vehement about it.''

"Wishful thinking, maybe? The superintendent and the rector seemed to think there are.''

"Yes, but they both, in their different ways, see a good deal more of the seedy side of Penzance than old Boleigh. He's by way of being a civic benefactor, on quite a large scale, I understand. Music, the visual arts, architectural preservation and renovation, that sort of thing. I shouldn't think he'd so much as know the name of a single contemporary pop musician.''

"Neither would I,'' I admitted. "I can name the four Beatles, but that's about where my expertise ends.''

"Count your blessings. At any rate, I switched to a different tack, asked him for the names of those five men who'd been so attracted to Lexa the night of his party.''

"I suppose he wanted to know why.''

"No, because I had a lovely fairy tale all ready.''

"Alan! You're learning bad habits from me. I'm sure you didn't tell lies when you were a CID detective.''

"You might be surprised. At any rate, I said Lexa had lost a ring that night at the party, and that her mother was very upset about it, now that Lexa was gone. Sentimental value, all that bosh. Of course, I asked first if it had been found when the caterers tidied up, and he said not. I said I had assumed that was the case, Boleigh being such a conscientious chap. I was sure he would have rung up, or told the police, I said.''

"The best butter.''

"Of course. Then I just happened to remember those five men. Said I thought one of them might have found the ring, put it in his pocket, meaning to phone Lexa— you can follow the line for yourself.''

"Brilliant. But why didn't you just tell him the truth?''

"Because he talks to a lot of people in the course of his philanthropy, and you never know what he might let slip. I don't want the whole town knowing we're looking into Lexa's death.''

"No, of course not. Sorry. Go on.''

"So he gave me their names, addresses, and telephone numbers.''

"And you came back here and got on the phone.''

"For a solid hour. Where were you, by the way?''

"I'll tell you later. Go on.''

"It took a good many calls, of course, because it's Saturday. All but one of them were out when I rang the first time, so it took several tries, and of course it was the fifth man, the last one I finally reached, who delivered the goods.''

"It always is. What story did you spin for them?''

"I started with my nice little ring fiction, in case they talked to Boleigh. If one must lie, it's best, I've found, to keep it simple.''

I nodded. Alan was right, though it's a lesson I have a hard time remembering. I tend to elaborate and then forget what I've said.

"From there I branched out with each of them, wondering if he'd happened to see Lexa since the party. Went on a bit about how lovely she was, how appealing, how I could understand any man wanting to see more of her. I rather left the impression that I was under her spell myself."

I sighed ostentatiously. "Remind me to look put upon if I should run into any of them. Did they buy it?"

"I think so. At any rate, all but one denied seeing her again, with great regret expressed. Two of them have live-in girlfriends, by the way."

"It figures. And the fifth?"

"The fifth, one James Barnet, met her on Thursday night at a hall just behind Wharf Road."

"The rave."

"And quite a lively little party, I gather."

"He told you what went on? I thought we agreed you look too much like a policeman to learn anything very useful."

"Apparently I looked more to Mr. Barnet like the dirty old man I was doing my best to impersonate. It helped that he'd been smoking a good deal of pot and was feeling very little pain."

"So that's what it is! I thought your clothes smelled odd."

"I'm surprised you didn't recognize the scent, and you a retired teacher."

"It hadn't made its way down to the fourth grade by the time I quit teaching. But yes, I knew the smell in those days from the high school kids. One forgets, mercifully. So what did he tell you about the rave?"

"Well, for a start, where to find it, more or less. The police can take it from there."

"Go on, what else?"

"He gave me a scenario of the evening. His memory is about as good as one might expect, given the drugs he took at the time and what he was taking this afternoon—not only cannabis, I suspect. However, after a somewhat tedious recital of exactly what I expected—music, lights, dancing, and so on—he got around to the drugs."

"Ecstasy."

"Yes, and others, as well, I gathered. Cocaine, heroin—as I said, quite a little party."

"I wonder this Barnet person has any brain left."

"I doubt he will have for much longer. But he did tell me one extremely interesting thing, something that gave me lots of ideas."

"Alan, if you don't tell me right this minute, I'm going to pour this bourbon on your head."

"I shall smell *really* interesting then. Very well. I have always believed in saving the best for last. He told me that Alexis met a number of people at the rave, among them a very attractive girl of about seventeen or eighteen. Blond and foxy, he said, and added that she was about Lexa's age, which tells you something of how observant he is."

"Don't blame the poor guy for that. She deliberately set out to look young that night. I talked to Eleanor about it. So who was she, this girl?"

"Well, that's where it gets very interesting indeed. Her name is Pamela, no surname, of course."

"Of course. Not at that age."

"Pamela and Lexa hit it off right away, and spent a good deal of time giggling, even dancing together occasionally. There's quite a lot of that at raves, you know. Solo dancing, same-sex pairs. It has little to do with what's to happen later in the evening, more with the general euphoria that the lights and the music and, of course, the drugs induce.''

I leaned forward intently. ''Did he say anything about Lexa taking drugs?''

''I asked. He didn't remember clearly, but assumed she did. He said she drank a lot of water, which people on ecstasy must do. Their mouths become very dry.''

''Lexa always drinks—drank—a lot of water.''

''Yes, and of course dancing makes one hot and thirsty, especially in a crowd with smoke in the air. But let me get to the interesting bit. Lexa and Pamela are getting on like a house afire, yes? Well, there was a bit of a dustup late in the evening, or early in the morning, actually.''

He paused to gauge the effect.

''Between Lexa and Pamela? Do hurry it up!''

''No, someone came to the club. An old cove, my informant said graciously, giving me a look that said he placed me in the same category. Mr. Barnet thought he looked familiar, but couldn't place him. Given Barnet's probable level of drug elevation at the time, and the obscuring effects of strobe lights and smoke, I'm a trifle surprised he could even venture a guess as to age and sex.

''He did remember quite clearly, however, that the gentleman in question was in a filthy temper, and that the object of his rage was…care to hazard a guess?''

''Lexa,'' I said with bitter satisfaction.

''Wrong. It was Lexa's new friend, Pamela.''

''But then… Alan, why are you so interested in this Pamela person?''

''Because she and the gentleman got into a shouting match, and Lexa tried to intervene. Apparently it worked for a little while. He sat at the table, bought everyone drinks—''

''Lexa didn't drink.''

"Water, orange juice, whatever. At any rate they talked for a while, and then the man lost his temper again. It ended with all three of them being chucked out of the club for creating a disturbance. Mr. Barnet was quite bitter about that. I suspect he'd had rather a different party aftermath in mind, and he blamed the gentleman for spoiling all the delightful plans. 'Pushes his way in, acting like he owns the place, like he owns the world' was his description of the gentleman's actions."

"What did Mr. Barnet do then? Did he try to go after Lexa?"

"No. It seems not to have occurred to him that the girls might be in danger, or perhaps he simply didn't care. At any rate, he eschewed the role of knight-errant and went home alone to sulk."

"And Lexa and Pamela Whoever went off with the 'old cove.'"

"We don't know that. We don't know anything more than that they left the club together."

"When?"

"Ah! The important question, isn't it? Unfortunately Mr. Barnet was floating a little too high to remember such a mundane detail as time. Late, he said, but when pressed he could come no closer. He also began to wonder why I wanted to know, and what it had to do with a missing ring, so I fell back on my lascivious interest in the mysterious Pamela."

"Oh, so you switched to Pamela. Fickle man."

"I had to," he said, suddenly serious. "Barnet knows that Lexa is dead. He may not be fully functional, but he watches the telly. I do believe he had forgotten until the second or third time I made him go over the altercation and what he saw as the two girls left the club with the unknown man. He got a bit weepy then, about Lexa, and I was able to make my escape.''

''With two descriptions that are about as much use as a do-it-yourself kit without the instructions.''

''With a little more than that, actually. He did say two small things I forgot to mention. One was that Pamela seemed well known at the club. The other was that the 'old cove' seemed, at the end, to have switched most of his furious attention from Pamela to Lexa.''

SIXTEEN

WELL, I WAS IMPRESSED enough with that to forgive Alan for his roundabout way of getting to the heart of the matter. His new information put my piddling little scraps of fact and gossip in the shade, all right. I made a quick trip up to Eleanor's room to give her our new information about the club, the girl Pamela, and the old man. Though tired and spent, Eleanor cheered up considerably at the idea that we were making progress. I promised to keep her informed and then left so she could get some rest and Alan and I could get some dinner.

I regaled Alan with my meager information over chicken tikka masala at the tandoori place Alan had mentioned.

"So Lexa was interested in shipwrecks," Alan commented at the end of my recitation.

"Well, maybe. Eleanor wasn't really paying attention to what Lexa said, remember. She may have been talking about something quite different and just happened to mention the wreck in passing."

"Possibly. Would you like a bit more raita, or some of the lime pickle?"

"Both, please. I need the raita to cool down the other." I spooned some of the yogurt and cucumber mixture over my curry, added a judicious modicum of the fiery-hot, but delicious, lime pickle, and took a large bite of the combination. Washed down with nice cold beer, good Indian food is one of my favorites.

When our food was all gone and we were soothing our overstimulated palates with another pair of beers, I pursued an idea. "I did just think at first that Lexa might have been talking about the wreck of the *Cita*. I don't remember reading about that when it first happened, but I suppose you, being Cornish by birth, read all about it."

"Of course! It was the best thing to happen to Scilly in many a long year. Tires, clothing, trainers, computer parts—"

"And don't forget the toilet seats."

"How could one?" Alan finished his beer and chuckled. "What made you think Lexa might be interested in the *Cita?*"

"I suppose because I just found out about it myself, and found it fascinating. But now I think I was wrong. I think she was interested in something quite different." I drained my own glass, set it down, and looked around. We had dined at the unfashionably early hour of seven, and the restaurant had been almost empty when we entered. Now it was filling up nicely, and there was plenty of loud, cheerful conversation to mask our voices.

Still, I lowered mine before I went on. "Alan, what if Lexa went to the library to learn something about smuggling? Not in Cornwall's past, I don't mean, but now? She was interested in drugs because of her mother's history. We think she was trying to find her father, the man who probably killed her mother. What if she found out something that made her believe smuggling was still going on here, not brandy and tobacco and lace, but drugs?"

Alan looked at me sharply, and then held up his hand. A hovering waiter appeared instantly.

"Our bill, please. I think they'd like our table, love," he said rather loudly to me. "There are people waiting."

The bill was presented, paid with mutual compliments and a large tip on Alan's part, and he steered me out the door and down the street.

"Sorry. Was I indiscreet?"

"Not really, but the waiter was paying close attention. I imagine he simply wanted us to leave, but it pays to be careful. Given your topic of conversation, I wanted to be quite sure no one overheard. No, I think we won't talk about it just yet."

Alan is sometimes overcautious. I've learned not to resent that. It offsets my impetuous tendencies. I walked sedately by his side all the way back to the hotel, confining my remarks to the beauty of the evening and, when we came to the seafront, the lulling sound of the waves. "I've always thought it would be lovely to have a house by the sea and fall asleep to that sound every night."

"And wonder, every stormy night, how much of your roof would still be there in the morning."

"I don't care. It's a sound to dream to."

I was very wide awake, however, when we had attained the privacy of our room. I refused Alan's offer of a drink and sat down in one of the easy chairs.

"Okay, so you believe there might be something in my theory?"

"Just possibly. While I was waiting for you to come back this afternoon, I rang up Colin and asked him to fill me in, in a general sort of way, on the sources of drugs in this part of the world."

"Ecstasy in particular."

"And the others. Most of them come from the same places. Colombia, some from Mexico, Holland, Belgium. Of course, they seldom come directly. A shipment of illegal drugs has often been to many ports of call before it finally reaches these shores.''

''You said the other day that most of it comes in by air.''

''And so it does, by air or by cargo ship. Innocent tourists are used as couriers sometimes, asked to take a package back to a friend or a relative. More often the transport's handled professionally, either in the air luggage of paid couriers or packed in the center of containers full of quite innocuous cargo. The Colombians used to ship cocaine in containers of roasted coffee beans, quite sure that the drug-sniffing dogs wouldn't be able to scent the drug over the powerful coffee aroma. They were wrong, so they took to burning the coffee that would be used to mask the drug. That didn't work, either; even the human handlers could tell burnt coffee when they smelt it, and they learned very quickly that drugs would be in the middle.''

''But still it comes in.''

''Oh, yes, we try our best, but everyone's understaffed, the police and Her Majesty's Customs alike. Far more slips through than we are able to intercept. But I learned something quite interesting today.''

''Oh, yes, Cornwall and drugs.''

''Yes. It seems rumors have been circulating for some time that there's more in the way of drug traffic in this quiet corner of England than might be expected. There are no major airports here, for one thing.''

''Plymouth is a major seaport, though.''

''Yes, and closely watched, for that reason. There's always been an efficient Customs operation at Plymouth—which is officially in Devon, by the way, not Cornwall. My sources say there's a good trickle coming in there, but something approaching a steady stream a bit farther west.''

"Around Penzance, for example."

"Perhaps."

I waited for him to say it, and when he didn't, I said it for him. "The old smugglers' caves."

"It would be a natural, wouldn't it? Drugs are the perfect cargo for your professional smuggler. Lightweight, easily rendered waterproof with plastic, extremely valuable."

"But everyone knows about the caves! Surely the authorities—"

"—are spread too thin, as I said. Dorothy, you've seen a small part of this coast, how rocky and steep it is. It's like that for most of the way from Plymouth right 'round the peninsula to Bude, at the northeast corner of the county, and it's all dotted with sea caves. A small force of men can't hope to patrol that length of promising territory. A smart man with a few high-speed, flat-bottomed boats and a crew who knew the area could run circles around a Customs force, especially considering the payoff. There's a great deal of money in this, a very great deal of money, indeed."

"And one young woman who got in the way…"

Alan didn't finish my sentence this time. He didn't have to. We both knew that if our scenario had any reality and Lexa had stumbled upon even a part of it, her fate had been sealed from the moment she set foot in Penzance.

"What do we do next?" I said after an unhappy little pause.

Alan stood and began to pace. "I go to Colin in the morning with what I've learned: the location of the club, and Pamela and the hot-tempered chap, one or both of whom may have been the last people to see Lexa alive. I'll tell them what we surmise, as well, what we've hypothesized just now. And I'll give them the new tape, of course.''

''What will they do with all that?''

''Treat it like any other report. Summarize it, feed it into HOLMES. Send someone to the rave club, try to find out who might have witnessed the encounter, preferably someone sufficiently in his or her right mind to give a better description than Mr. Barnet. They'll interrogate him, too, see if they can get any more out of him than I did. They'll be thorough, Dorothy, as thorough as they can be, given the fact that there are never enough staff, never enough hours in a day.''

''And we, meanwhile, will—what, Alan?''

''We'll do the same thing. Set about trying to find Pamela and the chap who just may have abducted both her and Lexa.''

SEVENTEEN

I GRIMACED AND ASKED, "How?"

Alan sighed, stopped pacing, and sat down. "That, of course, is the question. It's very much easier to do that sort of thing backed by authority and a large staff. We have very little to work with."

"We have a club where Pamela is known."

"And where we would stick out like a sore thumb."

"Then we go at opening time, before the crowds get there, and we talk to the owner."

"The owner is running an operation that is only marginally legal. Be sensible, Dorothy. What makes you think he'd be willing to tell us anything? The police, yes. Not a couple of old crocks who have no business there, and no authority to make him tell us anything. A pub, a tearoom, yes. There we might hope to make some progress. A rave club, no."

"I suppose you're right." I kicked off my shoes, perhaps a little harder than was strictly necessary, and sat on the bed with a vehement bounce. "I *hate* feeling old."

"Well," said my husband, sitting next to me on the bed and beginning to unbutton my shirt, "I have a cure in mind."

SUNDAY DAWNED CLEAR, warm, and beautiful. We woke early. "A fine day," said Alan, sitting up and looking out the window.

I stretched, yawned, and passed my hand idly along his back. "Lovely. I feel marvelous. Your cure was very effective." I sat up, too, swung my legs over the side, and ran both hands through my hair. It was a disheveled mess. "I need to wash my hair. Golly, you're right, it's a perfect day. Except—oh, Alan, I wish—"

"Yes. We both wish Lexa could enjoy it, too." He got up, came around to my side of the bed, and sat beside me, one arm around my shoulders. "Dorothy, if I learned anything in over forty years as a policeman, it is that one can't allow a nasty case to dominate one's life. There is sadness and evil in the world, yes. There is also goodness and beauty and justice. The one is as real as the other, and we must keep that fact firmly in mind or lose all sense of proportion."

"I know," I said a little drearily. "It just seems heartless, somehow, to revel in a glorious day with Lexa lying on a slab in the morgue."

Alan put his hand on my chin and turned my head so that I was looking directly at him. "Lexa is not lying on a slab in a morgue," he said very deliberately. "Her body may be, but the beauty and vitality that is Lexa is being well looked after, somewhere. You believe that as firmly as I do, and you mustn't forget it." He pulled me to my feet and gave me a little slap on the fanny. "Now into that shower, woman, and then come for a brisk walk on the beach. You need the cobwebs cleared out."

The walk did help. There was a fresh breeze coming off the sea, smelling of salt and fish. The waves, subdued and orderly today, rolled in, creamed onto the sand and pebbles, and retreated, leaving bits of seaweed behind. Their music today was the merest whisper, a classic, Mozartian sort of noise. The Sturm und Drang of the past few days, worthy of Beethoven at his frenzied best, was a mere memory.

"It's behaving itself today," I commented idly as we crunched along.

Alan nodded. "It has its moods, just like people. I've always found it hard not to think of the sea as a living, conscious creature."

"There's something eternal about it, too." I watched the waves, hypnotized by their relentless motion. "I wonder if primitive people ever worshiped the sea."

"The sea gods, at least, they did. Neptune and that lot. The sea provided the ancients with sustenance, but those old chaps knew what it could do when it was in a fury. It was wise to keep its gods placated."

"Good and evil. Beauty and ugliness. We can't get away from it, can we?"

"No, only learn to be grateful for the good and try to fight the evil."

Alan took my hand and we turned back to the hotel in a thoughtful mood.

He decided to go to the police station before breakfast to deliver my tape and make a report. He made a few notes to make sure he remembered everything, stuck them in his pocket, and rose. "I shouldn't be gone long at all, but go down if you're starving."

"No, I'll wait. I'd like to write up some of our ideas myself, try to get them in some sort of order."

"Paperwork, just like a policewoman. Hah! I knew you'd come 'round to it sooner or later."

I had barely begun to make sense of our lists, conversations, and random thoughts when he returned. The moment he opened the door, I knew he had bad news.

"What?"

"Nothing earth-shattering. Just—extremely disappointing. Look, I need some food, and so do you. Let's face this at breakfast."

I held my tongue until we had a meal in front of us. "All right, I can't stand it anymore."

"The case is being set aside."

"What?"

He nodded gloomily, ate some toast, and continued. "They've completed the autopsy. Lexa died of PMA, as I suspected. But there were no signs of violence on her body at all, Dorothy. No indication that she was taken to the cave by force. No indications of anyone's presence in the cave except hers and ours."

"But, Alan! Somebody had to have given her the drug! I tell you, she would never have taken it herself."

"I believe you, Dorothy. I think Superintendent Cardinnis is inclined to the same way of thinking. But he has no evidence of murder. A policeman has to rely on evidence, especially when he has a lot of other cases on his plate and his superiors have told him to concentrate on those."

"What cases?" I asked indignantly. "What's more important than Lexa's murder?"

"There was a big bank robbery last night. Barclay's in Market Jew Street. Several hundred thousand pounds. *And*—" He held up a finger as I opened my mouth to speak. "And—John Boleigh's granddaughter has gone missing."

That flattened me. "Oh. And a missing child takes first priority."

"Particularly the missing granddaughter of a wealthy, influential citizen."

"Yes." I pushed my plate away. Food had lost its appeal.

Alan pushed it back in front of me. "Eat."

"I don't *want* to eat. I'm depressed. Why are you always trying to make me eat something?"

"Because we have work to do, and need our strength." He piled his fork full of egg, bacon, and a triangle of fried bread, in that odd way of eating the English have, and conveyed it to his mouth. "Colin can't do much more with Lexa's case, at least not just now. That leaves it in our laps, doesn't it?"

I looked at him, mingled love and exasperation no doubt showing plainly on my mobile face. "Do you suppose I'll ever be able to get one jump ahead of you? Just when I think I've figured out what you're going to say or do next, you come up with a reaction I don't expect."

"Good. A little mystery never hurt a marriage. Now finish that breakfast. We need, among other things, to call on the Reverend Mr. Polwhistle, and what better place to find him than at church on Sunday morning?"

As soon as we got back to the room, we looked up the schedule of services at St. Martha's and walked over just in time for Matins. The bells were coming back into rounds as we walked in the front door.

In Shrebury we always go to a communion service, but then Shrebury Cathedral is very High Church. Alan had explained to me that Cornwall was evangelical country, with the Anglican churches far outnumbered by other denominations, so a more Protestant feeling prevailed at St. Martha's. It was an attractive church, and the choir was good, but I missed the more formal liturgy of the cathedral.

It seemed appropriate, though, that the sermon dealt with Satan and the other dark angels. I concentrated rather closely on the rector's words, for it had suddenly occurred to me that he was an important person in Penzance. He could know a lot about the drug scene, could even give us some ideas, perhaps.

I was less sanguine about that possibility a few minutes into his discourse. The Reverend Mr. Polwhistle had a tendency to rant a bit. Maybe he'd caught it from his evangelical colleagues. At any rate, I thought I could discern, in his remarks, somewhat more interest in the devils of this world than was quite healthy.

Ah, well, many people from Milton on down have found Satan rather an attractive figure. Charming fellow, just a trifle misguided. Mr. Polwhistle didn't take quite that tack. He painted the devil in the blackest possible terms, but he lingered lovingly over descriptions of his wicked nature in a way that made me shiver.

When the service was over, I toyed with the idea of merging with the crowd and slipping out, so as to avoid shaking the rector's hand at the front door, but Alan headed quite purposefully to the line of parishioners making their conventional greetings and I had little choice but to follow.

"Fine sermon, Rector," Alan said as we reached the head of the line.

"Ah, yes, you of all people would understand the works of the devil in the world."

Well, I hoped that was meant as a reference to Alan's former line of work, not his character.

Mr. Polwhistle kept his grip on Alan's hand and became very earnest. "He's abroad here in Penzance! We must seek out his servants and destroy them, before they destroy us!"

"Yes, indeed," murmured Alan, and managed to free himself. "Keep up the good work, sir."

And at last we were able to get ourselves down the

steps and into the pleasant garden at the front of the church.

"Is he quite all there, do you think?" I asked when we were well away.

"You may well ask! I don't remember quite so much hellfire in his sermons thirty-odd years ago. It's true he was only the curate then, and I suppose more or less under Mr. Trelawney's thumb."

"Well, he certainly seemed to be teetering close to the edge today."

"He's upset, of course. Careful, it's rather steep."

I held tightly to the railing of the steps leading down from St. Martha's churchyard to the street below. "I should say he's upset! And that's odd, in a way. I suppose he's fretting over a murder in his community, but how would he know it is a murder? We think it is, because we know of the connection to Lexa's mother's death, but I wouldn't think the police have publicized that aspect."

Alan considered carefully before he answered, half a block later. "Well, there are two possibilities. Offhand, I'd say he's the sort of chap to look on the darkest side of anything, and to leap to conclusions. A woman has died. Another woman died in exactly the same spot, many years ago. The rector would remember that, of course, and would remember that there were drugs involved then, because the newspapers made much of it at the time, along with a good deal of moaning about moral degeneration and the like. Meat and drink to the Polwhistles of this world. Given his preoccupation with drugs now, he'd be likely to assume that drugs were involved in this death, as well. Poor chap! I wonder if there's some personal tragedy behind his crusade?"

"Any sensible person deplores illegal drugs, Alan," I reminded him rather primly.

"You won't get a policeman to argue with you about that. Still, you and I don't go about preaching on the subject and invoking the name of the devil. All right, all right, we're not preachers by trade. I know."

"You said," I reminded him almost unwillingly, "that there might be two possibilities. Reasons he'd think Lexa's death was murder."

"Yes."

He looked at me. I nodded grimly. "I hoped that wasn't what you meant. He's certainly an important figure in Penzance, isn't he? And old enough to be the man at the rave club. If religious mania predisposes a man to murder—oh, mercy, Alan! I just thought of something else! Suppose a *clergyman* had an illegitimate child. Suppose drugs were involved. Suppose, thirty-odd years later, after he'd thought he'd covered it all up successfully and was safe from exposure, the child came to town, a conservative, evangelical town like Penzance…"

I stopped and looked at him suspiciously. "Had you already thought of all this? Is that why you stayed to talk to him?"

"You know my methods, Watson," said Alan lightly. "Really, you know, I think it's most unlikely. A possibility, but unlikely."

"You said there might be a personal tragedy behind his attitudes."

"I did. But the tragedy might well be growing up in a household with no sense of humor about religion."

He tilted his head to one side and looked at me consideringly. "Look, how would you feel if I suggested we take the rest of the day off? I have the feeling we've got to the stage of seeing bogeymen around every corner. We need a little perspective, especially if we have to go to that blasted rave club tonight."

"The rave club! But you said—"

"That was before the police parked the case. I think someone needs to talk to those people, and the sooner the better. We're a poor pair to do it, but better poor than none. We'll work out an approach. I leave that to you. I can occasionally invent a good lie, but you're the true virtuoso in that department. Now, what about an afternoon in Mousehole? The place will be crawling with tourists, of course, but it'll be a splendid antidote to the dubious Mr. Polwhistle."

"All right, you talked me into it. Should we wait until after lunch, or will there be someplace to eat there?"

"My dear, there are enough Cornish pasties in Mousehole to sink a battleship."

"Then let's go!"

EIGHTEEN

WE STOPPED AT the hotel and changed our church clothes for something more suitable. I looked in on Eleanor for a minute, but she was asleep and looked comfortable. With a clear conscience, then, I slathered sunscreen over exposed skin, clapped on a sensible wide-brimmed straw hat, and we set out.

Alan, on the way through Newlyn, detoured to show me his old house. "Just a fisherman's cottage."

It was attractive, though small, a solid structure of stuccoed stone painted a dazzling white, with window boxes and a bright-blue front door. Someday I would ask Alan how a Cornish girl happened to meet a Kentish hop farmer, but not now. Now I wanted to reconnect with the comfortable present.

"I think this is as near as we're likely to get," he said a few minutes later, pulling up to the curb and parking opposite a row of houses. He pointed to the sign saying "Mousehole." "It's a fair walk from here, but in a few yards there are steps down to the beach, where it'll be a bit cooler."

The concrete stairs were broad and well maintained, with a firm steel-pipe handrail. They weren't steep, either. I made it down with no more than a mild twinge or two from my knees.

"They look after tourists well in these parts."

"They know on which side their bread is buttered." Alan gestured ahead to the beach, which, sure enough, was full of activity. Families with small children waded in an inch or two of water at the edge of the sand, the toddlers squealing every time a wave broke over their toes. Two or three older children were building an elaborate sand castle, which necessitated endless trips to fetch water in plastic buckets.

I smiled at Alan. "They were tin when I was a little girl, the buckets, I mean. Sturdier for hauling water and wet sand. But I wasn't as good an architect as that crew."

"I thought you said you never saw the sea as a child."

"I didn't, but my parents had friends with a cottage on Lake Michigan. We'd go up there every summer for a week or so, and I adored it. It's so big it's basically an inland sea, except that the water's fresh. And it has huge sand dunes in some places. There was one called Tower Hill—goodness, I wonder if it's there still. Sands shift around so. Anyway, the thing to do was to climb up to the top, which is no mean trick in soft sand that slides out from under every step. Then, when you got to the top, you tucked yourself into a ball and rolled down, screaming all the way. Such fun!"

I saw on Alan's face the same look I'd felt on my own at Newlyn: regret for a past we hadn't shared and could never really communicate.

I tucked my hand under his arm, sighed, and then grinned. He quirked one eyebrow and grinned back. No use regretting what couldn't be helped.

If the beach had seemed crowded, Mousehole proper, when we reached it, was packed. I was beginning to think about lunch, so we found the nearest pasty shop, stood in line, and came away with two huge half-moon-shaped pies, hot and smelling wonderful, and a couple of soft drinks.

"Here, quick," said Alan, sprinting for a low wall over-looking the tiny harbor. Two women had just vacated their seats on the crowded wall; Alan seized the places for us.

We settled there in the sun, our legs dangling over the far edge, where the wall stretched ten or twelve feet down to the sands. Deserted by the tide, the harbor lay half empty of water; fishing boats painted in bright colors lay canted over forlornly, waiting for water to float them again. Dotted here and there, both on the sands and up on our level, were easels. Artists sat capturing the scene in oils or watercolor, oblivious to the curious stares of passersby. Tourists moved purposefully in and out of souvenir shops or stood, cameras raised, recording the day in their own more mechanical way. And everywhere the gulls strutted and swooped, raucously begging crumbs.

I took a bite of my pasty. It was incredibly good, like a sort of gravyless stew wrapped in flaky pastry. "Mmmm! I've had pasties before, but not like this. What's in them?"

"Beef, in these, though mutton's traditional. And the usual potatoes, turnips, onions. You can get all sorts now—chicken and broccoli, bacon and Stilton—anything. Your true Cornishman despises the modern versions. Won't even allow carrot in them, though women seem to like it."

"Well, I'm not Cornish, and I think they all sound delicious. I suppose the pastry's made with lard."

"What else?"

"What else, indeed?" I kept thoughts of cholesterol to myself. We eat sensibly most of the time; holidays are for breaking out of the mold. I resolved, though, to find a recipe for pasties and see if I couldn't modify it to be somewhat less lethal.

"We should come here at Christmas sometime and have some star-gazy pie."

"What on earth is that?"

So we sat there in the sun on the harbor wall and finished our pasties, and Alan told me the legend of the Mousehole cat and the great storm.

It was a long time ago, that winter storm, so long ago that nobody remembered exactly when. But it was a terrible time. The seas were so high and so dangerous that no fishing boat dared leave the protection of the harbor with its opening no bigger than a mousehole—from which the village derived its name. Within the harbor the boats were safe, but they could not go out to catch fish, and soon the people of Mousehole began to starve.

Then one day, two days before Christmas, Old Tom Bawcock had had enough. "Christmas, and no food!" he said to his cat. "It's not to be thought of. We're going out, and I'll come back with fish, or perish."

They nearly did perish, those two, but perhaps the cat, Mowzer, was a powerful force for good luck, because the storm abated after a time and the boat came safely back, loaded to the gunwales with fish. And as they approached the harbor mouth, Old Tom and his cat were greeted by a beautiful sight. There was a candle in every window in the village, and all the men stood on the harbor walls, lanterns in hand, to light home Old Tom and his faithful cat.

There was a great feast in the village that night, and the centerpieces of all the tables were huge fish pies, baked with the heads sticking out of the pastry, gazing at the beautiful stars. It was the night before Christmas Eve, and every December 23 since, the village has baked hundreds of star-gazy pies and lighted the harbor with thousands of lights, in loving memory of Old Tom and of Mowzer, the Mousehole cat.

"What a lovely story," I said when he had finished. "The classic fairy tale. The impossible task, the magic of some kind of goodwill that makes the task possible, the happy ending. I'm not sure about fish heads, though."

"Eating them is optional," said Alan with a chuckle. "There's a charming little book that retells the story with delightful illustrations. I'll find you one in a bookshop. Speaking of which, it's time we did some shopping. Mousehole, now, is as much an artists' colony as a fishing village, and there's some very fine work to be found amongst the touristy junk."

We strolled happily up the narrow, twisting lanes. I was glad Alan hadn't tried to bring the car any farther. Mousehole is no place to drive. It rises steeply from the sea, so such roads as there are have sharp switchbacks and corners blind as a moonless night. I watched, at one point, as the bus from Penzance arrived, turned into a dead-end street, and then backed, tortuously, with much grinding of gears and ever so slowly so as to avoid heedless pedestrians, in order to turn around and begin the return trip.

I nudged Alan and pointed to the bus driver. "There's one guy who has a worse job than a policeman."

"I think you're right about that."

We saw potteries displaying beautiful work. "Made from Cornish clay, possibly," Alan told me. "Some of the finest deposits of china clay in the world are up around St. Austell."

"I know that," I said smugly. "I read about it at the library."

Innumerable stores sold paintings and watercolors by local artists. The quality was variable, as one would expect, but there were some beautiful pictures I would have loved to take home, had the prices not been so high.

"It's good stuff, Dorothy, and the artists know the value of their work."

"Indeed," I said, sighing as I tore my gaze from one stormy seascape I could just see over my mantel at home.

The antique store drew me in, too. I had always enjoyed antique shopping back home in the States, but there the stores were filled mostly with interesting junk. This one carried the genuine article, with prices to match. I pulled my elbows in so as not to break anything as I wandered, looking longingly at Georgian silver candlesticks, Victorian mahogany lap desks, vases and platters made by Wedgwood and Royal Doulton and Spode.

I lingered longest over the jewelry case. There were a good many Victorian pieces, a gold-filigree bar brooch set with pearls, an enameled pansy with a tiny diamond dewdrop on one petal, a pair of gold-and-jet earrings I coveted. The loveliest thing of all was a gold cross, about an inch and a half long, set with red stones that were polished but not faceted.

"Cabochon rubies," said the dealer, who was lingering, hopeful of a sale. "A very old piece, that, sixteenth century, most likely. Beautiful workmanship. Came in only yesterday and won't stay long. Would you like me to get it out for you?"

"I doubt we could afford it."

"One can always look," said Alan, so it was removed from the case and laid reverently on a piece of blue velvet for our closer inspection.

I wouldn't have dared pick it up, but Alan hefted it and turned it over to inspect the back, which was solid gold. "It's very heavy," he commented. "Not all that comfortable hung around one's neck, I wouldn't have thought.''

''It was probably a decoration for a book at one time, or a reliquary, something of the kind,'' said the dealer. ''German work, I suspect. One can see that the loop at the top was added later.''

Alan looked at the tag, which had only a code number, in the coyly discreet tradition. ''A thousand pounds?'' he asked casually.

''Three, actually. The rubies are very fine. It would be much more if we had a provenance, but alas, with these very old pieces…'' He shook his head sadly. ''I ought to send it up to Sotheby's or Christie's to be sold at auction, but to tell the truth, I've lost my heart to it, and I'd like it to be sold from this shop. One of the finest pieces it's ever been my privilege to handle.''

I had refrained from gasping at the price, but my body language clearly indicated my feelings. The dealer saw that we weren't going to buy and put the cross back in the case. ''If you change your mind, you'd best do it soon. It won't stay long,'' he repeated, and we escaped.

But if the antique store was too rich for our blood, when we hit the bookshop, I had found my Mecca. ''This is the place, Alan. Go and have yourself a beer if you're tired, or hot, or whatever, but I want to browse here for a long time.''

''Go right ahead, my love. I'm in no hurry.''

There were cookbooks, all with pasty recipes, one entirely devoted to them. There were books about Cornwall's history and its present. There was a fine selection of used books, including some mysteries I'd never read and some old friends I didn't own. I felt like a kid in a candy store, turning from one shelf to another, adding to the growing stack of books piled up next to the cash register. I turned, holding up one especially intriguing find.

"Look, Alan, it's—oh, I'm so sorry! I thought you were my husband."

I had to look up at his face. He was at least as tall as Alan, and we were wedged close together in the narrow aisle.

"Ah, yes. Mrs.—ah—Nesbitt, I believe?"

The tall, black-haired man whose feet I was stepping on was, I was pretty sure, the mayor of Penzance.

"Oh, goodness, I do apologize, I—oh, *dear!*"

In my flurry of confusion, I dropped the book I was holding, also on the mayor's feet. It was a paperback, fortunately. He retrieved it with one long, slender hand and held it out to me with a gallant little nod. "I see you're interested in our infamous past, Mrs. Nesbitt."

I took back the book, a copy of one I'd read in the library, and tried to recover some of my aplomb. "Yes, I'm intrigued with the tales of smuggling and wrecking. By the way, I *am* Alan Nesbitt's wife—and how amazing that you remember—but I use my old name, Dorothy Martin. And I'm nothing like as good as you are at names; I've forgotten yours completely, except that you're the mayor. Is that what I should call you? Forgive an American's ignorance."

"Pendeen will do quite nicely, Percival Pendeen. No need for the title, except on formal occasions. In real life I own a shop, you know, very much like a mayor in a small American town, or so I understand."

"Yes, except for some reason small-town American mayors often tend to be undertakers. What sort of shop do you have, Mr. Pendeen?" I had edged my way out of the close quarters toward the cash register and now put my latest book on top of the pile, which threatened to topple. The mayor, following, looked at my selections with interest.

"My word, you do intend to read up on Cornish history, don't you? Quite a bloodthirsty bent in literature, Mrs. Martin!" There was something odd in his voice, I thought, some kind of satisfaction.

"Well, it's a fairly bloodthirsty history," I retorted. "Luring ships onto the rocks in order to loot them, smuggling, piracy—"

"Ah, that last was largely a figment of W. S. Gilbert's imagination."

"And the rest?"

"All too true, I fear." Again the hint of—what—smugness?

"But all in the past, of course." I shouldn't have said it, but his manner was beginning to irk me.

His eyes opened wide. He glanced again at my stack of books and patted my hand. "My dear lady, I see you also revel in crime novels, but you mustn't let your imagination run away with you. I do assure you, you won't find a more peaceable lot anywhere in the kingdom than the inhabitants of Cornwall."

His hand was very white and smooth and somehow repellent. I slid mine out from under as casually as I could, just as Alan appeared with a couple of books he had found.

"Nesbitt, good to see you! Been talking to your lovely wife. Mind you keep a close eye on her, now! She's a lady out for blood, I can see that! Cheerio, then."

"What on earth was that about?" asked Alan.

"I'm not sure. Are those all the books you want?" I turned to the cashier. "I think we're ready for the bitter truth. And I hope you have some sort of shopping bag. I forgot to bring a suitcase."

The young man grinned, added up the prices, and presented us with the total, which wasn't really too bad. The books filled two plastic bags. Each of us carrying one of them, Alan and I stepped out into the sunlight.

"All right, what didn't you want to tell me in there?" asked Alan when we had turned up a steep street that led only to people's houses and was thus almost deserted.

"I don't really know. Maybe nothing at all, but the mayor really acted rather peculiarly. Is he always that way—jokey, putting on a little too much mayoral good cheer?"

"You don't want much, do you, woman? I haven't laid eyes on the man in over thirty years, and I didn't know him well then."

"What does he do for a living? He said he had a shop."

"And so he does, or did when I lived in Penzance. Deals in antiques, I believe, the sort you looked at today, only more so. Very fancy prices, indeed. Louis the Fourteenth tables, French mantel clocks, ornate Italian inlay—you know the sort of thing."

"Imports," I said meaningfully.

"A good many of them, yes, I'd think so. Why? Don't tell me you're seeing bogeymen again!"

"Maybe. Alan, he was awfully interested in my interest in crime in Cornwall, past and present. And he never did answer my question, when I asked him what he sold. And-well—he's an important man in Penzance, and exactly what a young man would call an 'old cove.'"

NINETEEN

OUR EXCURSION to Mousehole lost its zest after that. Alan showed me where he would pick me up, at the last place before getting into the town where he could turn the car around, and trudged off with the heavier bag of books. I waited, sitting on a narrow stone wall, my own bag on the ground beside me. It wasn't a very comfortable seat, but my feet hurt.

My head didn't feel much better. Oh, it didn't hurt, though it was hot under my protective hat. It simply didn't seem to function. It might as well have been stuffed with clotted cream for all the good it was doing me.

The afternoon had been wonderful, just the tonic I needed, until Mr. Pendeen had come along. Then I had found myself caught up once more in a web of confusion and ridiculous suspicion. "Seeing bogeymen," Alan had said, and he was right.

As long as the police had been actively pursuing the case, we'd been free to go off on tangents. Now that they weren't, it was time for us to start acting sensibly, pursuing clues to Lexa's death, not bogeymen.

Seeing Alan approaching in the car, I took a deep breath, as if to provide my brain with oxygen, and began to think about the rave club.

"We have a godson," I announced to Alan as I sat down in the car.

He shot me a glance of surprise. "Yes, I have one or two, actually. We, together, don't actually—"

"A fictitious one."

"May I ask why we need such an invention?"

"He's an excuse. To get into the rave club tonight."

My husband has become accustomed to my flights of fancy. He simply grinned, looked carefully both ways, and pulled out into the heavy end-of-the-day-out traffic.

"He's a musician, you see. In—in London, I think. A drummer."

"Heaven help us. How old is he?"

"How old do you have to be to play in a club?"

"It depends. Twenty or so should be safe for most situations."

"Twenty, then. And he's thinking of moving to Penzance, to live with us."

"We live in Penzance. I see."

"Yes, well, we've just moved here," I said, improvising wildly. "We thought it was a nice place to retire to. And—let's see. We visited with young what's-his-name's parents not too long ago, and they're unhappy about his friends in London. Am I doing okay so far?"

"Sounds reasonable to me. Peter."

"Why?"

Alan shrugged, never taking his eyes off the road. "I've always liked the name. If you can invent a godson, I'm allowed to christen him."

"Peter it is. We've invited young Peter, then, to come and stay with us for a while, and his parents are hoping he'll be able to find work here, in a healthier sort of environment than London."

"And that is a debatable point if ever I heard one."

"The climate is better, anyway."

"The physical climate, perhaps. Fresh air, sunshine, the

lot. But the emotional climate..." Alan let the phrase trail off as he rubbed his hand down the back of his head, always a sign of distress. "Penzance has changed since I lived here."

"Well, dear, places do, in thirty-odd years. We've changed just a little ourselves."

"I didn't mean that sort of thing, though. Yes, of course there's been development, growth, the kind of change one expects. What I mean is something much more basic, a change in the feel of the place. It annoys me that I can't put my finger on it. There's just something wrong, some-how."

"Too much money around?" I suggested. "That's what the police superintendent thinks."

"It could be. Money corrupts nearly as well as power."

"Mr. Polwhistle would blame the devil, I suppose."

"And he might not be far wrong, Dorothy."

I looked at him. His face was perfectly serious.

"There's evil about somewhere, I'll swear to that. Except for fanatics like Mr. Polwhistle, we tend not to talk much about the devil anymore, unless as a joke. The subject is embarrassing, for some reason. But evil exists, and if those two concepts, evil and the devil, aren't the same thing, then my theology is skewed somewhere."

I had no answer for that, so we drove in silence.

Evil. We seemed to have talked about it a lot lately. Evil and good, and the necessity of keeping the vital balance between ignoring evil and becoming fascinated with it. Were we concentrating on it too much? I looked out the window. Alan had chosen a different way back to Penzance, a narrow country lane away from the crowded coast road. Here was the English countryside I loved so much, a seductively pretty scene that made it nearly impossible to believe anything dreadful had ever happened, could ever happen. Neat, lush fields, separated by low drystone walls, basked in the late-afternoon sun. Trees bent low over the road, sometimes caressing the roof of the car. Birds sang. The sky, a photographer's dream of deep blue with powder-puff clouds, arched serenely over all.

And in Penzance, on this bright-blue Sunday, Lexa's body lay cold and still in a refrigerated drawer, and the police worked extra shifts trying to track down a missing girl and a bank robber.

"I'd rather have Dickens," I said after a long silence.

Alan can often follow my thoughts, but his face told me he hadn't, this time.

"Filthy tenements. Fagin, Bill Sykes. Thieves, pickpockets, workhouses, starvation. You could see the evil in his books, touch it, smell it. You knew what to expect. It's less frightening that way than—" I waved my hand out the window.

"You sound a bit like Sherlock Holmes."

"I do?"

"In one of the stories, I can't remember which. He said he'd rather deal with the vilest alley in London than with the hidden wickedness of the country. Words to that effect. I think I agree. The evil that hides behind ordinary, respectable facades—oh, yes, that's much worse."

We turned onto a wider, busier road and said not another word all the way through Newlyn and back to the hotel.

I WOULD HAVE GIVEN a good deal not to have to go out that evening. A quiet drink, a leisurely, early dinner, then bed with one of my new books to put me to sleep—it sounded like an idyllic program. However, it was not to be.

"When do you think we ought to go?"

"Early, before many customers arrive, if we want to talk to the management. About ten, I'd think. Much later if we want to talk to the clientele. One o'clock, two."

I groaned and tried to remember the last time I'd voluntarily stayed up till two in the morning. I couldn't; it was too long ago. "It had better be early. If we make it too late I'll have to nap first, and then I'll be all muzzy and forget my lines."

"The fewer people there are about, the more conspicuous we'll be."

"We'll be conspicuous no matter when we go, and I make a whole lot better detective when I'm not walking in my sleep."

There was still a great deal of time to kill. We took our time about showering and changing. I was in something of a quandary about what to wear.

"Alan, I brought nothing I can wear to a teenagers' club. I don't even *own* anything that would be remotely suitable!"

"No micro minis? What a disappointment."

I glared at him.

"You wouldn't look at all bad in a short skirt, actually. I'm sure you know I married you for your legs. However, in the present emergency, if you've nothing appropriate, why don't you just wear something comfortable? We're playing anxious godparents, not would-be rockers."

So I put on a pair of conservative slacks and a sweater.

"Alan, I should check on Eleanor."

"Are you going to tell her our plans for this evening?"

"I think so. She'll want to know what we're doing on the case, especially if the police have told her they've shelved it."

"Not shelved, exactly. But they've probably told her they can release the body for burial."

"Oh, Alan! That will have been hard on her. I'll go up right away."

I tapped on her door and was told to come in. She was sitting quietly in her chair with a magazine in her lap, but I didn't think she'd been reading it.

"They came and told me I could make funeral arrangements" was her greeting. Her eyes were red, but she was in command of herself.

"Yes." I sat down next to her. "Would you like some help with that?"

"No, I've already talked to someone. A man named Polwhistle. I can't say I'd have chosen him for the job, but he met Lexa at that party. She told me about him because she thought I'd be amused by the name. He's better than a total stranger."

"I'd wondered if you'd want to take her back to London."

"No. She has—had—no church affiliations there. Oh, she was christened, of course. Betty saw to that, said it was the proper thing to do, but I doubt whether Lexa had been to church since. And at least this man knew her, if only briefly. It doesn't matter to me where she lies."

I was reminded of what Alan had said, about Lexa not really being in the morgue. I was tempted to say so, but Eleanor didn't share my beliefs and might not appreciate my parading them now.

"I'm not one to go visiting graves and all that morbid clap-trap," she went on, "even if I were going to be here to do it. Which I am not, not for long."

She might have meant "here in Penzance." I knew she didn't. "When is the service to be?"

"Tomorrow, two o'clock. No point in delay. It'll be a

simple graveside service, no nonsense about it." She sighed and said again, "None of it matters, does it? They've given me her things, clothes and that. I haven't had the heart to sort through them."

"I can help you with that, anyway. Shall I?"

"Yes. Yes, please. It would be very painful for me." She lapsed into silence for a moment, then said, "What does it mean, the police releasing her body and her belongings? I was afraid to ask, but they've abandoned the investigation, haven't they?"

I flinched inwardly, but I had promised to be honest with this woman. "Not abandoned. Deferred. They've had to shelve it for the moment because of the pressure of other work, and because there is no physical evidence that Lexa's death was caused by anything but an accident."

"That's bloody nonsense." She said it flatly, a statement of fact.

"I agree, and so does the superintendent, really, but he has to do what his superiors tell him. Eleanor, try not to worry too much. Alan and I are still actively working on it. In fact, we're going to that rave club tonight to see what we can find out. We're not going to let Lexa's murder go unpunished."

She smiled wanly. "I thought you wouldn't."

"You're tired. I'll leave you now, but would you like me to order you up some dinner before I go?"

"Thank you, no. I am still capable of using the telephone. It is one of the few functions left to me."

She spoke with some asperity. She hadn't given up, then. I smiled, promised to keep her informed, and left.

TWENTY

WE WENT DOWN to the bar, lingered there, then had a light dinner, but ate it with deliberation. Anything to stay awake until it was time to leave.

Shortly before ten we set out for where we hoped to find the rave club.

"You look odd, somehow," said Alan.

"I'm not wearing a hat. I feel naked without one, but there's no point in everyone at the club thinking I'm the Queen Mum."

"Oh, I don't think you look old enough for anyone to make that mistake," said my gallant husband. "Not quite."

Queen Elizabeth's mother has passed her hundredth birthday. "Thank you *very* much."

"Nor do you have quite the same quality of sweetness..." He grinned at my glare.

The truth was, we were acting silly to hide our anxiety, or at least I was. This endeavor was necessary, but I wasn't looking forward to it.

"The club's supposedly quite near the harbor," said Alan as we went out the door of the hotel. "It's in easy walking distance, and the night is lovely. Just look at those stars."

I rebelled. "We walked all afternoon, and on steep hills, too. If I'm going to be convincing tonight, I can't be thinking about how much my feet hurt. We're driving.''

"I can't guarantee a place to park.''

"One can never be guaranteed a place to park in England. We're driving, Alan. If you can't park close, you can drop me off, or I can walk a block or two if need be. Just not ten or twelve.''

So Alan got the car and we drove down Promenade Road, nearly deserted at this hour of a Sunday night. I tried to quell the butterflies in my stomach. I was feeling more and more uneasy about the whole thing. It suddenly seemed wildly unlikely that we would find out anything useful, and even if we did, were we showing our hand too soon, too blatantly?

The parking lot for the train and bus stations was nearly empty, and it was reasonably near the club, at least if Alan was right about where it was. "It may not be terribly easy to find, you know. Barnet, even half stoned, was cagey about telling me exactly which hall. But I scouted the area this morning as I was coming back from the police station, and I think it must be the Edward Hall, on a side street just off Wharf Road. It's rather an unsavory area, quite appropriate for this sort of thing.''

"Oh, we'll find it,'' I said, clutching Alan's arm a little more tightly. "If only by ear.''

That was the way it turned out. The place was quite efficiently soundproofed, but when the door opened to admit a group of kids just ahead of us, a wave of noise poured out. It was mostly percussion, the steady ba-boom, ba-boom in heartbeat tempo, a beat to be felt, viscerally, as much as heard.

I stopped, panicky. "Alan, there's no point going in there. We can't ask questions. We won't be able to hear the answers. Let's go back. This was a bad idea.''

"Cold feet?" he asked calmly.

I sighed. "Freezing."

"Come along, Granny. You were the one who came up with this scheme. It's too late to turn back now."

So, on the next tide of partygoers, we swept in.

We didn't get very far. For a little while I thought, maybe hoped, that we'd be thrown out. We were met in the vestibule by a skinny man in his thirties who stepped in front of us, barring our way. His punk haircut and the various metal objects hung here and there from nose, lip, eyebrows, and ears didn't make me feel one bit better. "Private club, innit?" he shouted above the blare of music from the hall proper. "Members only."

I would have turned tail, but Alan stood his ground. "We don't want to go in," he bellowed. "We want to speak to the manager."

"But you got to go in, like, to speak to him. 'Cause he's inside, in't he? And you can't go in, 'cause you're not members, are you?"

"How much?" Alan took out his wallet.

"Wotcher mean?" The gatekeeper's eyes fixed on the wallet, which had the edges of several ten-pound notes showing.

"How much to join the club?"

"'Unnerd quid."

I gasped.

"For what term?" asked Alan blandly.

The gatekeeper shrugged. "Life?"

Alan peeled off a couple of notes and gave them to the unsavory character. "This ought to do for ten minutes, then. How shall I know the manager?"

The twenty pounds disappeared into a blue-jeans pocket and the gatekeeper jerked his head toward the door into the hall.

"Just look for the oldest one in the room, mate. Except you lot, that is." He whinnied a disturbing laugh, took an oddly shaped cigarette out of his shirt pocket, and lit up, blowing the smoke in my face.

It was the first time in my life I'd ever knowingly inhaled marijuana. Even secondhand, the smoke made me giddy. I coughed wildly and clutched Alan's arm.

"Well done," he whispered in my ear. "Suits your role nicely."

"It wasn't an act," I croaked back at him, and we stepped through the doorway.

The scene inside the hall would have made Dante feel right at home. Though there were only a few patrons at this early hour, the noise—I refused to call it music—was at full volume. The throb from the huge speakers that hung over the stage was so intense as to be painful. Strobe lights splashed violent, pulsating color over the tables, dance floor, and dancers. The air was thick with heat and smoke and the smells of tobacco and marijuana and sweat. I fought nausea while I looked around for any sign of drug dealing. I could spot none, but I'm hardly an expert.

The stage itself, what one could see of it in the disorienting light, was bare of anything except a disc jockey seated at an elaborate console and a man standing at a microphone. I nudged Alan and pointed. He nodded. We moved around the dance floor to the stage and climbed up the steps.

The man at the mike, a tough-looking customer with a broken nose, a five-o'clock shadow, and muscles bulging under his shirt, busied himself with some sort of adjustment and paid no attention to us until Alan tapped his shoulder. Then he glanced at us, and did a double take. "Don't know where you two think you are," he screamed over the noise, "but you're not allowed on the stage."

"We need to talk to you," Alan screamed back. "Do you have an office, somewhere quiet?" He had another banknote in his hand, a twenty this time. He allowed the manager to see it for a moment before putting it back in his pocket.

The man nodded and pointed. We followed him off the stage and into a small room at the back of the hall. With the door shut, the sound level was almost bearable.

The manager threw himself into a chair behind a metal desk. He did not invite us to sit. "Look, I'm busy. You two refugees from the rest home have something to say, say it and get out of here."

I bit off an angry reply. Alan, veteran of a career in which he'd had to get used to rudeness, was better able to deal with it.

"Take that tone with me, young man, and you'll be the one who's out of there!"

"Hey, you're not the Bill, are you?"

The old problem: Alan looks and sometimes sounds like a policeman. "Not anymore," he said with perfect honesty, "though I have a fair number of friends who are. I'm not here to look into your operation, though, not this time. I want a few civil answers to civil questions, and I'm prepared to pay for your time."

"Right." It could not have been said more insolently, but the man leaned back in his chair, apparently ready to listen.

"We came in hoping to ask about employment."

"You?" His astonishment would have struck me funny if I hadn't been so nervous.

"Of course not, don't be an ass. Our godson is a drummer. We'd heard about this club—"

"How was that? We don't exactly advertise."

"Never mind how. We may, in your opinion, be old,

but we're not stupid. I can see, however, that your music is recorded, so I suppose we're wasting our time.''

"Wait a minute, wait a minute. Don't be in such a hurry.'' He could see that twenty pounds vanishing. ''It's too early for the band. Not enough people. But later on...'' He spread his hands. "The kid any good?''

"He plays in London.''

"What's he want to come down here for, then?''

I opened my mouth. No use letting Alan carry the whole burden. "We've persuaded him to look after us in our declining years," I said in a syrupy voice. "And he's just lost his girlfriend. She ran away with the lead guitarist. We thought there might be a better chance for him to find someone suitable in a smaller place, like Penzance.''

The manager lit a cigarette. At least this one contained tobacco, but I couldn't help coughing. He ignored me. "The loving grannies. Touching. Well, we get plenty of birds in here. He can take his pick. *If* we take him on. He have a band? We don't need solo drummers.''

"He knows people here. He can put one together,'' I said, still sweetly. "As for girls—someone told me there was a very pretty girl who came here a lot. Named Pamela something?''

The manager stood so suddenly his chair fell over. "Okay, out!''

"But what—?'' I began, bewildered.

"I don't know what you're up to, but I'm not having more trouble over Pamela Boleigh! After that shindy the other night, she's been barred from this club. We've already had the police here. I didn't care for that, I can tell you, and I don't care much for you, either, so get out!''

He opened the door and pointed.

He didn't even take Alan's money.

WE FOUND A back door and made our escape with more haste than grace. In the back alley, among the dustbins (which smell just as bad under that polite English name as do American garbage cans), we reconnoitered.

"Boleigh," I said.

Alan sighed. "His granddaughter, one assumes. It's not a common name in Penzance."

"Neither Tre, Pol, nor Pen."

"No. Cornish, all the same. His family have been here, or up north at least, for generations."

I ignored that. "So this is the granddaughter who's missing. I'd been imagining a child, a little girl."

"So had I. But coincidence can stretch only so far. The manager assumed at once that the Pamela we mentioned was Pamela Boleigh."

I clenched my hands into fists of frustration. "This makes the whole thing more complicated than ever. Pamela missing, Lexa dead—Alan, this could be much, much worse than we thought."

"And it was quite bad enough already."

I made a face that Alan probably couldn't see in the dark. "I said I preferred Dickens's obvious evil. I was wrong. That, in there, is unspeakable. I don't think I've ever in my life wanted so badly to get out of a situation. The whole place reeked of corruption and decadence. Did you spot any drugs? Except for the marijuana, I mean? I didn't see any, but then I don't know how to look."

"Nothing obvious. They're probably there, but the dealing won't start until later in the evening when the crowds arrive."

"Well, even without that, it was horrible."

"But we learned something."

"Nothing good."

"No." Alan sighed. "Let's get to the car, love."

The streets were dark and quiet. I couldn't hear the sea. We were near the harbor, where the waves were reduced to mere ripples by the protective walls and the boats within. I tried to take deep breaths of pure, clean air, but what I inhaled smelled of diesel fuel and, as we passed a dark, forbidding pub, of stale beer. The charm of Penzance had taken the night off.

"Alan, I'm not enjoying any of this at all."

"Neither am I, but enjoyment is not often a factor in this kind of work. Sometimes, at the end, there's a kind of righteous satisfaction. Sometimes not even that, when the villain gets off scot-free."

"But you kept at it, for forty years. And we have to keep at it this time, don't we?"

It wasn't a real question, and Alan didn't bother to answer. We climbed in the car.

"What now? Do you want to talk to Boleigh?"

"Not unless you think we must, Alan. It's late, and I've got a terrible headache from the noise and the smoke. Can't we let it wait until tomorrow?"

Alan sat. He didn't start the car. He didn't fasten his seat belt. He sat, pounding the steering wheel lightly with the heel of his hand.

"What?"

He stopped pounding and turned the key in the ignition. "Sorry. Didn't know I was fidgeting."

"Yes, but what were you fidgeting *about?*"

"Frustration. Dorothy, do you know how much I want to raid that pestilential club?"

"I have an idea. I also suspect you wouldn't be heartbroken if the manager just happened to trip during the proceedings and fall flat on his unlovely face. Because I feel the same way."

Alan pulled out of the parking lot onto Wharf Road and shook his head. "For a pair of law-abiding citizens..."

"We're perfectly normal," I said firmly. "What's more, if we can prove that Lexa died of illegal drugs from the rave club, we'll have a legitimate way to smash that man's face in. Figuratively, at least."

"It is," he said, "a considerable extra incentive."

By the time I'd taken a lengthy shower to rid myself of the smell of the club, Alan was asleep, but tired as I was, it took me quite a while to settle down. When I slept, I dreamed of Lexa and a shadowy Pamela being led off screaming to some terrible, unknown fate. I tried to run after them, but my legs were heavy and slow, after the manner of dreams.

I must have cried out in my sleep, for Alan touched me and I woke for a moment. As I moved nearer to him, I realized my pillow was wet with tears.

TWENTY-ONE

MORNING DAWNED, another gorgeous day in beautiful Cornwall. The breeze coming in the open window carried with it the murmur of a placid sea and the crying of the gulls, as well as the scents of flowers and salt water.

The beauty was, I thought sourly, a bright screen hiding darker corners. Today, the way I felt, the brightness was more than inappropriate: it was a personal affront. I sat up and pressed my fingertips to my throbbing temples. Alan, coming back from the bathroom, wordlessly handed me a washcloth wrung out in cold water. I collapsed back onto the pillow, the cloth over my eyes.

"I've ordered coffee," he said softly. "And orange juice. You need some sugar in your system."

"What I need is some peace of mind," I muttered. "And some aspirin."

"I can supply the aspirin, at least, but don't take too many on an empty stomach."

In due time, all the remedies beginning to work, I felt human enough to get dressed and think about facing the day.

"Mr. Boleigh first, I suppose," I said with little enthusiasm. "We have to go talk to him about his granddaughter."

"And perhaps you'd best look in on Mrs. Crosby?"

"Lord, yes. I don't know how I'm going to tell her that

the missing girl was with Lexa the night she died. She'll take it hard. She'll see as clearly as we do that it makes our job harder. Oh, and then I've promised her I'd help sort through Lexa's clothes and things, the stuff the police gave back and all. And we've said we wanted to look at her room, and of course there's the funeral this afternoon.'' I pressed my fingers to my head again. ''There's too much. I'll never be able to keep it all straight.''

''We need some organization. The day-to-day grind of police work consists almost entirely of writing up reports, you know, and we haven't kept ours up-to-date.''

''Ah, list making, yes. My favorite way of pretending I'm accomplishing something.'' I picked up the room-service menu and turned to the telephone.

While we were waiting for our breakfast to arrive, we dug out all our earlier lists and notes. They were meager in the extreme, but as we started in on our bacon and eggs we began to organize what little we had.

''Okay,'' I said with my mouth not quite full, fork in one hand and notebook in the other. ''We've checked off some of it. We found out why Lexa wanted to visit Cornwall, and what she did while she was here, at least in part. I think we need to follow up on that.'' I put down my fork and made a note.

Alan swallowed some toast. ''Yes, especially what she did all day Thursday. We know where she went in the evening, but what did she do before that?''

''The police probably know.''

''Almost certainly, but Colin is far too busy for me to pop in and bother him. Eleanor will tell us if she knows, and she might possibly remember something new.''

I added to the note. ''And I want to go back to the library, ask them what she looked up.''

''If they remember.''

"Remember Lexa? Are you kidding? If there was even one male librarian on duty that day, he'll be able to tell us where she sat, what she was wearing, and how many times she crossed her legs."

"You're feeling better."

"I guess I am," I said with a grin.

"And I agree with you. What they may not be able to tell us is what materials she consulted."

"True, but I'm betting." I added the word "library" to the notation. "Now, let's see. Oh, the cave. Remember, we want to go take another look at the cave." I took a deep breath, decided not to think about the cave until I actually had to face it, and continued. "And Lexa's room." I wrote busily.

"We can do that when we help Eleanor with Lexa's clothing. Does she want it packed up?"

"I don't know. I hope so. It's definitely a bad idea to keep it around. Eleanor's sensible; she'll probably want to give most of it away." I stopped, suddenly unable to speak. Tears began to trickle down my cheeks.

Alan waited until I'd sniffed and blown my nose before he quirked an interrogative eyebrow.

"I suddenly remembered the dress," I quavered. "That gorgeous dress I talked her into. She looked so beautiful in it, and she only got to wear it once...." More tears.

Alan is that rare male who knows how to deal with tears, at least with mine. He knows when sympathy is helpful and when it will only prolong the agony. In this case he cleared his throat and looked pointedly at the notebook. I pulled myself together.

"Very well, that seems to deal with the old list. Shall we add to it? We must talk to Boleigh about Pamela."

"Poor man."

"Indeed." Alan made no further comment, perhaps for

fear of setting me going again. "And perhaps we should speak again, more formally, to Mr. Polwhistle and Mr. Pendeen."

"You can do the mayor by yourself. He gives me the creeps."

Alan smiled. "I rather think he likes to dramatize himself a bit."

I studied the list, trying to think. "Would there be any point in talking again to the young men Lexa captivated the night of the party? Barnet and the rest?"

"You might get something out of them. I wasn't very popular with young Barnet, and I barely spoke to the rest."

"Okay, I'll put myself down for that, and you for Mr. Pendeen. Is there anybody else?"

We had been eating our breakfast in between remarks. Alan now pushed his plate away and took my notebook from me. "I think we've enough to do for now, don't you? For several days, in fact. We'll need to establish a schedule, but before we do, we'd better file a report."

"What *do* you mean? With the police?"

"No, with ourselves. We need to write down, systematically, what we know and what we need to know."

I groaned.

"The detective's unfailing response to paperwork," said Alan. "Here." He tore off a few pages. "We'll each write it out and then compare notes."

Ignoring my grumblings, he settled to the task, and after a histrionic sigh, I did, too.

It took a while, but when our two lists were boiled down, they amounted to more questions than answers.

"All right, we know Lexa came to Penzance to look for her father. We need to know who he is. We know she died in the same place her mother did—"

"Correction. We know she was found in the same place as her mother. We don't actually know where either of them died."

"Okay, okay. But we need to know what they were both doing there and how they got there. We know Lexa died of that drug, PMA, and we need to know where she got it and who gave it to her."

"If anyone did."

"She would not have taken it herself," I said stubbornly, and didn't wait for Alan's argument. "We know drugs were involved in both deaths, and we know there are drugs circulating in and around Penzance. We need to know where they're coming from."

"And if the police haven't been able to find that out, with the resources they have available, it isn't likely we will."

"You never know. Now, everything else we have is a question. What did Lexa learn at the library? What did she do all day Thursday, and where did she go after she left the rave club? Who was the man who quarreled with her and Pamela? Where is Pamela? And, going further afield into background material, what more, if anything, do the other four young men from the party know? Why is the Reverend Mr. Polwhistle obsessed with the devil? Is there anything suspicious about Mr. Pendeen and his importing business? Finally, what about the extra money Colin Cardinnis thinks is circulating in Penzance?"

I yawned, stretched, and threw the notebook on the table. "You know, I don't really understand about that last one. Surely, in this day and age, it's easier than ever to trace money."

"Not if the source doesn't want to be traced. It's very easy to hide behind layers of holding companies and foreign bank accounts. Once money gets into an account in the Cayman Islands, or in Geneva, the individual behind that money is all but invisible. Oh, it's *possible* to find him. Anything is possible, given sufficient time, resources, and international cooperation.''

I sighed. ''And of course the suspicion of a Penzance policeman that something funny's going on isn't likely to raise enough of any of those necessary things.''

''Not so long as it's only a suspicion.''

''So somebody's laundering money, and doing it very effectively.''

''If Colin is right about his uneasiness.''

''Well, there doesn't seem to be very much we can do about it, so let's get to work on something manageable. And I really do think, Alan, that our first duty is to talk to Mr. Boleigh. He'll be glad to see you, I imagine, and he might just have some useful information. If we can find Pamela, we'll take several giant steps forward.''

''Boleigh it is, then. Poor old Roley.''

''I thought his name was John.''

''That's his middle name. His first name is Roland. The nickname, I was told, was a leftover from school days. Apparently he was always a bit stout, even as a boy, and with his surname, of course—''

''Roley-Boleigh. Of course. Goodness, children can be cruel! No wonder he dropped his first name. I don't imagine anyone would dare call him that now, though.''

''Oh, affectionately, perhaps. I shouldn't have thought he'd mind anymore.''

''Probably not. I wish you hadn't told me, though, Alan. It would be awful if I slipped, especially now, when he must be worried sick.''

''You'll behave yourself. You almost always do. Are you ready?''

''As soon as I talk to Eleanor. I'll make that as short

as I decently can, but she'll probably be upset because of the funeral today. Alan, why don't you come with me? I really hate the thought of telling her about Pamela, and I could use some moral support.''

Eleanor was not alone. When we knocked on her door, it was answered by a woman in a nurse's uniform.

''Good morning,'' she said. ''May I help you?''

We introduced ourselves. ''We came to talk to Mrs. Crosby for a minute. You must be from hospice?''

''Yes. My name is Janet Banks. Come in, please. Mrs. Crosby has told me about you. We were just making some plans for today.''

''The funeral?''

''Yes, I've told Mrs. Crosby I'd be happy to drive her to the churchyard.''

Eleanor, sitting in the big armchair, looked unutterably weary. She nodded to us.

''Oh, we can do that. That is, if Eleanor would like to go with us?''

Eleanor nodded again, spiritlessly.

''Perhaps,'' said Alan to the nurse, ''you could accompany us, in case Mrs. Crosby should need your assistance.''

''Oh, of course. That's the sort of thing we always try to do. Now, you'd like to talk, so I'll be on my way. I'll be back at about one-thirty.''

''She seems like a nice woman,'' I said.

''Pleasant enough, I daresay.'' Eleanor looked at me briefly, then down at her lap. She had been crying.

I tried to steel myself to give her the bad news, but Alan grasped my elbow and took over. ''Eleanor, we realize this is a bad day for you, and we'd have preferred not to add to your burdens, but you need to know that the girl Pamela, the one Lexa met at the rave club, has disappeared.''

Even as tired, ill, and depressed as she was, Eleanor was quick. "That means she knows something. Pity no one found her to get her to tell it before she went missing.''

Her tone was scathing. Alan nodded. "A very great pity. But there are two ways to look at the situation. The other is that whereas we had only a Christian name before, we now know her identity, and the police are very actively looking for her. She may be found more quickly this way.''

"If she didn't know too much.'' Eleanor was not to be comforted.

"There is that possibility,'' Alan admitted. "We are on our way right now to talk to the girl's grandfather. He may be of some help.''

Eleanor nodded, sunk in misery once more, and we took our leave.

"She's not going to be with us much longer, is she?'' I said in a low tone when we were safely outside the room.

"Not unless we can come up with something to interest her in life for a little longer. I'm not entirely sure that would be a kindness.''

"The kindness would be to find Lexa's killer, so Eleanor can die in peace. Alan, whatever happens afterward, I'm sure it's better for people to die with their souls at rest.''

He smiled down at me. "I don't know that it makes one whit of difference to the dead, but I know *you'll* not rest till the questions are resolved. Shall we go talk to poor old Roley?''

"I'll get my hat.''

TWENTY-TWO

WE TELEPHONED FIRST. After some skirmishing with the functionary who answered the phone, we were told that yes, Mr. Boleigh was at home and would be pleased to see us. So we drove over to Bellevue, the elegant villa where Mr. Boleigh liked to throw elegant parties. It seemed, in the brilliant light of a September morning, to be an awfully big house for just him and his wife to be rattling around in.

Mr. Boleigh answered the door himself. "Please forgive our disorganization," he said somewhat stiffly. "My wife is with our daughter, who is prostrated, of course. So my secretary is having to take on Caroline's household duties as well as his normal ones, and at the same time try to keep the press at bay." He took a handkerchief out of his pocket and wiped his brow. "It's all rather difficult."

"I'm sorry, John." Alan grasped Boleigh's arm for a moment in a gesture of sympathy. "We're the ones who should apologize for the intrusion, but we thought we might be of some help. I'm sure the police are exploring every possible avenue, but is there any small thing we might do?"

I don't know if it was Alan's touch or the sympathy in his voice, but Boleigh's face crumpled and he dropped his polite facade. "I don't know. I can't think what's to be done. I stopped thinking like a policeman long ago, when I left the force. I was never much good at it anyway, as I expect you remember. Now I—oh, Lord, I can't seem to think at all!''

His face was ashen. He had seemed a healthy, hearty middle-aged man when we'd first met on St. Michael's Mount, and again at the party. Now he might have been eighty. I gave Alan a desperate look. He nodded.

''Now, John, this will never do. When did you last have any food?''

He gave us a bewildered look, as though he had forgotten what food was.

''Right. Dorothy, will you try to find the kitchen? John, sit down before you fall down, and tell me where you keep the whiskey.''

I scurried off toward the back premises and eventually, after a few false turns and dead ends, found the kitchen. It was empty. If the Boleighs kept a cook, he or she was off duty at the moment. I had no idea where the secretary might be, but I was here, and food, presumably, was here. I rummaged, found eggs, butter, bread, and tea. A skillet, a spatula, a teakettle and pot, and a toaster were all the equipment I needed, and very shortly I had a plate of scrambled eggs and several slices of toast. The tea was steeping in the pot. I found a large tray, rustled up a knife and fork, sugar, milk, and a small pot of marmalade, and carried the whole works back to the front of the house, where the sound of conversation led me to a room to the left of the front hall.

I plunked the tray down on a small table. ''There you are. Now, Mr. Boleigh, you'll have to stop talking and eat this right away. The plate is warm, but the kitchen's a long way from here, and cold eggs are an abomination unto the Lord.''

"I don't think—that is, you're being very kind, but—"

"I'm not being kind. I'm being terribly rude, and I've got some nerve, walking into your kitchen and messing it up. But now that I've done that, you might as well eat it—*while it's hot!*" I picked up the table, tray and all, and put it in front of his chair.

He sighed, picked up the fork, and took a bite. Alan and I turned our backs and walked to the other end of the room, which, now that I took the time to look at it, was a very fine library. Paneled in sage-green wood, it had what looked to my untutored eye like an Adam fireplace, with Wedgwood medallions. Built-in bookcases topped with graceful fan-shaped carvings held an assortment of books arranged by subject and then by author, so as to be easy to find. The books looked well read and well loved. This was a reader's library, not some decorator's dream with leather-bound books purchased by the yard.

The floor was covered with Persian rugs, their colors softened by time, their cost probably somewhere near that of our entire house, Alan's and mine. Soft, squashy leather chairs were dotted here and there, each with a floor lamp and a small table conveniently at hand. A sturdy but graceful writing table occupied the center of the room, and where the walls held no books, they displayed botanical prints.

"If the poor man can find peace anywhere, it ought to be here," I said in an undertone. "This is one of the loveliest, most soothing rooms I've ever seen."

"I don't know that he's able to accept peace just now," said Alan just as softly. "If ever I saw a tortured soul, it's John Boleigh. I got some whiskey into him. It helped his color but didn't do a thing for his state of mind."

We gave him several more minutes of privacy, then

turned back. He had eaten almost nothing, though he had
drunk some tea. His head was down and his eyes closed,
but he looked up at our approach.

"I'm sorry, Mrs.—er—"

"Dorothy, please. And don't apologize. I forced it on
you. I'm just sorry you don't feel able to eat."

"It's only that I'm so worried! She's such a lovely girl,
and only sixteen. There are such dangers out there for
pretty girls! Drugs, unsuitable boys..."

"It's a dangerous world, sadly. But she may have just
run off, you know. Teenagers do."

"Not Pamela!" It was the response I'd expected, the
automatic denial that a loved one would ever "do a thing
like that."

"No?" said Alan. "What sort of girl is she, John?
Quiet, studious?"

I opened my mouth and shut it again. If Alan was asking questions for which he knew at least part of the answers, he had a reason.

"No, not quiet. She enjoys dancing, music, all the
things young people do enjoy. But she's a good girl, Alan.
Not at all the wild sort."

"She's left school, I suppose."

"Yes, at sixteen, and why shouldn't she? School held
very little interest for her. She was far more sophisticated
than the other girls, and it's not as if she had to prepare
for a job. Her father is quite well-off, and of course her
mother, Sarah, is my daughter. I settled a considerable
sum on Sarah when she married, and on Pamela herself
at her sixteenth birthday. Both of them are also in my
will. Pamela has no need to earn her living, ever, even if
she doesn't marry well."

I made a mental note: spoiled rotten, both mother and

daughter. I wouldn't be surprised if Pamela had gone off with some fortune hunter.

Alan was evidently thinking along the same lines, for he said, "I suppose you and her parents have got in touch with her friends."

"Of course! That was the first thing we did when she didn't come home Saturday night, but no one had seen her."

"Saturday night? She spent Thursday and Friday night at home, then?"

"No. I'm telling this badly, I'm sorry. Thursday she went out dancing with some friends and told Sarah, her mother, that she'd probably go home with one of her girl-friends if they were up all night, and then spend Friday night with her, as well. She planned to be home by noon or thereabouts on Saturday."

"And her parents made no objection to this?"

"I suppose you think they should have done. That's because you've never met Pamela. You don't understand. She's a spirited girl; it's better to let her have her head. She's sensible enough when she's left to herself, but she won't be reined in. She's been out all night before, and never came to harm. So it wasn't until Saturday afternoon that her mother began to wonder, and not until nearly nightfall, when they hadn't heard from Pamela, that any-one began to really worry. Then, of course, they got on the phone, but all of Pamela's friends said they hadn't seen her for several days."

"Pamela hadn't said which girl she planned to stay with?"

"No. She liked to keep her arrangements flexible."

I'll just bet she did. I almost said it aloud. And what were the odds that the girlfriend was really a boyfriend?

"I knew nothing of this," Boleigh continued, "till Sunday morning, when Sarah rang up. I went straight to the police, which is what her parents should have done from the start, and they told me where Pamela had been seen Thursday night. I was appalled! Why would she go to such a place? And who was that man who made her so angry? Do the police know? Do *you* know, Alan?'' The poor man studied Alan's face intently.

Alan shook his head helplessly. ''I was hoping you might have some idea.''

''I never even imagined she'd go to a place like that. And where did she go from there? Alan, where is she? Why can't they find her? That girl they said she was with, Alexis Something—''

''Adams,'' I murmured. ''You met her.''

''Of course I met her! I'm not senile yet! You brought her to my party. She was very beautiful, and I suppose she was a friend of yours, but she was with Pamela, and now she's dead and Pamela is missing. Did she drag my granddaughter down with her?''

I was about to make an angry rejoinder when Boleigh put his head in his hands. ''They've got to find her, Alan. She's my youngest grandchild, the last there'll ever be. They've got to *find* her!''

He broke down completely. Alan and I looked at each other over his head. There were still questions we needed to ask, but Boleigh had endured all he could. Alan murmured something sympathetic and reassuring, and we tiptoed out of the room.

TWENTY-THREE

ALAN DROVE, not back to the hotel, but straight down the hill to the sea. We parked on the road at a point where a footbridge crossed the railway line, and went down to the beach to talk.

"Sixteen," I said. "That Barnet person thought she was maybe eighteen, but I suppose she tried to look older. Sixteen years old!" I sat on a handy rock. "What's happened to her, Alan? Has she been killed, too?"

He reached for his pipe, made the usual face when he found his pocket empty, and sat down beside me, hands clasped around one raised knee. "There are several lines of speculation. One, she's run away."

"I have to say that seems quite likely to me, no matter what John Boleigh says. The girl sounds like a menace to society *and* herself."

Alan nodded. "Overindulged, and that's throwing roses at it. If any daughter of mine, aged sixteen, had stayed out all night without my knowing exactly where she was and with whom—well, it simply wouldn't have happened. But it's a different world nowadays, and Pamela's discipline, or lack of it, is her family's problem, not ours. Our problem is to try to find her, and there are other, darker possibilities."

I enumerated them, trying hard to stay objective. "One,

she killed Lexa herself and has run from the police. Only why would she?''

''Motive is the least important consideration in any investigation. You know that. She'd been taking drugs; they both had. Who's to know what impulses might have surfaced?''

''In other words, you don't have a clue.''

''Right.''

I continued to list Pamela's possible fates. ''Two, she didn't kill Lexa, but she knows who did and has run from the murderer. And three, she knows who did and—well—didn't manage to run fast enough.''

''Any of those things. Add a drug overdose that killed her or made her amnesiac, and we have a reasonably complete list.''

''The police will have made the same list,'' I observed.

''Yes, and they'll be working at it methodically, according to procedural rules.''

''Will they find her?''

''Based on what I know of the force here, yes, they will, sooner or later. They'll be working hard at it, for one thing, because of John's prominence. That ought not to make a difference, but of course it does. Colin Cardinnis is only human, after all, and he knows the security of his job is in jeopardy if he doesn't do all he possibly can in this particular case.''

''Well, then, I don't see that there's much point to our looking for her, too. She was our best lead to Lexa's murderer before she disappeared, but now...'' I spread my hands. ''The police know she was at the rave club, and have begun tracing her from there.'' I was thinking out loud. ''If she and Lexa stayed together, that means they're tracing Lexa's movements, too. I really think we ought to leave that end of things to Cardinnis and crew.''

"I agree. Did you put your notebook in your handbag?"

"What do you think?" I rummaged and found it. We looked at it together. It made depressing reading.

"So many questions and so few answers," I moaned. "A number of people we can ask, though. Eleanor, people at the library, Pendeen, Polwhistle, and Lexa's conquests. Where should we start?"

Alan considered. "We can postpone the Reverend Mr. Polwhistle. We'll see him this afternoon at the funeral, so that line of inquiry might as well wait until then. That leaves five young men about whom we know very little, and Mr. Pendeen. He"—Alan looked at his watch— "ought to be easily found at this hour at his shop. Shall we go and see?"

I got up reluctantly. "Just as long as you don't leave me alone with him. He reminds me of Bela Lugosi."

We found Mr. Pendeen's antique store without difficulty in a pleasant little side street off the main shopping area. The store did, as Alan had suggested, remind me of the one in Mousehole, only on a larger scale. Pendeen's place carried no jewelry and only a little ornamental bric-a-brac. The bulk of his stock ran to exquisite furniture, from massive Baroque wardrobes down to spindly Victorian occasional tables. I didn't even bother to guess at prices. There were few things in the store I didn't covet, even though most of them wouldn't fit in our house and certainly not in our budget. Some of them, the more restrained Georgian pieces, would have looked gorgeous in John Boleigh's villa, though. I wondered if this was where he did his shopping.

The clerk was a woman. "Was there something you wished to see?" Her bored tone indicated clearly that she had sized us up expertly when we came in, dismissed us as not wealthy enough to buy anything in the place, and now wanted to get rid of us as quickly as possible. I let Alan deal with her.

"Please don't bother," he said with one of his most charming smiles. "We're here to see Mr. Pendeen, a business matter." He whisked me away toward the back of the store before the clerk could protest.

"How do you know where his office is?" I said under my breath.

"Where else could it be?"

Good point. I sent Alan on back by himself. "This stuff is gorgeous. Even if I can't buy, I can look. I'll join you eventually."

I did spend a little time wistfully looking at magnificent, museum-quality furniture I could never hope to own, but the exercise soon lost its appeal. I wondered what tack my husband was taking with Mr. Pendeen. I had no ideas, myself, about a productive approach. Why, after all, should he tell us anything? Particularly if he was involved in illegal activities.

Alan had been trained to deal with just that sort of situation, of course. It would be instructive to listen to him. I drifted toward the office door and was startled to hear Alan say, in quite a menacing tone, "Drugs."

"What about them?" said Mr. Pendeen. He sounded startled.

"How widespread are they in Penzance? How do they get in? What's being done to stop them?"

"I presume," he said dryly, "you are not referring to aspirin and antibiotics."

Alan apparently decided the question didn't require an answer. I stepped inside the door, very quietly.

Mr. Pendeen's back was to me. He made no indication

that he had heard me enter. His sleek black head remained still. Alan saw me, but made no sign.

"May I ask," said Mr. Pendeen, "what your interest is in the matter? Have you by chance turned to journalism in your retirement?"

"My interest is in Alexis Adams. She became a friend to my wife and me in the few days we were at the hotel together. I have been told that she was at a rave club the night she died. I believe that she took drugs, probably without knowing it, and that her tragic accident was a direct result of her drugged state."

"Can you prove any of this?"

"The police know that there were dangerous drugs in her body."

Oh, was it wise to reveal so much? My hands, held behind my back, clenched into tight fists. I deliberately relaxed them. Tension in a room can be as palpable as the sensation of someone's eyes on the back of one's neck. As that thought arose in my mind, I quickly averted my eyes from Mr. Pendeen's head.

His voice showed no sign that he knew I was there. "It is true," he said slowly, "that there is a drugs problem in Penzance. It has been growing for the past several years. It is also true that we suspect the raves to be a major center of distribution. We have not, however, been able to close down the club. We believe there is only one, though it changes location frequently. I have requested police raids, but on the appointed nights, either no rave has been found, or no drugs have been in evidence. It is not against the law to dance all night to loud music."

"Unfortunately, considering the music."

"Perhaps." There was a hint of a smile in the sound of his reply, but it faded with his next words. "Now you have had my response as mayor. You have, I believe, suggested that I might also have some information related to my expertise as an importer. I hope you did not imply by that what I fear you might have implied.''

My hands were clenched again. Again I stretched out my fingers. Alan answered calmly. ''I was afraid you might take it that way. No, I meant that you have some familiarity with shipments to Penzance, the way they're handled, dealings with Customs officials, and the like. How would someone wanting to smuggle drugs into England along this coast go about it?''

This time Pendeen laughed out loud. ''That, Nesbitt, is the sort of question no Cornishman would ever answer directly, as you ought to know. We have a reputation, do we not, for being closemouthed, for keeping our secrets. So I will say only that I, being a law-abiding citizen, have no idea how such things are done nowadays, or even if they are done. I do, of course, know a good deal about the smuggling methods of centuries past.''

And with that he turned to me, nodded politely, and said, ''I'm sure you'd be more comfortable sitting, Mrs. Martin, if you would like to join this fascinating conversation. As a stranger to the area, what strikes you as a promising method for modern smuggling?''

Well, if he'd intended to disconcert me, he'd succeeded, but I wouldn't give him the satisfaction of admitting it. I smiled. ''I'm sure I wouldn't know, Mr. Pendeen. Like you, I've read up about the old days, but floating brandy casks ashore sounds a little archaic for the twenty-first century. To tell the truth, I'm more interested in something entirely different that I've observed, if my husband will forgive me for changing the subject.'' I smiled again, showing as many teeth as possible and hoping Alan would read my expression. ''I couldn't help but notice that you have some very fine, and very expensive, antiques for sale. I've noticed other prices in town running on the high side, too. I admit that I'm just a little surprised.''

Alan frowned. I hurried on before he could interrupt me. ''From the reading I've been doing, I've gathered that most of Cornwall's industry died out quite some time ago, so that tourism is the major source of income now. And I've wondered how it is that Penzance seems so prosperous. One might almost imagine a rebirth of some sort. As mayor, do you have an explanation?''

''You're quite perceptive, Mrs. Martin. Ah, Nesbitt, you do indeed have your work cut out to keep up with your estimable wife. As for our fair city's prosperity, I hope I may say without undue immodesty that the council's policies under my leadership have been beneficial to the economic climate here. If there is any other explanation, I feel no need to seek it. I am simply grateful. Business is very good, indeed. And may I interest you, Mrs. Martin, in one of the pieces you have been good enough to admire?''

''Oh, I'm interested in them all, Mr. Pendeen. Unfortunately the budget of a retired schoolmarm and a retired policeman won't quite cover Louis the Sixteenth desks or Hepplewhite chairs.''

''Worse luck,'' Alan agreed, rising. ''Come, my dear. We really must leave this busy man to his work. Good of you to talk to us, Pendeen.''

''And what,'' I demanded as we drove to the hotel for lunch, ''did you make of that? Villain, or merely poseur?''

''Poseur, I think, but I'm not sure. He was playing with us, of course.''

''He knew I was there all the time, didn't he?''

Alan nodded. ''I saw his eyes twitch when you first came to the door.''

"But why the game? Is he up to something?"

Alan sighed as he slid the car into a parking space and pocketed the keys. "I think he's fully aware of his resemblance to Dracula, and uses it simply because it amuses him. It's probably good for business. 'Oh, my dear, simply the scariest man, I was afraid to leave the store without buying something, but really charming when I made up my mind, even took twenty percent off the price.'"

Alan's American accent is terrible, but his rendition of the socialite made me giggle anyway. "I wouldn't think, though, that the vampire routine would do much for his political ambitions."

"You as an American should know better than most people that politics is about nine-tenths show business."

With the usual accompaniment of creaks and groans, I extricated myself from the car. "Well, *as* an American, I also know that the other tenth is apt to be corruption. And I'm not convinced that the esteemed mayor isn't into something crooked right up to the chain of office he wears around his neck."

TWENTY-FOUR

WE HAD AN early lunch and then changed into our soberest clothes for Lexa's funeral. I was glad we had offered to take Eleanor, because all the fuss of getting her and her nurse settled in the car and then safely out of it again at the church kept me from thinking very much.

Eleanor was making a great effort. She had lost weight visibly, even in the few days we had known her, and her clothes hung on her, but she had applied her makeup carefully and made sure her wig was smoothly brushed and combed. She carried an elegant walking stick and tried not to show how heavily she was leaning on it as she walked across the grass to the open grave. Her nurse held her elbow lightly, ready to help if help was needed and wanted.

"Lexa would be proud of you," I whispered as Mr. Polwhistle appeared, his surplice and stole blowing in the brisk wind.

Eleanor tightened her lips in what might have been an attempt at a smile and fixed her eyes steadfastly forward.

The service began. The words from the Bible and the Book of Common Prayer, which ought to have been familiar and somewhat comforting, were instead from a modern translation that I found distracting, so I looked around as unobtrusively as I could.

I had expected that only Eleanor, Alan and I, and the

nurse would be present. I was surprised to see John Boleigh hovering a little distance away, with another man who looked vaguely familiar. I looked at Alan and raised my eyebrows.

"Cardinnis," he whispered under cover of a rather odd version of the Twenty-third Psalm which the tiny gathering was trying, with many stumbles, to recite.

Boleigh, I thought, looked almost as bad as Eleanor. Was he seeing his granddaughter lying there, praying she was alive and well, terrified that she was neither?

There were a few more readings, mercifully short, the Lord's Prayer, mercifully familiar, and then the words of committal, a blessing, and it was over. Eleanor turned away, refusing to cast earth or flowers on the body of the woman she had loved so devotedly, refusing, also, to weep. She held her head high, though her face, even through the makeup, was gray.

John Boleigh, Mr. Polwhistle, and Mr. Cardinnis all made attempts to speak to her. She ignored them, moving away as quickly as she could.

"We'd best get her back immediately," the nurse said to Alan. "She's near collapse, and she'll not want to do it with anyone watching."

"You go on," I said. "I'll have a word with Mr. Polwhistle and then walk home."

I hung around a corner of the churchyard for a few minutes, trying to be invisible or, at the worst, to look as if I were studying the old graves, while the priest spoke to Mr. Boleigh and the police superintendent. When they finally left—together, I noted, Boleigh talking agitatedly to Cardinnis—I hastened out of my secluded corner and caught up with Mr. Polwhistle on the church steps, just as he was about to go inside.

"Mr. Polwhistle?"

He peered nearsightedly back at me.

"It's Mrs. Martin, Mr. Polwhistle. Alan Nesbitt's wife. I was here just now for the funeral. I just wanted to say how grateful I was for the beautiful service." I've never avoided a little insincerity in a good cause.

"Thank you," he said quietly. "I saw you and your husband at the service. Such a shame there weren't more people to mourn such a beautiful girl, but I'm grateful if I was able to help her grieving mother in some small way."

"I'm sure it was a great comfort to her." Another lie. Nor did I correct him about Lexa's parentage. What did it matter?

"But was there some way I can help you?"

"Not really. I only wanted to thank you."

"No need." He hesitated and then went on. "I must admit I took something of a personal interest in the matter, though of course Alexis wasn't a parishioner. But I'm always particularly horrified when a young person dies from the misuse of drugs."

"Lexa's death wasn't a suicide, you know," I said hurriedly, and then wondered if I had given away some vital secret.

"No, the police assured me that it was almost certainly accidental, or I could not have buried her in consecrated ground, you know." Again he hesitated.

"Have you perhaps worked with teenagers, Mr. Polwhistle? You seem quite concerned about them." I was fishing, but there was something here. I could feel it.

"No, no." He shook his head sadly. "I have no talent for working with the young. I'm too old-fashioned, too stodgy. They don't understand me and I don't understand them. It's a terrible failing for a priest, and it has been a great sorrow to me over the years. Even with my own children—and grandchildren—'' He broke off.

I tried to probe for more. "Now I understand Pamela Boleigh is missing. Her grandfather seems terribly worried about her. Do you think she's run away?"

"I baptized Pamela," he said, his eyes focused on something I couldn't see. The past, perhaps. "She was the sweetest baby. I've known her all her life, and now—oh, who knows what evil may have befallen her? The devil, Mrs. Martin, the devil is abroad and at work!"

And he was off and running. I let the tirade run its course, and then pointedly looked at my watch. "Oh, I'm so sorry, I'm late! My husband's expecting me, and I must see how Mrs. Crosby is holding up. It was a pleasure to talk to you, and thank you again for a lovely service."

I shook his hand and went down the steps.

Once I was in the churchyard, though, and safely out of his sight, I studied the graves in earnest. It would be in the newer section, of course.

It didn't take long to find. "Susan Polwhistle," the stone read. "Beloved daughter of Susan and Gregory Polwhistle and granddaughter of the Reverend Samuel Polwhistle, rector of this church. Suffer the little children to come unto Me." The dates read, "1983-1996."

Thirteen. Mr. Polwhistle's granddaughter had died at the age of thirteen.

I was ready to bet every cent I had that she'd died of something related to drugs.

ALAN WAS WAITING for me back at the hotel. "Some tea, darling? Or a drink?"

"Tea, I think. We can make it up here, if that's all right with you. I don't want anything to eat."

He glanced at me and switched on the kettle. "Mr. Polwhistle was difficult, was he?"

"Not especially, except at the end when he got off on his hobbyhorse. I found out what the personal tragedy is."

"The tragedy? Oh, Polwhistle's, you mean? He isn't just cracked, then?"

"He's cracked on the subject of drugs because his granddaughter died at age thirteen."

"Of an overdose? He told you that?"

"He didn't actually tell me much of anything. I made some guesses from what little he did say, and found her headstone. If it wasn't from drugs, it was from something having to do with drugs. I'd stake my reputation as a snoop on it."

Alan sighed heavily. "It would certainly explain his mania on the subject. Poor man. Are you sure you wouldn't like a drink?"

"Not now. Alcohol's my drug of choice, but just now I feel like holding a crucifix in front of me to ward off anything down to and including aspirin. I'm even a little leery of caffeine."

"I'll make the tea weak."

It turned out to be not much more than fragrant hot water, but it was comforting all the same. "How's Eleanor?" I asked when I had finished my first cup and poured a second.

"'As well as can be expected' is the phrase, I believe. Miserable and weak, but holding her own, according to the nurse. She—Eleanor, I mean—gave me the key to Lexa's room before I left her. She said she simply wasn't up to sorting out anything, but she'd like it done as soon as possible."

"No time like the present, I suppose. I don't look forward to it, but that kind of thing just gets harder the longer you put it off." I drank the rest of the tea and got to my feet. "If you're not too tired?"

"We can have a nap later." It was the kind of remark that he would normally have accompanied with his best leer, but neither of us was in the mood just then.

We trudged up to the room Lexa had occupied for the last few days of her life. Alan unlocked the door and I entered with great reluctance.

The room had been kept clean. The hotel staff was too efficient not to do that, as soon as the police had given them permission. They had also tidied up, or else Lexa was a tidy person, but the room was still full of her personality. I, who had known her for such a short time, found the fading flowers on the bedside table, the sweater tossed over the arm of a chair, the perfume bottles and makeup in the bathroom almost unbearably pathetic. I could see that even entering the room would be impossible for Eleanor.

Alan said nothing, but opened a wardrobe door. "No suitcases in here. Try under the bed."

There were two large bags, one under each bed, with designer labels that screamed their cost. We each pulled one out and started to work.

"Did Eleanor say what she wanted done with the things?"

"Only that she never wanted to see any of them again. Charity, I suppose."

I nodded. Oxfam could make a fortune off these clothes.

"Oh, and she did say to keep the jewelry separate. I suppose some of it may be worth selling."

"Or else she wants to give it to Lexa's friends. I can't imagine, somehow, that she'd want to sell anything of Lexa's."

"You might be right."

We worked for a time in depressed silence. Lexa had brought no clothes inappropriate for a seaside resort. Her taste had been too good for that kind of ostentation. Everything she had, though, was of the very best quality. I inspected my hands carefully to make sure my nails were smooth and I had no rough fingertips before even touching her silk lingerie.

"Are the things from the police station here, Alan?"

He nodded. "In a box in the closet. I've gone through those, but kept them separate. I'd have thought it best to throw them away rather than give them to charity."

I shuddered and agreed.

The job didn't take long. Eleanor would have to face the same task on a much larger scale when she got back to Lexa's Knightsbridge flat, but we'd done what we could. We closed the bags and locked them. I stood holding the small jewel case with the few rings and earrings Lexa had brought to Penzance.

"Shall I take this over to Eleanor now? I hate to be responsible for it. I don't think there's anything of really fabulous value, but it's all good stuff, no fakes in the lot."

"You could knock and see if she's awake. If not, we can put it in the hotel safe."

Eleanor was in bed, but awake. The nurse had left. When I expressed surprise that Eleanor had been left alone, she snapped at me.

"When I want a keeper, I'll ask for one. I can manage for myself a little longer, thank you very much. I heard you next door. Have you finished?"

I didn't respond in kind. Eleanor was a good woman who'd had all she could take. "All done. You asked that we save her jewelry for you, so here it is." I handed her the box.

She opened the box and sifted through the contents. Then she glared at me. "Where's the rest of it?"

"That's all there was, Eleanor. We looked very carefully."

"That is *not* all there was. What have you done with the cross?"

TWENTY-FIVE

WELL, DARN IT, I'd had a tough day, too. I tried to hold on to my temper, but I confess I was somewhat brusque with Eleanor. "Everything we found is there. We even looked in the pockets of suitcases, all the little hiding places for jewelry. Is the cross you're talking about valuable? Would Lexa have put it in the hotel safe?"

Eleanor sank back onto the pillows, her brief anger spent. Her face was gray. "No, it wouldn't be in the safe. She wore it always, even when she was working, under her clothes. She would have been wearing it the night she died, probably tucked into the top of her tights. She'd hang it 'round her neck if she was wearing something with a high neckline, or in her bra if she was wearing one, even in a shoe if it wouldn't go anywhere else. She was never without it. Everyone she worked with knew about it. It ought to have been with the things the police returned."

"Eleanor, could it have been buried with her?"

"Not unless that priest lied to me. He said he'd take care of having her body properly dressed for burial, so I told him to take a dress from her room. He said she was— her body was wearing nothing at all. I should have seen to it myself! Dorothy, that cross belonged to her mother, to Betty, and it was all we had of her, and I want it back!

You're quite sure you didn't see it?'' Suspicion hardened her voice again.

"Eleanor, we did not take Lexa's cross. We didn't see it. We'll look again, of course, but I don't think we missed anything. What does it look like? Gold or silver?''

"Gold, set with garnets. It was about so big''—she held her fingers about an inch and a half apart—''and made to look old. Betty told me Lexa's father gave it to her, that first time they met. It was all he ever gave her, she would say, except for a baby. She used to wear it on a ribbon; a chain cut into her neck, she said, because the thing was so heavy. But she liked it, and when Lexa was born Betty passed it on to her. A baby couldn't wear it, of course, but Betty would pin it to the hood of the pram, or to Lexa's blanket. When Lexa became my responsibility, I put the cross away until she was old enough to understand how to look after it, and then gave it to her and told her the story.''

Eleanor blinked several times and turned her head away. ''She's worn it since she was ten. Until now.''

Alan and I looked at each other. Alan's look was a warning. He cleared his throat. ''We will certainly look for it, Eleanor, and see that you have it as soon as possible. A thing like that would be very noticeable.''

"You don't think a chambermaid stole it, do you? They all seem to be nice women; I'd hate to think…''

"I'm a reasonably nice woman, too, and you thought for a moment that I'd stolen it. No, it's all right. I know this has all been hard for you. We'll sort it out, I promise. Meanwhile, would you like some tea?''

Eleanor did not want tea. She wanted to rest. I was concerned about her condition, but she refused to let me call the nurse back, so there was nothing to do but leave her to her own devices and go back to our room.

"Alan, we'd better go back to that antique store right away! Somebody might buy it!"

My husband can be infuriatingly calm at times. He reached for the telephone. "There's a better way. Yes, operator, could you give me the number for the police station? You can connect me? Thank you."

"What are you going to do?"

He put a finger to his lips. "Hello? Alan Nesbitt here. I need to speak to Superintendent Cardinnis, please."

"But, Alan—"

"Hello? Oh, hello, Colin. I'll make this brief; I know how much you have on your plate. I hope you've managed to catch up with the bank robbers. Oh, what a pity; I *am* sorry, Colin. I'm calling about your other major headache, actually. Have you had any luck finding Pamela Boleigh? Yes, of course, early days yet. Well, you see, I think I may have some information about her. It's likely that she called on an antique shop in Mousehole on Saturday. Yes, to sell them a piece of jewelry of some considerable value."

The light dawned. Of course! Pamela stole it! Though how she knew Lexa had it, when it was hidden...or maybe Lexa gave it to her. She was riding a high, something she'd never experienced before. Her judgment would have been impaired. She might have taken it out to show Pamela, and then...oh, we didn't know enough. But Alan was being brilliant, anyway.

"...yes, it belonged to Alexis Adams, apparently. Mrs. Crosby can identify it. Very well, I'll be here."

He hung up the phone. "Colin will send someone to fetch the cross and bring it here. If it does turn out to be Lexa's, and it was brought in to the shop on Saturday, as the shopkeeper said..."

"Pamela, almost certainly. There's our motive, right

there. Unless…oh, Alan, it could have been the man from the club!''

''It could, though if he was responsible for Lexa's death, he'd have been very stupid to sell something so easily identified as hers, so soon after her death.''

''Criminals are not rocket scientists.''

''Most of them are not, which is fortunate for the police. However, it's pointless to speculate. The shopkeeper will remember who sold him the cross, the police will show him a photograph of Pamela, and we'll soon know.''

''Will they keep us informed?''

''I'm sure Colin will do his best. You must remember that he's working something like twenty hours out of the twenty-four. They've caught up with those bank robbers, but there's no sign of the stolen cash, so that investigation is still very much alive.''

''Was this what it was like when you were working, Alan?''

''The details changed as I moved up the ladder. The pressure was always the same. Crime never takes a holiday.''

Nor, apparently, can we, I thought with some resentment. Here we were in one of England's beauty spots, the famous West Country, and we couldn't get away from crime and tragedy. I had come to Penzance to help Alan resolve his feelings about an old crime, if I could, and now we were embroiled in several new ones.

Alan saw what I was thinking. ''Buck up, darling. I remind you that we mustn't make it our personal tragedy, or we'll lose our objectivity and our effectiveness. While we wait for Colin's information, what about a cream tea?''

I allowed myself to be seduced by food. We went to the wonderful tea shop down the street and I ate a great many things that were bad for me, but while Alan chatted about a possible jaunt to St. Ives, I kept thinking about that cross, and how soon we could know anything.

Alan finally gave up his efforts to distract me. "Very well," he said. "We may just as well go back to the hotel and wait for the phone to ring. You're acting like a cat on hot bricks."

"I know. I'm sorry. It's just that I think we should be there when they show Eleanor the cross. She has a strong sentimental attachment to it, and she'll be upset."

"Right you are. After you, love."

Colin had been busy while we idled. There was a message waiting for us.

Alan took it from the desk clerk and frowned. "When did this come in?"

"Not five minutes ago, sir."

"Good. Thank you."

"What?" I said, trying to look over Alan's shoulder.

"They have the cross. Colin's sending a sergeant over here with it any minute—and here she is, if I'm not mistaken."

The woman coming in the door was not in uniform, but her trim business suit might almost as well have had brass buttons, and she bore herself with military discipline.

"She'll have to loosen up some to be a good detective," I whispered to Alan. "She sticks out like a nun at a bikers' convention."

Alan smiled, apparently at the policewoman, and moved toward her with outstretched hand. "My name is Alan Nesbitt and this is my wife, Dorothy Martin. I believe you must be Detective Sergeant Blaine?"

"Yes, sir." She didn't salute, quite. "I'm relieved that you've returned. Superintendent Cardinnis said it would be best if you accompanied me to call on Mrs. Crosby. We have rung up to tell her we were coming.''

I wondered if that was the royal "we," or the one so infuriatingly used by some nurses, as in, "How are we today?'' I didn't dare ask. The sergeant's manner was so strictly business that I might instead have apologized for our dereliction of duty in leaving the hotel, if Alan hadn't favored me with the bland look that says ''Keep quiet.'' Instead I nodded and meekly followed the two of them to the elevator.

Alan let Sergeant Blaine handle the interview, only explaining, briefly, that we had recognized the cross from Eleanor's description as one we might have seen, and the police had brought it for her to identify.

She recognized it the moment Sergeant Blaine took it out of her pocket, even though it was enclosed in a small plastic bag. "Yes, of course that's Lexa's cross. What a relief!'' She held out her hand. ''Where did you find it?''

The sergeant did not answer the question. "Is there any way that you can identify it positively, Mrs. Crosby?''

Eleanor sighed. "How many pieces of jewelry have you ever seen that looked like that? Of course it's hers. Where did you find it?''

''It was found under circumstances that leave its ownership in doubt,'' said the sergeant firmly. ''I know you described it to us over the telephone, and to Mr. Nesbitt and Mrs. Martin. However, it would help greatly if there were some detail you could give us that would prove this piece belonged to your stepdaughter.''

"Dorothy, I'm not well enough for this,'' said Eleanor in exasperation. ''What is the woman talking about?''

''I suppose she means is there a scratch or something like that, some small mark that isn't obvious but that only Lexa, or you, would be likely to know about.''

"Why didn't she say so? Yes, there's a tiny *L* scratched just at the bottom of the ring the thing hangs by. Lexa did it when she was a teenager. Someone had told her that real gold was soft, and she got a pin to see if her cross was real gold. When it scratched easily, she added a short second scratch at the bottom because it made her initial. I scolded her when I found out about it, I can tell you. I've always thought the thing was probably worth a few pounds, if only for the gold. But you still haven't told me where it was found."

I looked at the sergeant. She nodded. "The scratch is there, and we have checked with some of Miss Adams's coworkers, who have confirmed that she always wore the cross. This was the property of the deceased, without doubt. You may tell Mrs. Crosby, if you wish."

I took a deep breath. "Alan and I saw it yesterday, Eleanor, by the purest chance. We were window-shopping at an antique store in Mousehole, and it caught my eye. Are you ready for a small shock?"

She frowned.

"The stones are rubies, not garnets. The dealer said it was sixteenth-century German work, and he had it priced at three thousand pounds."

She absorbed that in silence with only a widening of her eyes. Remarkable, I thought. Truly the English are schooled to be in command of their emotions.

"And how," she asked after a pause for consideration, "did Lexa's cross come to be in an antique shop in Mousehole?"

"We've speculated about that rather a good deal," said Alan. "I don't know if Sergeant Blaine can add anything to our guesses."

"It was brought in for sale two days ago, on Saturday.

The person who sold it matches the description of Pamela Boleigh, and the shopkeeper identified her photograph.''

"Pamela," said Eleanor, passing her tongue over her dry lips and turning to me. "That is the name of the girl who was with Lexa at the club. The one you told me about, who has gone missing."

I nodded.

"Then why," said Eleanor to the sergeant, "are you wasting time here when you might be out looking for that girl? For Lexa's murderer?"

TWENTY-SIX

NONE OF US tried to argue with her. There was no point in upsetting her further, and besides, she might well be right. I did insist on ordering up some tea, and Alan and I stayed with her to drink it and make sure she ate something.

Sergeant Blaine had taken the cross back to the police station, over Eleanor's bitter protests.

"It's the only thing of Lexa's that I want! Why am I not allowed to have it?"

"It is evidence in a crime investigation," Alan explained patiently. "It will be returned to you, but for now it must be examined by the forensics experts."

He didn't mention to her what he said to me when we were once more alone.

"You know, it's possible that Eleanor may never get that cross back."

"But why? It clearly belonged to Lexa, and her mother before her."

"Ah, yes, but how did the mother get it? Eleanor said it was a gift from Lexa's father, didn't she?"

"Yes, but—"

"And Lexa's father is emerging as a more and more unpleasant character, isn't he?"

I nodded, beginning to catch the drift.

"So where did he get it?"

"Yes, all right. If he stole it—but that would have been years ago! Isn't there a statute of limitations? Possession is nine points of the law, and all that."

"The laws are a trifle murky on the subject. There have been endless lawsuits, for example, about Nazi art treasures. Those things were looted perhaps sixty years ago and are now in the possession of legitimate buyers, or at least buyers whose lawyers will claim till the last trump that the works were bought in good faith. Of course, if the cross is a treasure trove, which it might well be, given its probable age, it belongs to the Crown, no matter who has possessed it since it was found."

I groaned. "Eleanor doesn't have the time to wait until some court makes a decision. It could take years, and she has weeks, or days."

Alan said nothing. There was nothing to be said, and nothing much to be done about it, either. I changed the subject. "The case against Pamela is looking worse, isn't it?"

"So much worse that the police have doubtless redoubled their efforts to find her. She is now not only a missing person, but a suspected thief, at the least, and murderess, at worst."

"Mr. Boleigh will be having seven fits, if he knows. How much will they tell him?"

"Virtually everything, I'd guess. If he were simply any ordinary John Bull, no, but given who he is, he'll have demanded constant and full reports, and he'll probably have got them."

"Would they part with some of that information to lowly beings like us?"

"*Whom* are you calling a lowly being, wench? I will remind you that I am, in these parts, The Chief, and am treated with due respect."

"Right. Will they tell you anything?"

He grinned. "Probably, if they're not too busy with other such Extremely Important Individuals. I'll ring up."

I went to the bathroom, and when I got back, Alan was just putting down the phone. His face had lost its good humor. "What's wrong?"

He sank down on the bed. "They've found her."

"Oh." There was no need to ask whether she was alive or dead. I sat beside him and took his hand. "Where?" I was terribly afraid he would say Pamela had been found in the same cave.

"Near Sheffield."

"Sheffield! What would she be doing way up north in Sheffield?"

"Not that Sheffield. This one's a village—well, scarcely that, a hamlet a little less than a mile from Mousehole."

"How?"

"It'll take an autopsy to be sure, but they found heroin and syringes in her car."

I stood up in sudden fury and began to pace. "So she over-dosed and died! The little *idiot!* All the money in the world, a doting family, and she goes and gets mixed up with drugs. With *heroin*, of all asinine things! And then she decides life isn't worth living. At age sixteen, when she's hardly lived at all! And now we'll never know how Lexa died, or anything about the cross, or—"

"Dorothy." Alan strode to the corner of the room where my pacing had taken me, and took both my arms in a strong grip. "Calm down."

When he uses that tone I obey, albeit reluctantly. I closed my mouth and glared at him.

"Listen to me. We *do not know* how Pamela died. If the pathologist finds that it was an overdose of heroin, we still won't know immediately who administered it, or whether the overdose was accidental or deliberate. But you have forgotten that the dead and their surroundings can speak, often eloquently. Before you dive in off the deep end, wait for a little more information.''

"Yes, well, exactly what are the police doing about this?''

He detailed procedures, detailed them until I was sick of the whole subject.

"And if they'd done all that a lot sooner,'' I said when he'd finished, "Pamela Boleigh might still be alive!''

"What makes you think so?''

"It's obvious, isn't it? If they'd found her—''

"If you must blame someone, blame Pamela's incredibly casual parents! By the time anyone knew she was missing, she'd already been dead for hours. Colin could tell me that much even before the autopsy. She died sometime between Saturday afternoon and Sunday morning. Tell me what the police could have done about that.''

He was as nearly angry with me as I had ever known him to be, and I realized, finally, that the anger wasn't all on account of my misguided ranting. He, too, was wishing that things were different, that Pamela was still alive.

"Okay. I was wrong and I admit it, and I'm sorry. I get carried away, I guess. But do you mind if I ask a sensible sort of question?''

"You're quite sure it's sensible?''

"I think so. It's just that I don't understand why it took them so long to find Pamela's car. I know there's a lot of countryside out there, but surely a strange car would stick out a mile if this Sheffield is as tiny as you say. Wouldn't somebody have reported it?''

He relaxed a little. "They would, and they did, or rather he did, as soon as he saw it. There's a disused quarry about a quarter-mile outside Sheffield, with a road to it that's little more than a track now. The quarry itself has filled with water, and is sometimes used by the locals as a bathing pool. None of the fine evangelical folk of Sheffield would use it on a Sunday, of course, but this afternoon a farmer found himself hot and tired after working in the sun and decided to cool off with a dip in the quarry. He saw Pamela's car parked just off the track, thought it was odd, and went to investigate.''

"Poor man."

"Yes, he probably found it unpleasant. The weather's been quite hot."

I sighed. "So okay, I suppose nobody's to blame, but the fact still remains that our best source of information can't tell us anything now."

"Except what the forensics team can come up with. You keep forgetting them."

"They're not very exciting, and they take so long. All those tests and everything. Oh, I know they're important, but I'm impatient."

"I never," said my long-suffering husband, "would have noticed."

"What's the weather supposed to do tomorrow?"

Alan raised his eyebrows at the change of subject. "More of the same, I believe."

"No thunderstorms? No hurricanes from America, or typhoons, or monsoons?"

"None of the above is predicted."

"Then let's go back out to the cave. We've never done that; other things kept getting in the way."

"Why do you keep harping on that cave? The police will have searched it thoroughly, and you hate the place."

"I don't hate it. I think it's fascinating. I'm just scared

to go inside, that's all, and I wouldn't admit that much to anyone but you. I'm ashamed.''

"Phobias are nothing to be ashamed of, Dorothy."

"That's easy for you to say. You don't have any."

Alan smiled a small, secret smile. Aha, I thought. There's something he hasn't told me.

I wouldn't ask. If he ever wanted to tell me, he would. But somehow the thought that my strong, bulky, fearless cop had an intimate knowledge of irrational fear made me feel better. If Alan, of all people, was phobic, then anybody might be, without shame.

"Anyway, I'm going to the cave, period. Now for heaven's sake let's go down and have a drink. We've earned it after a day like today."

"I thought you'd gone off alcohol."

"A momentary aberration. Anyone's entitled to a few of them."

"And to a civilized libation or two. After you, my dear."

TWENTY-SEVEN

TUESDAY MORNING was another day of perfect weather, sunny, not too hot, not too windy, puffy little clouds in a picture-postcard sky. We'd had only one bad day, really, and that had been sent to us from America. I was being forced to abandon my clichéd ideas about England's weather.

"A great day for the cave," I said cheerily to Alan over our first cups of tea, brewed in the room.

Alan looked at me with a suspicion that was entirely justified. Any morning that I'm cheerful before I have two cups of coffee in me, something's up.

"You don't want to go, do you?"

"We've been over that. No, I don't, not much. Yes, I'm going. Are you just about ready for breakfast?"

I don't always know when to be tactful and keep my mouth shut, but Alan almost always does. He smiled and said, "Quite ready."

We ordered a large breakfast. I was hungry, and determined this time to keep my food decently in my stomach where it belonged. I did not, after all, have to enter the cave, and just standing at the entrance surrounded by fresh air couldn't possibly bother me.

Right.

We got ready as soon as we'd finished eating. I dressed in layers in case the sun became too warm later, and brought along the sunscreen in case I had to remove the layers. I had already slathered some all over my face and chosen my widest-brimmed hat. "Okay, Captain Kidd, lead on."

"Captain Kidd? Aren't you getting pirates mixed up with smugglers?"

"Whatever. Let's go."

Alan took us by different roads than the ones we had used before. It seemed years ago that I had first seen Prussia Cove, but it had really been only four days. "We haven't been here quite a week," I said in the middle of Alan's explanation about some aspect of the landscape.

"I know. It seems much longer, doesn't it?"

"A lifetime."

"That's why I brought you this way. I wanted you to see a little more of the area than just the seaside. Cornwall has a lot to offer. It's a pity we'll have to go home soon."

"Oh, but not before we see the end of this business!"

"I hope not, but we can't neglect our other responsibilities forever."

No. A house, two cats, a volunteer job, Alan's consulting jobs—no, Alan was right. We'd have to go home soon. I said a silent prayer that we, or the police, would solve Lexa's murder before that, and tried to pay attention to the features Alan was pointing out.

"I'm sorry, what did you say?"

"One of the old mines," he repeated patiently. "There are a number of them hereabouts. And those fields, over there, are known as Carter's Downs."

That grabbed me, as he'd known it would. "Not really! The same Carters, the smugglers, do you think?"

"No one seems to know, but it would be logical, wouldn't it? This is very much their part of the world, the old rogues. We're only a little over a mile from their old haunts.''

"Prussia Cove? I thought it was much farther. Confused by the different route, I suppose.''

We got to the top of the cliff in just a few minutes, and the small parking area near Bessie's Cove was deserted. We would have privacy for our search of the cave that I was beginning to think of as "Lexa's Cave.''

"I don't want to seem a doubting Thomas,'' said Alan when we had reached our resting place halfway down the cliff path, ''but what exactly is it you want me to look for here?''

I shook my head. "I wish I knew. And you know how much I wish I could help with the search.''

Alan dismissed that with a wave of his hand.

'It's just this nagging feeling at the back of my head. There has to be a reason why both Betty and Lexa came here, or were brought here. There has to be a connection, and I've had this notion that there has to be a clue here somewhere.''

"I'm sure I can't imagine what.''

"Neither can I, and the whole idea is probably as irrational as my claustrophobia.''

"Well, never mind.'' He patted my knee. "It's a lovely day for the seaside. It's a pity we didn't bring our bathing suits and a picnic lunch. We are, after all, on what was meant to be a holiday.''

I swallowed my temper. He didn't mean to sound patronizing, and I'd admitted, myself, that the whole outing was probably futile. I stood. "Yes, well, let's get it over with, and then, if we can't think of anything useful to do, we'll try to have some fun.''

"I was joking, my dear,'' he said mildly. "Neither of us is likely to have much fun until this is over. Nor was

I poking fun at you. You've been right too often, and what is popularly known as intuition is always based on something rational. Who knows what we might find?"

That was better, and I smiled my appreciation, but he couldn't quite keep the skepticism out of his voice.

The sea, today, was far out. A great expanse of rock was exposed to view. "When is high tide, do you know?" I asked Alan as we went on down. "I didn't think to ask anybody."

"Ah, that shows you up for the inland woman that you are. I checked the tide tables at the front desk. They don't list Prussia Cove, but one can extrapolate from Penzance and Marazion—"

"You're showing off. Just tell me."

"Merciless woman. About three this afternoon."

"And it's—what—ten or so?"

"Closer to nine-thirty. Only just past dead water."

"That has an ominous sound, I must say. No, I was kidding, I know what it means." At least I thought I did. In the Ngaio Marsh book of the same name, which, incidentally, had been set in Cornwall, it had seemed to be a rather macabre synonym for low tide. Maybe, I thought, determined to look on the bright side, it was standard Cornish usage, and that's why Alan had thought of it now.

We had reached the gently sloping rocks of the shore. I stood and peered out to sea, squinting against the brilliantly sparkling waves. "That boat out there had better stay well offshore for the next few hours, then. It's pretty big. I wouldn't think there'd be enough water to float it anywhere close to the coast for quite a while."

"Her," said Alan. "A boat is a her or a she, not an it. But you're quite right. Not only dead water, but spring tide as well."

I sighed ostentatiously. "All right, you're dying to ex-pound. Very well, I'll listen."

"I won't go into a long lecture about the sun and the moon and gravitational pull and all that. Suffice it to say that at springs, the high tides are higher and the low tides lower than at any other time. So the sea is extraordinarily far out just now, and this afternoon the tide will be extra high."

"Got it. Bad for the boat, good for us, at least until the tide starts coming in. Hadn't we better get moving?"

"Your wish is my command."

We rounded the little point. The rocks were not only bare of water, but quite dry in the sun. I peered into the cave, wondering if I could muster up the courage to go in, at least a little way. I really did want to see.

I nearly shrieked. "Alan, not again!" I pointed.

"No, love." He grasped me around the shoulders in his most reassuring hug. "Just seaweed. The tide was extra high last night, remember."

I got my breathing back in order. "Right. Stupid of me. But I don't think I'll come any farther. That stuff looks slippery, and—oh, darn it, I hate to say so, but my legs are rubbery already. I'll sit here and watch, if I won't block your light too much."

"I brought a torch. I'll report if I find anything of interest."

I'll say one thing for training as a policeman—Alan was nothing if not thorough. Starting at the entrance to the cave, he examined every crevice in the floor, every protruding ridge of the rocky walls, even the crannies of the ceiling. He picked up stones and shells and fragments of seaweed and pored over them with his flashlight like a jeweler appraising a diamond.

I grew a little bored with the process. There was quite

obviously nothing to find. Alan was right; this was a wild-goose chase. I turned my gaze out to sea.

"Alan, that boat's coming in closer! Very close! I sure hope whoever's in charge of it—I mean her—knows what he's doing!"

"Let's have a look—damn!"

There was a slither and a loud, thumping crash. I jumped and looked back into the cave, just in time to see my husband disappearing into a hole at the back of the cave.

TWENTY-EIGHT

I WAS OFF THAT ROCK and into the cave in what seemed like microseconds. "Alan! Alan! Where are you? Are you all right? *Alan!*"

Then he was there in front of me, a trifle disheveled, more than a little dirty, and oozing blood from several small cuts on his hands and face.

"I'm not hurt. Took a tumble, that's all. I must say I feel a fool."

"You scared me to death. What *happened?*"

"What happened," he said, brushing himself off and getting blood on his clothes in the process, "is that I discovered, quite by accident, what's remarkable about this particular cave. The light's none too good, and I'm afraid I broke the torch, but come and see. That is, if—Dorothy, whatever are you doing in here?"

I hadn't thought about it till that moment. I was in a cave, actually at the very back, or what had seemed the back until a moment ago. I didn't stop to analyze how I'd managed to get there. "I don't know. I think you scared the claustrophobia out of me. But where were you? And how did that hole, or passage, or whatever it is just suddenly appear? I swear I didn't hear anybody say 'Open, Sesame.'"

"No, there's a far more prosaic explanation. You called to me and startled me. I slipped on that blasted seaweed and grabbed at anything I could grab to try to save myself. I can't say I succeeded very well at that." He looked ruefully at his hands. I was glad he couldn't see his face.

"The trouble was that the rock I caught hold of moved, most unexpectedly, I must say."

"Ooh! A secret panel, a pivot—"

"Nothing of the sort. Simply a large slab of rock, balanced rather carefully, I suspect, so that one man could shift it. At any rate, one man did! And lucky not to be killed, I must say. If it had fallen on me, I'd not be telling you the tale."

He pointed. I shuddered. The rough-hewn slab of rock that had crashed to the floor was probably four by five feet and at least five inches thick. I marveled that Alan had been able to move it at all, no matter how carefully it might have been balanced. It was certain that we would never be able to move it back.

"Fortunately, it fell one way, I slithered the other, and I ended up *there*—in one of the old mine shafts."

"Oh." Mixed-up visions of pirates, smugglers, and Ali Baba faded, to be replaced by something as ordinary as a disused mine shaft. "I guess you were lucky not to take a bad fall. It might have gone down really deep."

"No, these shafts were almost horizontal, remember? It probably once went back many hundred feet, and may still, for all I know. I couldn't see back very far, what with the poor light and the star bursts in front of my eyes."

I shuddered again, and not only at the thought of Alan's injuries. That shaft, going back into the cliff, maybe for hundreds of feet...

"Alan, if you want to show me that shaft, you'd better do it fast. I'm not sure how much longer the shock value will keep me sane in here."

"Then don't chance it. You go back to the entrance and wait. I can show you just as well there."

"How can you show me what's in that shaft if I go away like a craven coward?"

"Because," said Alan, verging on impatience, "I'll bring bits of it out. Now go."

I went. I'd read somewhere, in a Josephine Tey book I thought, that it was better not to fight a phobia. Maybe if I got in and out of this cave without an attack, I could try another cave sometime. Maybe I could conquer the irrational fear altogether.

Feeling slightly light-headed, I went and sat on my rock, watching the boat, much closer now. I ought to have been worried about it, I suppose, but the adrenaline rush had left me limp and unable to worry about anything much

It was a few minutes before Alan came out and sat beside me, and what he showed me put all other thoughts out of my head. I looked up with eyes and mouth both wide open.

"Yes, I thought you'd be interested. There are dozens of bundles just like this back in that hole."

"But—but—banknotes? Why on earth would anyone use a cave as a stash for money? It would mildew. Even for a miser, it makes a stupid bank."

Then I hit myself on the head. "Bank! Oh, Alan, you married an idiot! The bank robbery!"

He sat back and enjoyed my reaction. "Precisely. The notes have had no time to mildew because they've been there for only a few days. And that's not all, Dorothy. There are quite a few plastic bags in there, some full of white powder, some of something lumpy I think are tablets, though I couldn't tell for sure in that light. And then there was this."

He took something out of his pocket. "It was in a crevice. It flashed in the light from my torch just before the wretched thing broke, so I poked about for it."

It was a broken chain made of heavy, flat, elaborately wrought links that looked very much like gold, even though the thing was awfully grubby. Every second link was set with a large, unattractive gray bead.

I studied it curiously. "It looks like part of a worn-out chain of office for a Lord Mayor or someone like that. What on earth would it be doing in the cave? And what are those ugly gray things?"

"Pearls," said Alan. "Dead pearls. Pearls must be worn to stay beautiful, you know. They need the oil from the skin or they become dry and dead. The design is Renaissance, just like the chains of office. You're right about that. But I don't think, somehow, that this chain ever graced the neck of a civic official."

"What, then?" I held it out where the light would strike it better and looked more closely.

"How about a chain for a cross? A gold cross perhaps, set with rubies?"

I looked up at him then, mouth agape once more. "Lexa's cross? But—Alan, look at that boat!"

The boat I'd been watching was so close now that we could hear the roar of its motor. It was a yacht, maybe forty feet or so, a lovely, trim craft, and it was headed straight in to shore at what sounded like full throttle.

"The fool! He'll have it on the rocks—"

Even as Alan spoke, there came a hideous cracking sound as the boat struck a hidden rock, some hundred yards from where we stood watching. The boat stopped with a shudder, though its engine continued to roar. Then the engine stopped, too, and we could clearly see the bubbles rising as the boat filled with water, and hear the creaks and groans of her death throes.

She was resting in what seemed to be a few feet of water, perhaps fifty yards offshore. It was hard to tell just how deep the water was. I had no idea how much water a boat like that drew. It seemed that whoever was aboard her could easily reach shore, but there was no sign of any human activity.

Alan had already begun stripping off his clothes. "They may have been stunned by the crash. I'll have to swim out and see. Can you climb the cliff alone?"

"Of course! I'll get the cell phone and call for help."

"Here's the car key. And oh—better take this with you." He handed me the bundle of money. I jammed it into my pocket without a second thought, collected my walking stick, and made for the cliff, while Alan took off at a run for the wreck.

I got up that steep, rocky path at a pace that astounded me, arthritis notwithstanding. Once at the car, though, it took me several infuriating minutes to reach the police, and then they said that they were not the proper people to deal with the problem, but that they would alert the lifeboat service. I jammed one fist in my pocket in a fine display of temper, and encountered inspiration. "Fine. Do you want me to give them the money, too?"

"What money would that be, madam?"

"The missing bank loot. We found it in the cave, or we think that's what it is. I did tell you, didn't I, that this is Mrs. Alan Nesbitt calling?"

There is a time to use one's own name, and a time to drop that of anyone else who might prove useful.

"We'll send someone right out, madam. Wait there."

"No, I'm going back down to help Alan. Believe me,

several of your people know the place!'' I turned off the cell phone and slipped it into my pocket, and headed back.

Going down the cliff was more painful, and slower, but I made it with no mishaps and hurried across the slippery black rocks to the site of the wreck. I hadn't gone far before I saw Alan. He climbed up out of the water, and, to my surprise, he was alone and began walking toward me. I stepped up my pace.

When we met I was too winded to say more than ''What's happening?''

''Here, catch your breath first,'' Alan said, and sneezed.

He was shivering. I pulled off my windbreaker and gave it to him. ''Here, put it on before you freeze. Is he all right? Whoever was sailing the boat, I mean.''

''He's dead.''

''Alan!''

''If you can, love, let's get back to my clothes. The water's a trifle chilly.''

I would just bet it was. We walked back to the rock where Alan had left his clothes, and I contained myself until he had climbed into them and was relatively warm.

''All right, then. I called the police. They're coming, along with a lifeboat crew.''

''The lifeboat won't be necessary. I don't suppose you brought the mobile with you?''

I handed it over. Alan punched in a few numbers, counterordered the lifeboat, and then sat on the rock with me to await the police.

''All right, tell me.''

''There was only the one man on board. I did a pretty thorough search for crew, but there was no one else. The boat's beyond repair, I think. Sad, really. A lovely vessel.''

''But the man, Alan! The captain, or pilot, or whatever

you call him. I suppose he fell when the boat crashed, and hit his head or something.''

''There were no injuries to his head.''

There was something so odd in his tone that I asked no questions, simply waited for him to go on.

He took a deep breath and then let it out in a long sigh. ''It's John Boleigh's boat, Dorothy. He's been shot through the heart.''

TWENTY-NINE

I ABSORBED THAT in silence. Finally I asked a question. "You said there was no one else on the boat?"

"No one."

"And we saw no one leave, either before or after she crashed. At least I didn't."

"Nor I. And the gun was in his hand."

I slipped my arm around Alan's waist; he hugged my shoulders close. We sat in the warm sun. Around us the waves lapped and the gulls cried.

"Was he dead before the boat crashed? Is that why he lost control and rammed the rocks?"

"How can I know? The forensics men will make what they can of the boat, but time of death can't be determined precisely enough to know which happened first. I can make a guess, though, and I suspect it's pretty close to yours.

"I think he took his boat out, brooding about his granddaughter, perhaps considering suicide. Then something tipped the balance for him. He headed the boat for shore, revved up the engines, perhaps set some mechanism for maintaining course."

"An autopilot, sort of?"

"Something like that. I don't know. Some of these slap-up yachts have some pretty fancy toys attached. But somehow he fixed the course, and then took his gun and..."

I swallowed. "I can almost understand why he might have wanted to die. He was besotted with that grand-daughter of his. But why did he take that beautiful yacht with him?"

"Again, how is one to know? But did you happen to see the name of the boat?"

"No."

"No, of course not. The name panel was on the stern, which you never saw. But I did, when I was looking for a ladder to climb aboard."

"Well?"

"She was the *Pamela*."

THE POLICE ARRIVED not long after that, and a controlled pandemonium set in. When the first detachment found out they were dealing with the death of John Boleigh, they called out the reserves, including Superintendent Cardin-nis. He greeted me politely, and then he and Alan went away to do a lot of talking. They explored the cave and then came out and talked some more. Most of the crew spent their time, at first, getting Mr. Boleigh's body out of the boat and safely up the cliff. Once that was accom-plished, they sent for yet more reinforcements, this time including a couple of tugboats that made efforts either to refloat the *Pamela* or push her yet farther up on the rocks. I couldn't tell which, and so far as I could see, they made no progress at all in either direction. A grounded forty-foot yacht doesn't move at all easily.

Eventually the first group of policemen tired of watch-ing the marine types at their work, and went back to the cave. Presently they emerged carrying large plastic bags full, I presumed, of money and mysterious white powder and pills.

No one paid much attention to me. I am, after all, a

woman, and though the English are wonderfully polite to women, they have not yet quite realized that we are more than simply decorative adjuncts to our husbands.

That was all right with me in the present circumstances. I sat comfortably warm in the sun, hoping my sunscreen was still working, and I thought.

I thought about a wealthy man and his yacht. I thought about his granddaughter, dead of a drug overdose, and his great, if overindulgent, love for her.

I thought about two women found dead, over thirty years apart, also with illegal drugs in their bodies, and found in the same cave only a few yards from where I sat.

I thought about a valuable cross set with rubies and a ruined chain set with dead pearls.

I thought about a story my husband had told me and a book I had read in the library.

When the men had done all the talking and exploring and examining and so forth that they apparently meant to do that day, Alan and Superintendent Cardinnis came back to my rock.

"Any success?"

"Quite a lot, Mrs. Martin, at least in one respect," said Cardinnis. He wasn't quite beaming, but I was certain he would have been if it hadn't been for Mr. Boleigh's unfortunate demise. "The money you two found is certainly from the bank robbery, and there was a nice little stash of heroin, cocaine, and MDMA hidden in there as well. The Chief certainly does live up to his reputation! I don't know how he does it, I must say."

The words "pure accident" hovered on my lips, but I forbore to utter them.

"We've not been so lucky with the boat, not yet, at any rate. When the tide comes in, we may be able to refloat her and tow her ashore, and then she may have something to tell us.

"But we've been neglecting you, I fear. Is there anything you'd care to add to your husband's account?"

Well, of course I couldn't know what I might add until I knew what he'd told them—but I didn't say that, either. I simply smiled and adjusted my hat. I find my hats handy for all sorts of reasons, not the least being that men often admire them while discounting the head under them. It can be useful to be underestimated.

"I don't imagine I do. Alan is very thorough. I do have one question, though, for my own satisfaction."

"Of course." Cardinnis smiled indulgently.

"Alan and I were not, I'm afraid, able to get much out of the manager of the rave club. He took a dislike to us. I can't imagine why. But just out of curiosity, did your people ask him who the elderly gentleman was, the one who joined Lexa and Pamela that night?"

"They did." Cardinnis looked surprised. "The chap said he didn't know the man."

"I've been very curious about that incident. It doesn't seem to fit anything very well. Would it be a terrible burden for your men to ask the manager again? Perhaps his memory might have improved."

Cardinnis still looked puzzled, but he promised he would do that. I saw him wink at Alan, who smiled back, but then looked at me, a speculative frown on his face.

"It may be tomorrow before I can spare anyone, Mrs. Martin. We've got rather a lot to do today, I'm afraid."

"Of course you do. Tomorrow will be splendid." Any delay, in fact, increased the likelihood of an honest answer. I stood and flexed my shoulders. "Alan, do you suppose we could go back to the hotel? If I have to sit on that rock any longer, various portions of my anatomy will never be the same. Besides, it's long past lunchtime and I'm hungry.''

Alan looked a little shocked. I knew he thought I was unfeeling, thinking about my posterior and my stomach when poor Mr. Boleigh was dead. But I hadn't known the man well, I hadn't seen him with a bullet hole in him, and I had an agenda of my own.

However, Alan responded with his usual courtesy. ''Of course. I've kept you here far too long. Unless there's anything else we can do, Colin?''

''No, no, you've been a very great help. I'll never be able to thank you enough for finding that money. It's a great load off my mind. I'll ring you, Mrs. Martin, as soon as I have an answer to your question.''

''Thank you, Superintendent.'' I waved and we trudged toward the cliff path.

''Pure luck,'' I murmured in Alan's ear.

''Mmm?''

''Finding that money. Nothing but luck. You were accepting that poor man's praise as if you'd done something remarkable.''

''One must preserve one's image,'' he said imperturbably. ''And it wasn't luck at all.''

''Of course it was!''

''No, indeed. It was due entirely to your intuitive insistence that I was there in the first place, and in fact due to your agitated cry that I fell against that confounded stone door. I've you to thank.''

I grunted. The path was getting steep. ''And I suppose you told Colin that.''

''Certainly not. One cannot admit to reliance upon intuition. No, don't turn around, you'll fall! I may deserve a smart slap, but you mind your step.''

We were quiet on the way back to town. I don't know

what Alan was thinking about, but I was putting together the pieces of a very complicated puzzle.

I came up out of my brown study when we got to the roundabout just at the edge of town. "Alan, I don't want to go back to the hotel yet."

"My dear, I thought you were hungry."

"I am, but there's something I want to do first. Swing by Mr. Pendeen's antique store, will you?"

Yes, Mr. Pendeen was in, we were informed by the starchy clerk. He was very busy. She doubted he could see us.

I signaled Alan with my eyes. Obligingly, he engaged the clerk in conversation about a small desk in the window. We had seen it and were interested. Was it mahogany? Ah, rosewood! And made, he supposed, around...

I slipped away and made for the back of the store.

Mr. Pendeen was genuinely busy, but he'd made the mistake of not quite closing his office door. Two men who I suspected were political cronies sat in the chairs in front of the desk, smoking pipes and talking. I tapped on the office door and walked in, uninvited.

"Oh, I'm so sorry! I didn't mean to interrupt, but I have a very quick question I thought you might be able to answer for me, Mr. Pendeen. I can come back later if—"

I relied on the mayor having better manners than mine. I was right. "No, no, come in, Mrs. Martin. I am rather busy, but—"

"Yes, of course, and it really is a quick question, I promise. I suppose it's none of my business, to tell the truth, but when Alan and I visited Mr. Boleigh the other day, I couldn't help noticing that he has such lovely antiques in his home. I wondered if he inherited them, or perhaps bought them from you, or..." I let the question trail off and crossed my fingers, hoping Mr. Pendeen was eager enough to get rid of me that he wouldn't stop to wonder why I wanted to know.

"Oh, no, his family had very little money and certainly no priceless heirlooms. His immediate family, that is. It was when his uncle died and left him that fabulous inheritance that he began to buy lovely pieces from me, and from other dealers, of course. I think I may say that some of his choicest pieces came from me, however."

"Goodness, the uncle must have left a great deal of money."

"Not money, dear lady. Art treasures, you know, a remarkable collection. Fetched incredible prices at Christie's and Sotheby's, and from private collectors, as well. Now, if that really was all…"

"It was, and I do thank you. My apologies for the intrusion." I nodded deferentially to each of the men in turn and beat it out of there before Pendeen could start thinking clearly.

"I was looking for the rest room," I said in response to the clerk's lifted eyebrows. "You don't seem to have one, and I'm sorry, Alan, but I really must—um—"

He nodded gravely and whisked me out to the car. "All right, what was that little charade all about?"

"Alan, have you ever done jigsaw puzzles?"

"In my youth."

"Then you may remember that, as you near the end, you become convinced that there aren't enough pieces left to finish the thing. In particular, that piece you need with the corner of the house and the little bit of sky, the one shaped sort of like a horse, must have gotten lost. It isn't anywhere. And then you're down to three pieces, and you turn the last one the right way 'round, and there it is, house and sky, horse-shaped, and you can't understand why you didn't see it before.''

''I seem to remember something of the sort.''

''Well, I've just found the next-to-last piece.''

''Indeed.''

There was a pause.

''I suppose the last piece will be the answer you get from Colin Cardinnis? About the man at the rave club?''

''If it's the right answer, yes. If it's the wrong answer, the whole puzzle falls apart.''

''And do you intend to tell me about it, or is this an Ellery Queen novel? 'You have all the necessary information to solve the problem,' et cetera.''

''Don't be silly. Of course I'll tell you, but if you don't mind I'd like to have lunch first, or tea, or whatever we can get at this hour. Then I'll sit down and work it all out in my own mind to make sure I won't make a fool of myself when I try it out on you. And if it all holds together, including Colin's piece, when we get it—well, then I think we should go see Eleanor Crosby.''

THIRTY

"THE DAYS ARE drawing in," said Alan, looking out the window of our room at the tireless sea and the serene, cloudless sky. Though it was only a little after six, the sky was beginning to take on that opaque look that comes just before light fades and the first stars appear.

"'Light thickens, and'...and I can't remember the rest."

"It's unlucky to quote from *Macbeth*."

"Only in the theater, or so I've always understood." I rearranged the dishes and silverware on my tea tray. I'd been doing that, I realized, for quite some time. I pushed the tray away. "Alan, it does all make sense, doesn't it?"

He turned away from the window. "Granted the one supposition, the rest hangs together. I find it hard to believe...but you could be right. We'll soon know, I suppose."

I picked up the evening paper, a national daily. Issued from London with a noon deadline, it had nothing about the death of a prominent Penzance man, but the event had headlined the local television news an hour or so earlier. Alan and I had turned the set off.

I was reading the same item for the fourth time. I still had no idea what it said. I threw down the paper.

I'd sketched out everything for him, my conclusions and the reasoning that had led up to them. I was almost convinced I was right, though I wasn't a bit happy about it. But I wished I *knew*.

The phone rang. I jumped, nearly upsetting the tea table. Alan looked at me. I shook my head. He picked up the phone.

"Nesbitt here. Yes, Colin."

I hadn't thought my nerves could get any tighter. I was wrong.

"Yes. I see. Yes, a bit of a shocker. Oh, well, that's good news, anyway. Thank you so much. No, don't bother, you've a great deal to do. I'll tell her, and thank you again."

I didn't need his few words of explanation to tell me I was right. I stood up, suddenly almost calm now that it was nearly over. "We'd better tell Eleanor. She may have heard of Boleigh's death, and she'll be wondering what it means."

"Yes. It's a terrible story, but she deserves to be told."

We tapped on Eleanor's door, got no answer, and opened it quietly. She was dozing in bed, a supper tray in her lap. She had eaten almost nothing.

"Eleanor," I said softly.

She woke at once. "Oh. I thought you were the maid, to take away the tray."

"You haven't eaten."

"I'm not hungry. Would you mind moving that thing?"

Alan set the tray on the tea table.

"You know something," said Eleanor. Her voice had sharpened. "I can see it in your faces. What's happened now?"

"Something *has* happened, Eleanor, several things, in fact, but we came to you because we think we've unraveled most of the story."

"Which story?"

"The whole story," said Alan. "Betty, Lexa, Pamela—the lot."

Eleanor frowned. "You say you *think* you know. Can you prove it?"

"Some of it can be proved, not all. When we've finished I think you'll agree that proof is a secondary consideration. Suppose I let Dorothy tell you."

"Very well, but I warn you I want proof, proof that will stand up in court! I want this devil punished!"

"Yes, we understand. Dorothy?"

We pulled chairs up to the bedside and I began.

"I started thinking today, really thinking and not just chasing ideas around in my head. I thought about Betty and a beautiful old cross given to her by her lover, Lexa's father. And I began wondering where he might have gotten such a thing, thirty-odd years ago.

"It's over four hundred years old and extremely valuable, and not of English manufacture. Well, of course, there are many ways such a thing could have come to these shores, maybe centuries back, so that didn't give me much to go on. But then Alan found a broken chain, an elaborate one of similar age, in the cave where Betty and Lexa died. There's a hidden part to that cave, you see, an old mine shaft, actually, that Alan found quite by accident, just this morning. That started all kinds of wild ideas buzzing around.

"What if pirates had hidden their plunder there, ages ago? That cross and chain could well have been a part of such a hoard. Or there was another theory, less romantic but maybe more likely.

"Lexa spent some time in the library when she first came to Penzance, and talked to you about a shipwreck. I read a few things about shipwrecks, too, and one little item I remembered was that a German ship was wrecked near Penzance, sometime close to the end of World War Two. That reminded me of something Alan had said about Nazi art treasures, and I put two and two together. Suppose that wrecked ship had been carrying some of those looted treasures out of Germany to some safer place? I read somewhere that the Nazis did that as the war heated up, hoping to save them if their German strongholds were badly damaged. Just suppose someone had seen that ship wrecked, seen it before anyone else, and had known a place to hide the treasures? Or the treasures might even have drifted to the cave on the currents—things do, in that area—and been found by our someone, who then went to look for more. And suppose that someone had died before he could do anything further with his booty, and it was found only twenty odd years later, by Betty's lover?''

''Pure speculation, said Eleanor restlessly,

''Not quite. There was that chain, remember.''

''Precious little to support such an elaborate story.''

''You're right. There's more, but I have to tell this my own way. Do you mind if I help myself to some of your water?''

Eleanor waved an elegant hand, thin to the point of transparency, and I opened her untouched bottle of water, poured some into her untouched glass, and continued.

''You see, the chain wasn't the only thing Alan found in that mine shaft. He also found quite a cache of drugs and a great deal of money, banknotes. The police have determined that the money was from that bank robbery the other day, and the drugs are probably heroin, cocaine, and ecstasy.''

I had her entire attention now. ''And then something happened, something that helped me put the whole thing together. A yacht that had been cruising in the bay suddenly set a course straight for shore and crashed into underwater rocks at high speed. While I went to phone for help, Alan swam out and boarded her, and found that John Boleigh had been at the controls. He was dead of a gunshot wound, the gun in his hand.''

"He'd killed himself?"

"It looks that way. Of course, we won't know for sure until the police check some things, and in fact we may never know, unless the police can get the yacht off the rocks."

"Some luck there, possibly," Alan put in. "Cardinnis mentioned it when he phoned. With the spring tide, they've been able to float her enough to tow her to shore. They'll be able to search her in safety now."

"Good. But you were pretty sure, weren't you, Alan? About the suicide?"

"Not sure, no." He spread his hands. "It seems the most likely solution."

"He'd lost his granddaughter," said Eleanor. "I can understand."

"I think there may have been more to it than that, Eleanor. Quite a lot more, in fact. When I'd had a chance to think over the whole business clearly, I had two questions. I asked one of the mayor of Penzance, who is also an antique dealer, and the other of the police. The answer to both was the answer I expected."

"Well? Get on with it!"

I was not going to be rushed. This story had to be told properly.

"I asked Mr. Pendeen—that's the mayor—how Mr. Boleigh had made his money. I didn't put it quite that way, of course, but Mr. Pendeen told me that an uncle of Mr. Boleigh had left him a fortune. That was more or less what Alan had said. But when I mentioned money, Mr. Pendeen corrected me. Eleanor, Mr. Boleigh was left, according to the mayor, not money but a fabulous collection of art treasures.''

I let that one sink in for a moment and then went on. ''My second question had to do with the man seen with Lexa and Pamela Boleigh at the rave club. The police did a little more checking on it and came back with the information that the man was, as I had finally suspected, Mr. Boleigh. Pamela's grandfather. *And*—'' I paused for effect. ''*And,* as the manager has only just been willing to tell us, having learned of Mr. Boleigh's death, Boleigh was the owner of the club.''

Eleanor looked at me in stark incomprehension for a moment, and then she burst out, ''He killed them! The bloody bastard killed both of them!''

''If he did, Eleanor, he's beyond the reach of human justice now. You see why Alan said that proof didn't matter quite so much. But—no, wait. Alan, I think you might send down for some brandy. I know I could use it, and I'm sure Eleanor could.'' I turned to her. ''If you're allowed alcohol, that is?''

''Probably not, but what does it matter?''

''Indeed.''

''But I want to know everything. I don't understand!''

''Yes, I want to tell you everything. But it's a pretty painful story, so if you don't mind, I'd rather wait till our drinks get here.''

THIRTY-ONE

WE SETTLED, drinks in hand. Afternoon had faded to evening. Alan had drawn the drapes and turned on lamps. The room looked as cozy and comfortable as the beginning of a fairy tale. In a way, it was appropriate, because the tale I had to tell certainly had a number of ogres in it. I began the story accordingly.

"Once upon a time there was a very pretty girl named Betty Adams. She was a pleasant girl, but not always wise in her choice of friends. She lived in London, but one day she went to Penzance for a weekend with some of those not-so-wonderful friends. She made more friends, oh, very quickly, and one of them was a man named John Boleigh. He was married and had at least one child, a daughter probably about five or six years old, but he didn't tell Betty that. He probably didn't tell her his real name, either. He met her at a party where a lot of drugs were circulating, and both of them smoked a good deal of marijuana. They both became amorous, and he became indiscreet, as well. He took Betty to a place where they could have some privacy, perhaps a deserted house at the top of a cliff, perhaps only his car. They made love, and then he began to talk.

"He told Betty that he was a policeman, but that he wouldn't need to go on working much longer, because of a piece of incredibly good luck. He had found, he said, yes, found at the bottom of this very cliff, a cache of fabulous treasures. Paintings, sculpture, religious artifacts, jewels—a king's ransom. He had to sell them slowly, he said, but when he had enough money, he'd be free.

"Though she sometimes did foolish things, Betty was no fool, even under the influence of a drug. She didn't believe him. So he pulled out, from somewhere he kept it handy so he could gloat over it now and then, the smallest of the things he had found, a lovely ruby-studded cross. He handed it to her. 'Here, take it. Keep it. There's plenty more where that came from.'"

I took another sip of brandy. The next part was hard.

"Eventually he took her back to her friends, and she went home to London with a souvenir of her trip. Two souvenirs, in fact though she didn't know for a few weeks that she was pregnant.

"You know all of this part, how she decided that, since the baby's father, Lexa's father, was rich, he should help with support. How she went back to Penzance, leaving behind the cross but not her memory of the story.

"Somehow she found Boleigh, I don't know how. At any rate, she did, probably at another party. She got him off to himself and told him about Lexa.

"Boleigh, meanwhile, had begun his career of patron of the arts. He had probably sold most of his treasures, most likely through some highly dubious channels. He had put it about that they'd been auctioned respectably, to explain why he was now a very wealthy man indeed. He had a position and a reputation to maintain, as well as a growing family.

"Betty represented embarrassment, but more, she represented danger. Betty knew things she should not. He had to get rid of her somehow. He could pay her off, yes, but how was he to know she wouldn't keep coming back and back? She had the means of blackmail readily at hand.''

"She would never have done such a thing!''

Eleanor would have continued, but I held up my hand. "No, I don't think she would, but you have to remember Boleigh didn't know her. He'd met her exactly once. How was he to know? To him she was a threat, nothing more nor less.

"We'll never know exactly what happened, except that he, or someone, gave her some LSD, enough to hamper her judgment severely. Maybe he made the mistake of taking her out to the cliff house again, as a nice, lonely spot to dispose of someone, and she recognized the place and tried, despite the stormy weather, to fly over the cliff to find the treasure cave. I suspect that's the answer, but maybe he pushed her into the sea at some other spot and the currents carried her back to the cave after several days of stormy weather. At any rate, he must have had a nasty shock when her body was found. Even if all the treasure was gone by that time, he might have left some trace of his treasure raids to the cave, and questions could well be asked.

"However, nothing came of it, and for over thirty years he prospered. Not, perhaps, entirely as he had planned.

"He'd had to sell his treasures on the black market. No matter what their origin, Nazi loot or pirate's booty, they couldn't be sold openly. And the old saw is, unfortunately, all too true. One cannot touch pitch and not be soiled.

"His partners in crime figured out where the treasures had been found, I don't know how. Maybe they hauled out some of the larger pieces themselves. At any rate, they, or some of their associates, began to see the possibilities of a lovely, hidden place that was easily accessible by sea. They approached Boleigh about using the cave for a little storage of their own, and hinted that perhaps, since he liked to use a little in the way of drugs now and then, he'd be interested in getting into distribution himself.

"I think, by then, that he'd probably stopped using drugs completely. His community position and his family were of growing importance to him, and he'd never taken more than a little pot. He didn't want to fall in with their scheme. At least that's what I believe. But the criminals who wanted to use him didn't care about his scruples, and they had a mighty hold over him. They knew the origin of his wealth. So Boleigh found himself in the drug business."

Eleanor made an inarticulate noise. Alan pushed her brandy glass into her hands and made her take a sip. I took a pull of mine, too. The story was becoming more and more unsavory.

"The business wasn't all bad. He made a lot of money from it, was able to spend more and more on his pet charities, buy more and more niceties for his lovely home, lavish more and more gifts on his children and, by now, grandchildren. He also bought, on the sly, an old building, turning it into a rave club where the drugs could be distributed and where, incidentally, he could make a lot more money even without the lucrative little sideline. He was, I suspect, able to persuade himself that the drugs hurt only those foolish enough to buy them, and that those people were, in any case, the dregs of society.

"Then two things happened in quick succession. Lexa came to town, looking the image of her mother, and met him. Not only that, but she was being escorted by a retired chief constable, and Boleigh overheard her talking about drugs! He'd scarcely taken that in when he found out that his beloved granddaughter Pamela was frequenting the rave club and taking drugs."

Eleanor's hands clenched. "So he lured both of them out of the club and killed them! Wherever he is now, I hope he's paying for his devilment!"

"He may have done that, but I don't think so. This is what I think happened."

I fortified myself with the last few drops of brandy.

"He was with the girls at the club. Then the three of them went out. I'm sure the manager only appeared to throw out Boleigh, who was his boss, after all, but he, the manager I mean, must have made it clear that things would be better for everyone if Boleigh left. Boleigh had given Lexa what I imagine he thought was ecstasy, probably two or three tablets of it dropped into her water or orange juice or whatever she was drinking. I'm sure he gave Pamela nothing, but she had undoubtedly taken some ecstasy—or something—of her own accord.

"Boleigh, of course, had taken no drugs, and he was a good deal older than the girls. I believe they, flying high, feeling on top of the world, got away from him easily. I think Lexa, who had guessed part of the story just as I did, got Pamela, her now-bosom-buddy Pamela, to drive her out to the cave, maybe to show her where her mother had been, or maybe because Lexa had guessed part of the treasure story. Lexa knew, from her library research, roughly where Bessie's Cove was, and of course Pamela knew the area thoroughly. She was born here.

"How those two got down the cliff path in the dark and the wind I don't know. They were high on drugs, of course, and sometimes the belief that one is invincible helps make it so. Anyway, they did, and they found the cave. If I'm right about the tides and the time they might have arrived, the tide was going out. They would have had no trouble.

"Then what happened—who knows? I suspect that

Lexa, in drug-induced exuberance, told Pamela the whole story and showed her the cross. I don't know how Pamela reacted, but I imagine that at some point the girls fell asleep in the cave. They would have been warm enough, especially Lexa, because of the drug. At least Pamela slept. In Lexa, the drug went on doing its deadly work. And in the morning, when Pamela woke, Lexa—didn't.''

Eleanor swallowed hard again. I wished I had more brandy.

"Pamela was down from her high by that time, very far down, very depressed, and very frightened. Frightened of her grandfather, who had been furiously angry, frightened of being there with Lexa's body, frightened of everything. She was cold, too. She scrambled up the cliff, Luna's cross with her. I don't know what she did the rest of Friday, but on Saturday she took the cross to Mousehole to sell, possibly to buy some heroin. And we know the rest.''

Eleanor lay silent.

"The money?" Alan prompted.

"Oh, yes. I think the crooks who planned the bank robbery were the same ones who were running the drugs. Anyway, they somehow had some information about the cave. It wasn't too hard to persuade Boleigh to let them use the cave for a temporary stash.

"When Boleigh went out this morning on his yacht, he might have been planning to remove the money and give it back. He might have planned to steal it himself and flee the country. His life in Penzance certainly lay in ruins. Or, knowing all he did, he might have planned suicide from the first. He had loved Pamela deeply, and he knew that he had only himself to blame for her destruction.''

"Then," said Eleanor finally, "then you believe he killed none of them?''

"Not directly, no. Indirectly, he killed all of them, as well as Mr. Polwhistle's granddaughter and possibly a good many more people over the years, people he'd never met. Those 'society dregs' he cared about so little. Except at the end. He cared then, I think."

I could find a little sympathy in my heart for him, but I didn't say so. I doubted Eleanor felt the same way.

ALAN TOOK MY TALE to the police the next day. It was a mass of speculation, of course, and Colin took it as such. There were a few things they could check, and they would, if only to rule out other possibilities.

We left Penzance that same day. I vowed I'd never come back.

"No, Dorothy. Don't say that. It's not the fault of the place. Good and evil, remember. Cornwall is beautiful. So are most of its people. We'll go back one day."

"Climb back on the horse that threw you? Well, perhaps." But our home and our cats and even the rain that still persisted looked very good to me.

Colin Cardinnis called in a couple of days to say that Eleanor, feeling she could no longer trespass on the hotelkeepers' good nature, had gone to a nursing home. I thought about writing to her, couldn't think of what to say, and left it too late. We heard of her death two weeks after we left Penzance.

"She looked very peaceful," the nurse said. "They often do."

"She was at peace, I think." That was all I could say.

It was weeks later that I got a small package in the mail, with a letter from a law firm.

"It's Lexa's cross," I said to Alan. I had difficulty speaking, and blew my nose. "Apparently the police decided it *was* Eleanor's property, and she'd left a note asking that it be given to me. Alan, I don't want it!''

"Sell it, then. Christie's will get a good price for you. Give the money to a drug rehabilitation program.''

"Good from evil?'' I demanded, still sniffing.

"One can only hope, my dear. One can only hope.''

GLARE ICE

A CLAIRE WATKINS MYSTERY
MARY LOGUE

November in Wisconsin is much too cold for deputy sheriff
Claire Watkins to dive into the frigid waters of Lake Pepin
to pull a man from a submerged automobile. The victim
is Buck Owens, apparently tied to the driver's seat while
his car sank through the thin ice.

Claire had seen Buck's girlfriend, Stephanie Klaus, earlier this
week, her face badly bruised. Claire doesn't suspect her of his
murder—but does think that whoever did this to Stephanie
killed Buck, as well. When Stephanie is found beaten again
nearly to death and too terrified to talk, Claire makes a
shocking discovery that puts a face on the killer.

**"...a powerful sense of place and...a refreshing break from
the standard modern female protagonist..."
—*Publishers Weekly***

Available December 2002 at your favorite retail outlet.

WML442

A Romantic Way To **DIE**

A SHERIFF DAN RHODES MYSTERY

Bill Crider

When a romance convention comes to Blacklin County, Texas, Sheriff Dan Rhodes is not quite sure what all the fuss is about—though his wife, Ivy, happily demands he use his badge to cut in line to get the autograph of the show's star: the very buff cover model Terry Don Coslin, a hometown boy turned hunk of the century.

But not even great pecs, gorgeous hair, kissable lips and thousands of devoted fans can protect Terry Don from the deadly intent of a killer. Now Rhodes must make his way into the breathless, steamy, backstabbing, sweet savage world of the happily ever after.

"Crider fans will welcome this..."
—Publishers Weekly

Available December 2002 at your favorite retail outlet.

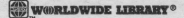

WBC440